December Road
Seasons of Love and War
Book 2

by

Brenda Ashworth Barry

Published by
Melange Books, LLC
White Bear Lake, MN 55110
www.melange-books.com

December Road ~ Copyright © 2014 by Brenda Ashworth Barry

ISBN: 978-1-68046-003-2

Cover Art by Caroline Andrus

Dedication

First, I'd like to thank my wonderful husband, Matthew Barry for being supportive and helping me with all the ins and outs of the military.

Next, I'd like to thank my reading buddy and dear friend, Cindy Watson. Life is never boring.

I want to give a shout out to my group of friends who are there for me through thick and thin and support me through all the craziness. You ladies BETA read and help support my fan page. Mona, my BFF, Vicky, Lisa, Shannon, Colleen, and Susan. Thank you and I love you.

Thank you to my wonderful friend and Editor, Joyce. You are the best.

And to Frank and Kellie; you have both been there by my side. I love you.

To all my friends and family who have read my book and called me up or sent me messages of how much they love my story. You mean the world to me.

To my parents—I love you very much.

And of course, to my brother Chuck who gave me tons of love and encouragement to write in the first place. From the day I came home and you were standing there with my notebook in hand, almost begging me to finish a small story I had written. Thank you Charles Cole Ashworth for being the most wonderful brother a girl could ever ask for and pushing me to continue to write.

To my brother Joe who served in the military, during the Vietnam War. Thank you for being the brave man that you were and still are.

Last but not least, to my family at Melange. I am so very blessed to be a part of this wonderful group.

Chapter One

"Get away from me, you sonofabitch! I'll kill you!" Kaylob hit the nurse so hard she nearly fell to the floor.

Beth Ann's heartbeat sounded like a jackhammer inside her head as she froze near the doorway and watched Kaylob's worst combat outburst since he'd arrived at the VA hospital. Her stomach twisted and she couldn't seem to breathe.

Dr. Richardson pushed his way between the nurse and Kaylob and somehow managed to give him an injection.

"What the hell are you doing to me? Let me out of here!" Kaylob sounded like a wounded animal. "I'll break your neck!"

The nurse ran out the door and returned seconds later with an orderly.

"Calm down, son," Dr. Richardson ordered while he struggled to restrain Kaylob. "You're not in Vietnam anymore. You're at the VA hospital in San Francisco."

Kaylob didn't seem to hear the doctor's words or notice Beth Ann. His arms flailed in every direction fighting to escape his bed.

Weak-kneed, Beth Ann turned her face toward the wall, unable to watch any longer. But scuffling sounds made her look again. Kaylob had grabbed the thin doctor around the neck and was squeezing hard. Beth Ann almost screamed when she saw the doctors face go red as he tried gasping for air. The nurse and the orderly both jumped onto the bed and tried to pry Kaylob's hands from the doctor's throat.

"Get him off!" yelled the nurse, tugging at Kaylob's hands.

"He's strong as hell," the orderly shouted.

Beth Ann's entire body trembled watching the orderly struggle to free Dr. Richardson from Kaylob's grasp. Luckily, for the doctor, the sedative kicked in, and Kaylob's eyes fluttered as he fell back on the bed.

1

"I'll kill you," he mumbled. "Bastards…" Then he fell silent.

The short, round nurse shook her head and bent over, resting her hands on her knees. "He's one strong man," she said, trying to catch her breath.

The orderly patted Dr. Richardson's back. "You okay, Doc?"

The doctor nodded his face still red.

Beth Ann's mind was spinning from the flurry of activity around her. She was going to fall if she didn't sit down soon. Her gut tightened at the knowledge that Kaylob hadn't recognized her. What in God's name happened over there that would make him act that way? The Kaylob she knew would never hit a woman or fly into a rage and try to choke a doctor—that much she knew for sure. She watched while the nurse and orderly tucked blankets around Kaylob's sleeping body.

"He should rest comfortably for a couple hours now," the nurse said reassuringly, looking at Beth Ann. She and the orderly started toward the door, then the nurse stopped and turned to speak to the doctor. "Do you want one of us to stay while you finish up?"

"No," Dr. Richardson replied, smiling weakly as the color returned to his face. "I should be fine now." He looked concerned and pushed his glasses back in place then faced Beth Ann. "You may want to rethink staying here. It's not safe, and if he keeps this up, I'm afraid we may have to *make* you go."

"No, I can't leave him!" Beth Ann said, shaking her head. "Please don't make me. I wasn't here when he woke up just now—that probably upset him. I'm sure my being here will help him."

The doctor nodded reluctantly, then he looked Beth Ann straight in the eyes and said, "I know you want to help, but we don't want you to get hurt— and we don't want to be held accountable if you *do* get injured. If you want to stay, you'll have to sign a waiver to absolve us of all responsibility."

"I'll sign whatever you want me to," Beth Ann said resolutely.

"Okay," the doctor agreed with a sigh. "I'll have the paperwork brought to you immediately." He turned to look at Kaylob and shook his head. "He should be comfortable now. We just don't know if he'll ever be the same. I sure hope he calms down. The last thing we want to do is restrain someone who's been in a POW camp."

Restrain him? No, they couldn't do that especially after everything he must have gone through. It could make things worse. Beth Ann moved beside the bed after the doctor left and gently caressed Kaylob's forehead, running her fingers through his matted, blond hair.

She touched the dimple on his chin and whispered, "I love you, Mr. O'Brien. I've loved you since I was eleven years old, and that's never going to change."

She had just watched her gentle-natured childhood sweetheart fly into an uncontrollable rage, which must have started in his sleep after she had stepped out to use the restroom. The surprising thing was that his fury had continued after he was fully awake.

Good God, what had they done to him in that horrible place? It must be worse than anything she'd imagined.

Minutes later she heard footsteps enter the room and turned to see the tall nurse motioning for her to step outside. What now? As soon as Beth Ann stepped into the hallway, the nurse handed her a piece of paper.

"This guy has called twice and you told us to hold all calls," the nurse said. "He says you need to call him now. He also said if he didn't hear from you today, he'd be seeing you tomorrow."

The nurse left and Beth Ann didn't even need to look at the paper in her hand to know that it was Blake's number. He couldn't come to the hospital. What the hell was he thinking? She had to call him—and right away. She found a payphone and dialed Blake's number, but Dana answered.

"Hi, Dana, this is Beth Ann. Is Blake there?" Dana was Blake's housekeeper and almost like a little sister to him.

"Hi, Beth Ann. No, he's not here." Dana paused then added, "I'll be sure to tell him you called though. He said he's coming to see you if you didn't call him. He's awfully angry."

"I've tried to call before, but he's never home. Could you please tell him I'll try again in the morning before he leaves for work?"

"I will," Dana said.

"I'm so sorry to put you in the middle of all this."

"It's okay. I miss you, Beth Ann."

"I miss you too." Beth Ann felt tears welling up.

After she hung up, Beth Ann felt her stomach tighten, not only because she could hear the hurt in Dana's voice, but also because of the possibility that Blake might show up.

When she got back to Kaylob's room, she sat next to the bed and dozed off until a sound woke her. She looked up to see Jackie touching her shoulder. Beth Ann glanced at the clock on the wall and realized she had been asleep for over two hours.

"How is he?" Jackie asked softly.

"He had a rough morning, so they gave him a sedative," Beth Ann replied. "But he seems to be okay now."

"I'm glad." Jackie leaned over and kissed her son's forehead. "What happened?"

"He thought he was back in the jungle being tortured. He didn't seem to recognize me at all." A tear rolled down Beth Ann's cheek.

Jackie gently wiped the tear away, then she bent down and gave Beth Ann a hug. "Don't worry, honey. He's going to get better." She straightened and took Beth Ann's hand. "We need to talk in private. Let's go out in the hall."

Beth Ann followed her out of the room. The worry lines she saw on Jackie's round face told her something was wrong.

Jackie kept her voice low. "Your mom called me this morning and said Blake has been calling the house and going on about how you need to get back home. You might want to get in touch with him." After a pause she added, "He also said something about coming here."

"I know," Beth Ann said. "I tried to call him about two hours ago, but he wasn't home."

With Blake's celebrity status, she wondered if he would be able to get by security and hoped they wouldn't let him in. It was scary to think about how something like that would affect Kaylob. Even scarier was the thought of how Blake would act if he did show up. He had always been a hothead and a lot more jealous than Kaylob.

Jackie looked down at Beth Ann's left hand. "I'm afraid Kaylob will see this ring and find out that you're engaged to another man."

Beth Ann gasped. "Oh my gosh! I forgot about the ring. I need to take it off. While I'm at it, I also need to get cleaned up and change my clothes."

Jackie studied Beth Ann's face. "So you've decided to stay with Kaylob? I hope you know I'm not trying to pressure you. I just thought I should point it out."

Beth Ann shook her head. There was really nothing to decide. "Kaylob's back and he's always been the love of my life. Of course I'm staying with him."

Relief flooded Jackie's face, and she reached out and hugged Beth Ann again. "I'm so glad. Now you go do whatever you need to do, and get something to eat while you're at it. I'll stay here with Kaylob."

Beth Ann grabbed her bag and hurried down the hall to the ladies room. The cleaning staff had apparently just cleaned the room, because the smell of Pine-Sol was very strong. As she pulled the engagement ring from her finger, she felt a sharp pain in her heart. She hated the thought of hurting Blake. He hadn't been just her fiancé; he had been her confidant, her friend, and her shoulder to lean on. She put her hands over her face and cried—for Blake, for what Kaylob had been through, and for the thing she was about to do.

Her mind raced trying to think of a way to make Blake understand. She had already told him to cancel the wedding. Wasn't that a clear enough sign that she wanted to break it off? She knew better, not with Blake, and in truth, it wasn't fair to him. She would simply have to lay it all on the line—but doing that without hurting him would be impossible. How would he react? Would he flip out? She'd never gone through anything like this before, and there was no how-to book for this situation.

She stuffed the ring into her makeup bag and wiped the tears from her cheeks. Glancing in the mirror, she could see she was a mess. Her face showed obvious signs of stress and exhaustion, and her brown eyes were swollen and red. She turned on the water and splashed her face, then brushed her teeth and decided to put her hair in a French braid.

While she wove strands of her curly red hair into the braid, another troubling thought struck. What if the paparazzi somehow got inside the hospital? Those damned reporters knew about Kaylob's return and there's no telling what they would say. They were always skulking around taking pictures of her and Blake—something she definitely wouldn't miss.

The mere thought of it caused her head to throb, so she downed two aspirins and decided that eating breakfast would be a good idea. At least it might temporarily take her mind off everything that was happening.

When she got back to the room two hours later, Kaylob was still asleep. Jackie glanced up from the scarf she was knitting and smiled. Her silver hair made her look much older, but her deep brown eyes at least showed life again. Maybe now with Kaylob home, Jackie would be able to take off those extra pounds that caused her blood pressure to rise and would stop looking so old for her age. It was nice to see her smiling. Beth Ann knew Jackie had always suffered with depression and that Kaylob had tried so hard to make it better for her. That was just the way he was, always kind, caring and giving.

As far as Beth Ann was concerned, Kaylob was the most beautiful man in world—even with all his scars, pale skin and messed-up hair. He made her heart soar like no one else.

Suddenly, Kaylob cried out in his sleep. "Let me out, you bastards!"

Beth Ann rushed to his side. Kaylob lashed out, his fist almost grazing her cheek.

Jackie jumped up and ran toward the door. "I'll get help."

"Kaylob, honey, it's okay," Beth Ann said, gently touching his face.

He clutched her wrist, dragging her down to him.

"Kaylob, no!" *Jesus he's got my neck.* Beth Ann tried to scream but couldn't because he was choking her. "Kaylob, it's me—Beth Ann! Let go." She struggled to pry his hands from her throat.

5

Chapter Two

A second later, he opened his eyes and dropped his hands. "Oh my God," he said, his blue eyes filled with tears. "I'm a goddamn monster."

Beth Ann coughed and fought to get air back in her lungs. She didn't want Kaylob to see how frightened she was, nor did she want the hospital to know he had choked her.

"It's okay, honey, you didn't know it was me," she said, still gasping for air as she ran her hand down her hair and clothes, trying to make it look as if nothing had happened.

Kaylob lifted her wrist and saw the marks he had inflicted. His eyes went to her throat, and tears flooded down his face. All she could to do was lean over and kiss his head, but he looked away.

"I'm so sorry, Beth Ann. I'm such a mess. I wouldn't be surprised if you walked away and never looked back. It's not safe to be around me."

"Kaylob Shawn O'Brien, don't you dare talk like that." Beth Ann wrapped him in her arms as he buried his face in her chest and wept. It took everything she had not to break down with him. This kind of pain was something she'd never seen in him before.

After a few moments, the nurse came back into the room with Jackie. The minute Jackie saw Kaylob, her face transformed from fear to grief. Beth Ann raised her hand discreetly to stop her from saying anything. Seconds later, when Harold, Kaylob's dad, walked into the room, Jackie took him by the arm and they all left.

Beth Ann felt as if her heart would explode with anguish over what Kaylob had been through. She had never felt him die even when the Army had declared him dead, but nobody would listen to her, even after all her visions and nightmares.

Everyone thought I was insane. Hell, I *thought I was insane.*

Well, one person had listened. Thank God for him.

The next morning, Beth Ann slipped quietly out of the room to call Blake. She knew she had to break it off with him once and for all. Now she understood what people meant when they said, ending a relationship was never easy. Sadly, doing it over the phone seemed like the wrong thing to do, but what other choice did she have? She made her way to the pay phone again, called Blake's number collect and listened as the operator connected the call.

Blake's voice was as cold as ice. "Hello, Beth Ann."

"Hi, Blake." Her mind raced as she tried desperately to think of what to say, but he saved her the trouble.

"When the hell are you coming home, and why haven't you returned my calls?" His Texas drawl was thick.

"Blake, I can't come home and I have called you but you weren't there," Beth Ann said, trying to sound firm. "Kaylob's in bad shape. Jesus, you know he was a POW, and I have to be here for him. He's barely hanging on." Before he could respond, she continued. "And please *don't* come here. Kaylob's already been through so much, and I won't let him be subjected to any more pain."

There was a long pause before Blake finally said, "Okay. Out of respect for his situation, I'll stay away—for now. But I won't stay away indefinitely. You can be there for a while, but I want you home as soon as possible." His voice softened as he added, "I miss you."

"I understand," Beth Ann said, "but I'm not coming back to the townhouse. I can't just leave him."

"Like hell!" His anger returned. "I'm telling you, Beth Ann. I'll put up with you staying for only so long, then I'm coming to get you. We're engaged, in case you forgot."

"Blake, I need to tell you something about that." Beth Ann struggled to maintain her courage.

"No! You don't need to tell me anything!" Blake's voice sent shivers down Beth Ann's spine. "You heard what I said, and I meant every word! I love you and hope Kaylob gets better, but I want you *home*."

The phone went dead before Beth Ann could say anything else. She stood staring at the receiver. She hadn't even had the chance to break up with him— but he *had* to know that's what she'd been about to do, didn't he? He wasn't stupid. She had told him straight out that she wasn't coming home. And as soon as she'd found out Kaylob was alive, she had told him to cancel the wedding. He was just refusing to believe what he knew deep inside.

Over the next several days, Beth Ann kept a constant vigil by Kaylob's bedside. She was grateful that Blake didn't call again, but she hadn't ruled out the possibility of him showing up at the hospital. That thought made her stomach roll.

She also discovered that humming and singing to Kaylob seemed to soothe his spirit. As she was singing a special melody for him, a young hospital assistant waltzed in with magazines and a big smile. Oh Lord, one of them had a photo of Beth Ann plastered on the front with a headline that read, TONY NOMINEE TORN BETWEEN MOST ELIGIBLE BACHELOR AND CHILDHOOD SWEETHEART WAR HERO.

Beth Ann grabbed the magazine from her hand and tossed it in the garbage, then she asked the girl to step outside. The look on the poor girl's face made Beth Ann feel awful. She looked about sixteen and was chewing her bottom lip and shuffling her feet.

Beth Ann touched her arm and said, "I'm sorry, sweetie, but we're sheltering him from certain things. You've done such a good job and all. I'm sorry for upsetting you."

The girl nodded with a tremulous smile. "I understand and I'm sorry. I'll make sure not to bring any more of those magazines, just books."

After that, Beth Ann notified the nursing staff and hoped that would keep the gossip magazines away, along with any phone calls.

Late one afternoon, Beth Ann sat with Kaylob and watched him sleeping peacefully. This was rare anymore, so when Jackie walked in the room, Beth Ann held a finger to her lips.

Jackie stood looking down at her son, then she leaned over and brushed the hair out of Beth Ann's eyes. "Go take a break, honey. Get something to eat or take a walk."

"I don't know if I should leave him," Beth Ann said. "He's been having so many nightmares. I just never know when they'll hit. I signed that paper releasing the hospital of liability."

"That's good, dear. But I can take care of my son."

"I didn't mean to suggest you couldn't." Beth Ann put a hand on Jackie's arm. "Okay, I'll take a walk and be back soon. Someone is supposed to come and get him for X-rays any minute."

Once Beth Ann stepped outside into the fresh air, she was glad she'd taken Jackie up on her offer. The breeze whispered promises of winter, which had always arrived late in the Bay Area. The fog slowly rolled across the bay as the sunlight faded and left behind golden streaks that glistened through the trees. She walked for a short time and collected her thoughts. After a few minutes, she sat down on a bench and closed her eyes to whisper a prayer of thanks. *Dear God, thank you so much for returning Kaylob to me. I should have known you were listening. I know you must not like me anymore, and I'm sorry. I was so mad, but thank you anyway. Amen.*

After enjoying the fresh air as long as she could allow herself, she headed back to the room. She stopped in the doorway when she heard Jackie on the phone, not wanting to interrupt.

"Yes, Beth Ann is here with him and hasn't left his side." Jackie paused to listen to whoever was on the other end of the phone. "I know. Harold is here, but he's down in the cafeteria eating right now." Another pause. "Yes, he's being supportive for once."

Jackie was sitting with her back to Beth Ann, looking out the window. Kaylob wasn't in the bed, so they must have taken him for X-rays. Beth Ann didn't mean to eavesdrop, but she couldn't help but overhear.

"I know, Lillian. I miss you so much, but how is New York?" She paused. "I know. I want to see you too." She went silent. "I'm so sorry, it's never been fair you deserve to see Kaylob. I'm glad the nurse came and asked if your call could be put through." Her voice cracked. "I wish you could come too."

A nurse came walking down the hallway toward the room, so Beth Ann had to let her presence be known.

"Kaylob's on his way back from his tests and x-rays," the nurse said. "They're right behind me.

Beth Ann went in the room and Jackie hung up the phone. Kaylob arrived a minute later and a nurse and orderly transferred him from the gurney to the bed. He was completely out of it and seemed in pain. Jackie appeared anxious to leave, and Beth Ann wondered what that phone call had been all about.

"Try to get some sleep," Jackie said and gave her a quick hug.

After Jackie left, Beth Ann sat guard, afraid to leave Kaylob's side. She looked at the horror story played out on his body and wanted to heal every bruise, scar, and broken bone. Even his hair was thinner from the burns on his scalp. There was one area on his ribs covered with a large Ace bandage. She lifted the sheet to see if he had any other injuries but Kaylob stirred from his sleep and interrupted her.

He opened his beautiful blue eyes and gently took her hand. "Sweetheart, I'm not sure if they allow that sort of thing in the hospital." He winked with a smile. "But if you go lock the door tight, maybe we could find a way. Hell, who knows? That just might cure me."

Beth Ann chuckled, which felt good after all the stress. It was nice to see his humor hadn't been stolen away. But after just a few minutes of flirting and joking around, his eyes drifted closed again and he went back to sleep.

Beth Ann's thoughts returned to Jackie's phone conversation. She had a suspicion about it, and if she was right, it was a potential earthquake of an eight-point magnitude on the scale of emotions. Now wasn't the time to open that can of corn.

One thing Beth Ann knew for certain, she and Kaylob needed to be in each other's arms; because that was the place they had always called home.

* * * *

Blake sat at the desk in his office, trying to concentrate on some paperwork, but all he could think about was why the hell he was sitting there instead of going after his fiancée. He'd never loved anyone but Beth Ann, and he'd loved her since they were kids. He couldn't bear the thought of going back to an empty house and seeing all her clothes still hanging in the closet.

A knock on the door brought him back to reality. "Blake, you have a phone call on line one," his secretary Melissa said. "It's Mr. Duncan."

Melissa was the daughter of a business associate, Vincent Allen. Her dad had thought it would be good for his little girl to have a real job so she could learn responsibility and not grow up taking things for granted. Blake had hired her as a favor to his client and it had worked out well. Not only was Melissa a good secretary, she had been sweet and supportive since Beth Ann had left, always there trying to lift his spirits.

"Tell him I'm on a conference call and I'll call him later," Blake said glumly.

After Melissa closed the door, Blake pounded his fist on his desk. The decision had been made! It was time to go to San Francisco and *make* Beth Ann come home. He'd throw her over his shoulder if he had to. Unfortunately, the company plane was in use but he could drive there in about eight hours if he left now. He picked up the files on his desk and stuffed them into his briefcase.

Melissa smiled as he emerged from his office, but her smile faltered when he announced, "I need you to call all my clients and tell them I had an emergency. I'm going to San Francisco."

Melissa's eyes grew wide. "San Francisco? Are you going to go see Beth Ann?"

"You're damned right," Blake said, "and I'll be bringing her back with me, too. I'm going home to pack. I'll be gone for a few days."

Melissa stood and walked around her desk. "Do you think that's a good idea? Don't you think you should you respect Beth Ann's wishes?"

Blake looked at Melissa, his eyes narrowing. "I don't think that's any of your business, darlin. Just please do what I asked. I'll call you tomorrow morning." He gave her a partial smile, then turned toward the door and left.

* * * *

Later that day, while Beth Ann was napping by Kaylob's bed, something jarred her awake.

"*Ahhhh*...Get away from me, you sonofabitch!" Kaylob yelled and began thrashing around in the bed.

"Kaylob, wake up!" Beth Ann tried to catch one of his hands but couldn't. She frantically pushed the emergency button beside the bed then ran to the door and yelled down the hallway. "Help!"

When she looked at Kaylob again, he was ripping the IV out of his arm. "Get the hell away from me! I'll kill you, goddamn it!"

Beth Ann watched helplessly as pillows hit the floor, followed by a table that went crashing across the room as Kaylob tried to get out of bed.

"You goddamned pigs! I'll kill you all!"

A nurse and two orderlies came running into the room and rushed to where Kaylob had fallen to the floor beside the bed. The orderlies grabbed Kaylob, and the nurse took Beth Ann by the arm and led her out of the room.

"Please wait out here until we get him settled," she said. She hurried back into the room, leaving Beth Ann alone in the hallway, feeling numb and powerless.

Another crash came from inside the room and made her head spin. Feeling faint, she leaned against the wall and slowly slid to the floor where she wrapped her arms around her knees and began to cry. How much more could she take? Between Blake's threats and Kaylob's heartbreaking outbursts, she didn't know what to do.

A few seconds later, Dr. Richardson rushed by Beth Ann and entered Kaylob's room. There were no more crashes for several minutes. As Beth Ann waited, still huddled on the floor, one of the orderlies stepped out and looked down at her.

"My name is Stewart," he said kindly, his deep brown eyes showing concern. "We've given Kaylob a sedative, so he'll be out of it for a while. You should be able to go in soon, but I really think it would be best for you to go home. He's dangerous, both to himself and to others. It could take quite some time for him to return to normal."

"Are you crazy?" Beth Ann looked up defiantly. "No way I'm leaving him. I signed that damned paper and I'm staying, do you hear me? Nobody can make me leave."

Stewart bent over and helped her to her feet. "I understand," he said. "It's your choice. I just wanted you to know the truth. It might get worse before it gets better, and—"

"I'm staying. And Kaylob *will* get better."

He must have been well over six feet tall and she knew he could easily carry her out. But she remained firm.

Stewart nodded and sighed. "Again, it's your choice."

After he had gone back into the room, Beth Ann leaned against the wall again. She'd had no idea it was going to be this bad, but no matter how bad it got; she was determined to stay by Kaylob's side.

As she stood trying to collect herself, she saw Jackie and Harold coming down the hall. Harold was holding a newspaper and a coffee cup while Jackie carried two cups. Harold tucked the paper under his arm and surprised Beth Ann by giving her a warm hug. Kaylob's dad rarely showed emotions.

She told them what had happened and how Stewart had tried to get her to leave. Jackie was visibly upset, and Harold's brown eyes slanted with anger.

"That young man had no right to tell you that," Harold said. "He can't know what will happen. Kaylob *will* get better—and soon."

He turned and marched back down the hallway. As Beth Ann watched him go, Jackie said, "He really does love Kaylob. I just wish he'd been able to show that while he was growing up."

Beth Ann had often wondered if Harold loved his son. He was rarely around when Kaylob was growing up, and when he was all he did was bark orders for all the things he wanted Kaylob to do. Kaylob had worked more than any of the other kids she knew. And unlike Kaylob, Harold hardly ever smiled. They didn't even look alike—Harold was short with dark hair and Kaylob muscular, tall and blond.

Fifteen minutes later, Dr. Richardson came out in the hall and said, "Mrs. O'Brien, it might be a while before Kaylob is emotionally stable again." He glanced at Beth Ann and shook his head. "You can't get close to him when he's having that kind of rage. It's not safe."

Jackie latched on to Beth Ann's hand. "How long do you think Kaylob will go through this, doctor?"

"It's hard to say. With Vietnam Syndrome, it can last for years. We just don't know. It depends on the person and what they went through." He looked at Beth Ann again. "Maybe it would be best for you to go home and see where this goes, for your own good."

"No. I'm not leaving his side." Beth Ann's face heated. "You'll have to carry me out of here." She held the doctor's stare and stood her ground. "I signed those papers and was told I could stay. I don't want to hear anything about me leaving again."

He nodded. "Okay, it's up to you. But he may continue to have night terrors and flashbacks for a while, and you can also expect personality change, anger and rage. He might not want to be around people either. Sometimes they isolate themselves."

A nurse approached and handed some pamphlets to the doctor that he gave to Jackie and Beth Ann. They were filled with information about Vietnam Syndrome, which she would read them later.

Jackie took off in search of Harold, but Beth Ann had only one place she wanted to be—by Kaylob's side. She would fight for him, just like he had fought for his country.

Alone in the room with Kaylob, Beth Ann wanted to lie beside him and hold him but was afraid of what the hospital would say. To hell with it, she would do it anyway. Gingerly, she climbed next to him and lay her head across his heart, then she gazed at him and saw his eyes open. He cradled her face, giving her a long, lingering kiss.

"I love you, Beth Ann, with all my heart," he said, just before he drifted back to sleep.

She cuddled with him for over an hour, listening to his heartbeat and touching his chest and arms. After a while, what she needed was to stretch her legs, so she eased herself off the bed and went down the hall to the restroom. On the way back to the room, she decided to call her two best friends in Riverside, Frankie Russo and Carol Thomas. Then she called her very best friend in the world, Lisa Lane.

Hours later, while Beth Ann was reading, Kaylob reached out for her with trembling hands, his forehead covered with sweat. This once-strong man now needed her for comfort. She vowed to give him everything he needed. It was time for her to be a brave soldier of a different kind.

Beth Ann believed with all her heart that he would make it through this. Their dreams were at stake, the future they had been planning since childhood. He wanted to be a chef and open a restaurant. She had become the Broadway star she had dreamed of as a child, but her dream had always included having Kaylob by her side. They had planned to grow old together. Kaylob wanted children, but that conversation would have to come at another time, even if it was just with herself.

* * * *

Hours later Blake pulled out his overnight bag and neatly packed enough clothes for three days, making sure everything was color coordinated. He just *had* to see Beth Ann. He couldn't stand it anymore. Everyone in the free world had been calling him constantly—except her. Once he had her alone in the hotel, he'd be able to prove how much they really loved each other. She'd touched his heart in a way he never even knew he needed.

He folded the last shirt into the bag when the phone rang once. He knew Dana must have answered it. A moment later, there was a knock at his door.

"Come in," he called, not looking up from packing.

"Beth Ann is on the phone," Dana said as she opened the door and stared at the bag on the bed. "She wants to talk to you."

Blake closed his bag, picked up the phone and said, "Hello?"

"You can't come here," Beth Ann said firmly. "Please don't do this."

"How did you know I was coming?" Blake demanded. "Who told you?"

"It doesn't matter who told me," Beth Ann replied. "What matters is that you can't come here, Blake!"

"Like hell I can't! You're engaged to me, and that's the end of it."

"Blake, if you come here I'll never forgive you!" Beth Ann's voice rose. "You don't understand what a fragile state Kaylob's in." There was a long pause, then she said, "I need to end things between us, Blake. I'm not coming back and—"

Blake slammed the receiver down, then he picked up the phone and threw it across the room. There was no way in hell he'd let her end things over the telephone. God, he needed a drink—maybe more than one. He stormed downstairs to get drunk enough to forget that his heart had just been blasted.

Chapter Three

A few days later, Beth Ann was finally beginning to feel a bit safer since Blake hadn't shown up at the hospital. The only time she left Kaylob's side was to eat, go to the bathroom, or stretch her legs. The nurses tried to encourage her to rest, and one nurse even offered her an unused On-Call Room, but Beth Ann insisted that she needed to stay by the man she loved.

Although it was slow going, Kaylob's condition began to improve. Every time he started to yell, Beth Ann would sing to him—and it worked wonders. The staff was amazed to see how it relaxed him. However, lack of sleep and Kaylob's outbursts were definitely beginning to strip the sheen off Beth Ann's spirit.

One morning when Beth Ann returned from walking up and down the hallway to stretch her legs, she entered the room to an uplifting sight. Kaylob was sitting up eating a cookie, laughing with the orderly named Stewart. Beth Ann stood transfixed in the doorway, watching until their eyes met.

Kaylob winked and gave her a loving smile, then he wiggled his index finger to call her over. "Sweetheart," he said, "you look really tired. I think you could use a nap."

"I'm okay." Beth Ann forced a smile. "I've been sleeping on the two chairs by the bed." After Stewart had excused himself and left the room, she sat beside Kaylob on the edge of the bed.

He took one of her hands in his and kissed her palm. "Please Beth Ann, don't make me have to get out of this bed and carry you. Stewart tells me you haven't had any real sleep since you came here. Sleeping on those metal chairs can't be comfortable."

It took several minutes of insistence from Kaylob, but Beth Ann finally agreed to get some rest. Just as she got to her feet, a nurse walked in and Beth Ann saw her give Kaylob a sly wink and knew they had all worked out this scheme together. Kaylob just raised his eyebrows to acknowledge that Beth Ann's suspicions were correct. He lifted her hand to give it one last kiss but stopped short, his eyes widening.

"I seem to remember a ring on your finger before, and it wasn't mine. And neither of them is there now." He looked up at her, his blue eyes turning serious. "I guess there are still some things we need to talk about."

Beth Ann nodded and leaned over to kiss his forehead. "Yes, we have a lot to catch up on," she whispered, "but I think we should wait until you're out of the hospital."

Her heart was in her throat, but she wasn't about to cause Kaylob more pain by talking about any other man—and especially not about Blake. Heck, she didn't even know he had seen the ring. Why hadn't she taken it off sooner?

The nurse cleared her throat, no doubt waiting for Beth Ann. The staff had arranged for Beth Ann to rest in an old On-Call Room that had been used for doctors in the past. Now that Kaylob was feeling better, she could get some sleep. The nurse led her to the room and opened the door. Relief and elation filled Beth Ann when she saw a little twin bed with civilian pillows and real pillowcases. As soon as her body hit the bed, she was out.

Later on when she awoke, she couldn't remember where she was. *Had everything been a dream*? After a few seconds, she got her bearings and flicked on the table lamp. Beside it, she found a note left by Carmen, the head nurse with the green eyes and large... never mind.

*You are welcome to take a shower. I
put your stuff in the closet. Hope you
rested well. This room is not used by
doctors since they have a newer one,
so it's yours to use anytime you want. I
left the key to the room in the
bathroom near your makeup bag. And
don't worry about Kaylob. I'm more
than happy to take extra time with him.
Carmen*

Well, of course she was. Most women had always been willing. Putting floozies aside, taking a daily shower definitely sounded wonderful. Beth Ann couldn't remember the last time she'd taken one. She'd just been washing up in the bathroom.

A glance at the alarm clock informed her she'd been asleep for six hours. When she jumped into the inviting spray, it felt like Heaven. She stood under the stream for at least fifteen minutes and let the warm water rush over her. It made her feel human again.

After she was dried off, she opened her makeup bag and noticed Blake's ring. Oh God, she had to call him and she had to do it now. She couldn't avoid the unavoidable. She had to try to talk reasonably with him and hoped he wouldn't hang up again.

Since childhood, Blake had always been charming. When she'd seen him on the opening night of her show and he'd kissed her, it had been nice, but she was still suffering over Kaylob. But when she saw him five months later, she had been more than ready for a distraction, but his devotion to her had made her grow to love him.

But not the way she loved Kaylob.

Once she was done with her makeup, she took a deep breath, let it out, and tried to prepare emotionally for the conversation with Blake. A few seconds later, she stepped out of the On-Call Room and went back to the payphone and called collect.

"Hello, Beth Ann," he drawled.

"Blake," she said in a soft voice, glancing around at the people coming and going. "We need to talk."

His voice was measured. "What do you want from me this time? To kick me down to my knees?"

"Blake, please," she said. "I'm so sorry. I don't want to hurt you."

"Please don't then. Answer this for me—have I made you happy?"

"Yes, you made me very happy. You're a fantastic man, and I've enjoyed my time with you. But... I can't be with you." She took a deep breath so she could continue. "There's no amount of time I could take that would ever change my mind. I'm going to have Frankie and Carol pick up my stuff."

"No they won't, because I won't let them in." His voice was getting louder. "Don't I deserve more than this? You're not gonna walk away like I meant nothing! That's bullshit. I won't accept you breaking up with me over the phone."

He was right. He deserved more, but she needed to end things with him now and couldn't leave Kaylob's side to do it in person. For now, she would just have Frankie pick up a few of her clothes and see Blake later. Jesus, this was a mess. A couple of people walked by, which made it even harder to say the things she needed to say. She huddled into the corner of the payphone, trying to hide the tears streaming down her face.

"Blake, you mean a lot to me and always will, but... I'm so very sorry. I'll have Frankie pick up *some* of my clothes."

"Goddamn it, Beth Ann! I love you so much. Don't do this to me..."

When his voice cracked, her heart splintered and made it twice as hard to tell him the whole truth, so she didn't. She couldn't hurt him more by telling him that she'd always loved Kaylob more.

He was silent for a minute, then he said, "You don't know how much he's changed. I've read about guys when they come home from war. He's gonna be different. He could be—"

"Yes, he's different," she said, "but he's still Kaylob. I don't want to talk about him with you. It only hurts you, and I don't want to do that."

She heard him sigh, obviously trying to control his emotions. She rubbed her hand through her hair.

"Blake, I promise we'll talk face to face. Just not now." When he didn't answer she said, "I want you to find someone who'll give you everything you need and deserve. But you have to understand that it can't be me."

A dial tone was all she got in reply. Tears stung her eyes, and a lump formed in her throat that slid down to her stomach. She went back into the On-Call Room and tried to fix her makeup stained eyes, then she took a deep, cleansing breath before heading back to Kaylob's room.

When she got to the door, she heard Kaylob laughing and saw Nurse Jezebel fluffing his pillows. The nurse touched his arm and wiggled her behind when she left, giving a nod to Beth Ann. Some things never change. Beth Ann felt herself turning a familiar green color, one she hadn't expected to wear so soon. When she looked at Kaylob, she could tell he was trying to suppress his laughter, but he failed miserably.

"Very funny, Mr. O'Brien," she said, arching an eyebrow.

He winked at her. "What did you like more, when she touched my arm or when she shook her behind?"

"I like that I let her live," Beth Ann said.

She sat in the chair beside his bed, and he rubbed his thumb under her eyes, his mood changed instantly. He picked up her left hand and stared at her bare finger.

"You're gonna have to come clean with me sooner or later," he said.

Beth Ann gazed at him. "As soon as we get out of here and have some real privacy, I'll tell you everything." She fidgeted in her seat.

He nodded and pulled her closer. "Relax, sweetheart. I love you and nothing's ever going to change that. But, I'm wondering if you're still in love with me?"

Beth Ann moved her face towards his. "Mr. O'Brien, I've always been in love with you and nothing will ever change that." She moved her face even closer and held his gaze.

"Ah, baby," he said, just above a whisper.

His breath on her mouth and his sweet words left her dazed. When their lips touched, she emptied every emotion from her heart and soul into that one kiss. His gasp for air confirmed what she suspected; he was turned on. Their tongues danced in harmony and he deepened the kiss. Nobody had ever kissed her like Kaylob. They were twin flames with a connection that could never be broken. But would he be as loving once he found out about Blake? Would his kisses be as sweet?

When Kaylob was sleeping again, Beth Ann decided to take a walk outside so she could try to collect her thoughts. The morning had proven to be a roller coaster of emotions, but at least she'd gotten some sleep. She headed toward the elevators and was startled to see some familiar and beloved faces coming up the hallway. Carol, Frankie and her former neighbor, Jack Schell, must have seen her at the same moment, because they sprinted toward her.

"How are you doing, Beth Ann?" Frankie pulled her into his arms, his forehead crinkled in worry.

That almost brought tears to Beth Ann's eyes. Being with her best friends was a dose of love she needed desperately. When Carol and Jack moved into the circle and embraced her too, she couldn't hold back the tears.

She pointed to Kaylob's room, her voice just shy of a whisper, "He had barely fallen asleep when I left."

But when she looked up, Kaylob was standing in the doorway. He seemed surprised at first to see his friends, but when he saw Frankie with his arms still around Beth Ann, his expression changed to hurt mixed with a hint of anger. He turned and stepped back into his room.

"How about I meet you guys at the cafeteria in a few minutes?" Beth Ann said.

Jack and Carol agreed, but they both looked distressed as they headed away. Frankie lingered behind and glanced at Kaylob's room then back to Beth Ann.

"You haven't told him about Blake yet, have you?"

Beth Ann shook her head. "Not until we're out of here. But from the look he just gave you, I can see I need to tell him right now that it wasn't you."

"Good idea." Frankie sighed, and gave her arm a gentle squeeze then took off to join the others.

When Beth Ann walked back into Kaylob's room, it felt as though someone had turned on the air conditioner full blast. Her attempt at checking Kaylob's emotional temperature was met with a cold rejection of her outstretched hand.

"So it was Frankie?" he said, glancing down at her hand.

"No, Kaylob. It was not Frankie." She covered the ring-less finger.

"Then who…?"

"We have plenty time to talk." She paused. "I just don't think this is the place for us to have a heart-to-heart talk. It seems like you're getting better, so hopefully you'll be released soon. And right now, I need to go to the cafeteria. Our friends are waiting for us there."

He took a deep breath. "Okay, let's go."

He stood and started to slip on his robe, but he lost his balance. Beth Ann tried to help but he waved her away. "I guess I can't even put on my own robe!"

In the next instant, the water pitcher flew across the room and crashed against the wall, drenching her in the splash.

Chapter Four

"Shit...." Kaylob looked at the ground then back at Beth Ann. "I'm sorry, baby." He took his robe and started drying her off.

Still in distress, she moved to the sink and grabbed some paper towels. She felt her heart dive at the thought of his mood swings.

"Kaylob, I was just trying to help you."

His face fell as he watched her. "I apologize. Hell, I guess I'm insane now." He moved next to her and lifted her chin. "Can you forgive me?"

She nodded. "Of course. Let's go. Everybody's waiting." She took his hand and kissed his cheek.

On the way to the cafeteria, they stopped at the nurse's station to tell them about the mess in the room.

Once they stepped inside the elevator Kaylob turned towards her and pulled her into his arms.

"I love you." He melted a kiss across her mouth.

That was all it took for her to forget about the last few minutes. "I love you too," she whispered into his lips and heard him growl. She recognized that growl and had to chuckle.

Once they arrived at the cafeteria, their three friends came over to greet Kaylob.

Carol hugged him first. "Welcome home, you big lug."

Jack was already tearing up. "I'm so glad you're home." He shook Kaylob's hand, but Kaylob pulled him into a hug.

Frankie and Kaylob stood there for a minute before Frankie said, "We cool, bro?" He studied Kaylob's face.

Kaylob pretended to punch him in the arm and they laughed. Beth Ann sighed in relief.

While they sat at one of the large tables, sharing stories and laughing about Frankie's lifestyle, it almost seemed like old times. Frankie and Kaylob started in about sports, which was like a foreign language to the other three in the group, so they ended up talking about music and dancing.

As the conversations went on, Beth Ann noticed Carol seemed different. It was as if her rebellious nature had been tempered, leaving a soothing calmness behind. She was also positively glowing.

"What's going on with you, Carol?" Beth Ann asked finally. "Something's changed."

She noticed a blush spread across Carol's beautiful mocha skin. She had always been so stunning with her long lean legs and fabulous dance skills. Beth Ann had met Carol in Riverside at the Lakeside School of Performing Arts where Carol had been one of their best teachers.

"Could it be possible that you finally have a special someone in your life?" Beth Ann moved her eyes back and forth between Carol and Frankie.

Carol shook her head. "It's not Frankie."

"Okay, who is he then? Do I know him?"

"No, you don't know her."

"But..." Confusion mixed with surprise washed over Beth Ann. "You've talked about guys..." She lowered her voice and glanced cautiously at Kaylob then back at Carol. "We've compared notes. And look at how you've talked about Frankie and how good-looking he is."

"I notice beautiful people. Frankie is tall, dark and handsome. His Italian skin and those dark green eyes... I mean, for a guy, he's really sexy." She looked at Frankie and winked. "I was going to tell you anyway because we've had pictures taken by those camera snoopers." "And..." She almost whispered. "I didn't want you to find out from a gossip magazine."

All the clues suddenly became clear to Beth Ann. "Was I the last to know?" she asked.

Kaylob winked. "Looks that way, sweetheart. I had my suspicions, but it wasn't my place to say anything."

Beth Ann frowned at Frankie. "I suppose you and Jack both knew."

They both nodded and Carol said, "You'll meet her soon enough. She's moved in with me. I love her."

"Well, that's great news," Beth Ann said, taking Carol's hand. "I'm happy for both of you. What's her name?"

"It's Shelia, and she's from Tacoma. You know the one from Washington that I was always running off to see. She's thirty-three and wonderful."

"Mrs. Robinson, are you trying to seduce me?" Frankie cracked, prompting Carol to smack him with the back of her hand.

Beth Ann laughed. "I watched *The Graduate*."

Frankie chuckled. "I lived *The Graduate*." He looked at Kaylob and grinned. "From what I hear, so did Kaylob back in Jr. High School."

Kaylob gave Frankie a playful punch, then he immediately stared into his coffee cup as if there was something important inside.

Carol laughed. "You're going to love her, and she's not that much older— only eight years. She taught at the University of Washington. We met at a fundraiser in Santa Barbara. She left her job to move in with me a few weeks ago, and we're hoping she gets a job at the University of California in Riverside soon."

"Wow," Beth Ann exclaimed. "That was fast."

Carol laughed again. "Not really, but that's another story."

Jack cracked up. "I always knew you were one of us. It takes one to know one."

Jack was a cute little guy with brown curly hair and a flair for fashion. He had been her favorite neighbor at her old apartment in Riverside. His tall, refined partner, Lenard, was the complete opposite of Jack, and Beth Ann loved them both.

After an hour or so, Beth Ann noticed that Kaylob looked tired. She was about to ask him if he wanted to leave when a big crash came from the kitchen. Kaylob was out of his chair so fast that it crashed to the floor, then he fell to the ground and covered his head.

Everyone at the table froze as Beth Ann got up to go to him. When he looked up at her, his eyes reminded her of a wild animal.

She put a comforting hand on his back. "Honey, it's okay. Someone dropped something in the kitchen."

Frankie moved beside her to help Kaylob up. A look of relief and embarrassment swept across Kaylob's face when he took Frankie's hand.

"I'm feeling a little rundown. Maybe it's time for me to go back to my room." He paused and looked at his friends, his face flushed. "I'm sorry, guys. Thanks for coming all this way to see me."

Frankie put his hand on Kaylob's shoulder. "Of course we couldn't wait." Everyone smiled and nodded.

When they arrived back at Kaylob's room, each person took turns saying their goodbyes.

Frankie hugged him twice and said, "I'm so glad your home, bro. I've missed you. Call if you need anything."

After Kaylob was settled back in bed, Beth Ann rejoined her friends in the hallway. Carol scrunched her forehead and asked, "Is he gonna be okay?"

"Yes, it just takes time." Beth Ann gave her a tiny smile.

Frankie touched her cheek. "If you need anything, you call, okay? I can take a few days away from school."

Beth Ann hugged him. "Thanks, but he'll be back to normal in no time. He's just been through a lot. Don't worry, I'll be fine."

Carol and Frankie nodded and started to leave, but Jack lingered behind.

"Go ahead, I'll catch up," he said. After they were around the corner, he stepped closer to Beth Ann.

"What about Blake, honey? What are you going to do?"

"I broke up with him. Jack. It was so awful. He wouldn't accept it. Would you please ask Frankie to go pick up some of my clothes for me?"

Jack nodded. "I feel bad for Blake, but Kaylob is the one you're meant to be with. Everybody knows that." His face softened. "Don't worry about Blake. I know he must be hurt, but what Kaylob is going through must be a hundred times worse."

Beth Ann took his hand. "More like a million times. I've had to turn into a soldier of another kind. I'll fight for Kaylob to win this war. Our entire future and all our hopes and dreams are at stake."

Jack moved his hand to her face. "You've grown up so much over the last few years. Kaylob's going to be surprised and proud at your maturity."

"Thank you, Jack." They hugged and Beth Ann watched him walk away, trying to swallow back her emotions.

I have grown up she thought as she placed her hand across her heart.

Chapter Five

The days melted by like a candle in the sun. Beth Ann and Kaylob both wondered when he would be released. He was stronger and had gained weight, so it shouldn't be too much longer. With all the time on their hands, they had time to make plans but hadn't. The only significant choice they'd made was to postpone any conversations about what had happened while they'd been apart. Of course, they got some fine kissing in. If Beth Ann had her way, that was how they'd spend the rest of the time there—lip sucking and making out.

The rest of the world nibbled at the outside of their shell, occasionally coming inside when needed. More than a few times, she had to ditch magazines that had stories about her and Blake. She had agreed to let their hometown paper, *The Novato Advance* come in and do a story on Kaylob, which had included plenty of their history. She had told them not to ask anything about her life while he was gone. Even so, the gossip papers were going to love the information and would twist everything.

Every time she thought about Blake, a pain rippled through her chest. There was no doubt that if he read the article, he'd be more than a little upset. In all honesty, she was still worried about him showing up at the hospital. So Friday morning while Kaylob slept, she tiptoed out and made a call. She used her change this time so she wouldn't have to call collect.

"Hello, Tanner residence," Dana answered.

"Hi, Dana. It's me, Beth Ann."

"Oh, hi, Beth Ann." Dana's tone was quiet.

"Is Blake there?"

"No, he's gone for a few days. He said he needed to get out of town, so he went to Vegas."

"Oh, good. I hope he has fun." Beth Ann paused. "He's always loved Vegas."

"I hope so. He's been so angry and drinking so much. But he said he wasn't coming to the hospital."

Beth Ann was relieved to hear that and went on to tell Dana about the article. She also reminded her about the wedding gown and asked her to put any delivered packages in the spare room. Just before they hung up, she was sure Dana was crying, which made her feel like crap. Dana had always been so sweet and had made Beth Ann feel at home. At least she knew Dana would watch over Blake. She had always been so protective.

Later that afternoon, Beth Ann sat by Kaylob's bed, trying to keep her eyes open and finally feeling some peace of mind, even if only for a day. Just as she was nodding off, she looked up to see a tall guy in an army uniform standing in the doorway. Her eyes followed his uniform up to his face and she saw a very handsome man with dark hair and olive skin.

He smiled. "You're Beth Ann, O'Brien's fiancée, right?"

"Yes, that's me." She nodded.

"Ah, the redhead. Your pictures don't do you justice." A smile slid across his rugged face. "You were right. He's alive and looking mighty damn good."

"John!" She stood up and gave him a huge grin. John Patterson was one of the few people she had confided in about her visions and dreams of Kaylob. He was the only person who'd been willing to believe Kaylob might still be alive and hadn't thought Beth Ann was completely out of her mind. He strode over to her and gave her a giant hug.

"It's good to finally meet you, Beth Ann."

"You too, John." She swallowed back tears. "Thank you for coming."

After he released her, Beth Ann noticed Kaylob's eyes were wide open and looking right at the man in uniform. He shifted in bed, holding out his hand.

"Patterson, Jesus! I was wondering if you were alive. I wanted to ask, but with all that was going on…I guess I was afraid of what they'd tell me."

"O'Brien, I can't believe my eyes." John shook his hand. "It's good to see you. Man, you're a sight."

Kaylob sat up on the edge of his bed. He looked at Beth Ann and nodded toward his robe. She grabbed it and helped him put it on.

"Thanks, sweetheart."

She touched his hand and moved out of the way. Kaylob stood with a sheen of tears in his eyes. And when John pulled Kaylob into a hug, she had to force back the lump in her own throat.

John backed up and looked Kaylob directly in the eyes. "How do I ever thank you for saving my life? I wouldn't be standing here if it weren't for you." His voice quivered.

"Hey, seeing you…" Kaylob swallowed. "That's all the thanks I need. For over two years, I didn't know if you were alive or dead."

Beth Ann felt horrible for not telling him something sooner. "I'm so sorry, honey. I should have told you John was alive. I didn't know you thought he was dead."

Kaylob touched her hand and smiled. "Not your fault, sweetheart."

John nodded. "I met your parents last year when I made a trip to your hometown. Novato's a cute little place." He turned to look at Beth Ann. "I've had many conversations with your girl here. She always thought you were alive."

She smiled. "Yes, I did."

Kaylob squeezed her hand. "Yeah, she's pretty special."

John looked back and forth between the two of them. "As soon as I got to the POW camp where they were holding you, I was stunned. The place was exactly how Beth Ann had described it. She's really something." John paused before going on. "But when I got there, they said you hadn't been found. Now I know they thought you were someone else. Leave it to the Army to screw that up. Jesus, man, when I found out you were alive, I couldn't wait to come and see you."

Kaylob looked from Beth Ann to John and grinned. "Thanks bud. I'm sure as hell glad you came. This has made my day."

John backed up toward the door. "A few other guys are here to see you too, O'Brien." He motioned for them to come in.

The guy that came in first was in a wheelchair. Kaylob's jaw dropped.

"Well, I'll be dammed." Kaylob walked over and put his arm around the man, then he glanced over at Beth Ann. "Beth Ann, this is Chris Donavan from Bravo Company."

She went over to shake his hand. "Nice to meet you, Chris."

"You too." Chris grinned and looked up at Kaylob. "Nice to see you in the land of the living, O'Brien."

"Man, you don't even know how often I wondered if you guys made it out alive." Kaylob's face looked serious.

Two more guys walked in and stood in the doorway looking at Kaylob. He was clearly shocked to see them.

"Well, I'll be double dammed. If this isn't Christmas, I don't know what is. Johnston and Langston, I can't believe this." Kaylob walked over and shook their hands.

Johnston took Kaylob's arm. "You look like hell, O'Brien. But at least you're alive, and that looks damn good."

They all laughed. Kaylob led him over to Beth Ann and introduced them.

"So you're the redhead that's always right." He took Beth Ann's hand and raised his eyebrows with a chuckle. "I heard all about you every minute of every day. I'm Mike, by the way."

Beth Ann felt her cheeks flush when she shook his hand. "Always right?" She arched an eyebrow at Kaylob. "Nice to meet you, Mike. I suppose I'm mostly right." She glanced over at John and grinned. "Right, John?"

He nodded. "True statement. But a long story."

"Hey, don't forget me," the other guy said. "I'm Andy Langston, and I'm the one who kept O'Brien in line." He smiled at Kaylob then stepped over and shook Beth Ann's hand.

"Nice to meet you, Andy." Beth Ann chuckled.

After he quit shaking her hand, Andy turned and put his hand on Kaylob's shoulder. "Good to see you, man. You're looking better than I thought you would after spending over two years at that resort. I heard you were in one of the best kinds."

Kaylob threw his head back in laughter. "Yeah, best pampering you could ever get."

The laughter gave way to an awkward silence. Then Mike cleared his throat and said, "None of us would be alive if it wasn't for you." He swiped away the tears and pointed to his friend in the wheelchair. "Go ahead, Chris. We got your back."

Chris Donavan clutched the arms of the wheelchair while he fought to stand. With a look of deep concentration, he managed to get to his feet. After a few wobbly seconds and with sheer determination, he took two steps to Kaylob and hugged him.

"I love ya, O'Brien." His eyes pooled. "I can tell you that I'm alive and getting the chance to walk again because of you."

Kaylob returned his hug but was too choked up to say anything.

Chris and Nick helped him sit back down. Beth Ann swallowed her own tears, and the look on Kaylob's face made her really understand completely for the first time why he'd had to go back to the war again. The memory of the tantrum she'd thrown when Kaylob told her he'd volunteered to go back for a second tour made her feel ashamed of her selfishness.

Although, that might have been the best tantrum she'd ever thrown, because it had led to the most beautiful days of her life. In the process of making up, they'd made love for seven beautiful days, their first time after waiting so many years. Just thinking of those days made her wonder if they would ever have them back again. Would he ever be that same beautiful man he was back then? The man who'd given her seven roses for their seven glorious nights together and had named every one of them.

Of course, he would be—why was she even asking that?

Her thoughts were interrupted when John moved close and put his arm around her shoulder. "So, Beth Ann, how about dumping this big guy and marrying me instead?"

Kaylob gave him a playful shove, then all the guys busted up.

"So what happened with the girl in that picture?" Kaylob asked John.

"Oh, you know, nothing much. I married her and she's going to have my baby in three months. I guess you might say that after almost losing my life, I had a wake-up call. I realized that she loved me and hell, I love her too. A very wise man once told me that when you find the right one, there's no need to look around anymore." He winked at Kaylob.

"Ha—good for you, Patterson." Kaylob placed his hand on his shoulder. "Congratulations."

Beth Ann gave John a hug. "I'm happy for you too."

"Thank you both. For more than you know." He glanced at Kaylob, and the look was one of love, respect, and honor all wrapped up in one. "I wouldn't be getting a chance at fatherhood without you."

Beth Ann looked around the room and saw all the guys fighting back emotions. Okay, that did it. Her eyeballs were officially leaking. She excused herself and left to go to the restroom.

When she returned, they were all sharing stories about different things they'd gone through. Mike talked about his stress disorder and how his wife had found him standing on the roof of the house one night, yelling and scaring the children.

"She just couldn't handle my outbursts anymore and left with the kids," he said quietly. "I don't blame her."

Beth Ann felt awful for him. There was nothing Kaylob could do to make her walk away from him. How could she do that to her husband?

Before the guys left, they handed over a bundle of letters from the men of Bravo Company. Beth Ann learned that Kaylob had not only rescued, possibly, ten guys, but also a chain of men who had gone on to rescue others. Without Kaylob, that chain of rescues might never have happened. John explained that Kaylob was responsible for saving more lives than he would ever know.

After the men left, Kaylob pulled Beth Ann into his arms coaxed her to lie with him on the bed. He gave her a lingering kiss as more tears fell from her eyes.

"Ah, don't cry, baby," Kaylob whispered.

"These are good tears," she said. "I'm so proud of you."

"Thank you, Beth Ann." He lifted her hand to his lips and pressed a kiss into her palm. "I know things have been hard for you. I hope you can forgive me."

"There's nothing I need to forgive," she said, melting into his arms. The man holding her at that moment was *her* Kaylob—the man she had loved since childhood.

* * * *

Beth Ann was more than ready for Kaylob to be released from the hospital. But while one part of her was excited, another part was terrified. What if, once Kaylob found out about Blake, he walked away and never looked back? What would she do? Surely, Kaylob would understand, wouldn't he?

If the truth be known, she had been angry with Kaylob for leaving her again, and when he had been declared dead she fell apart. But all that was over now and she couldn't lose him again. Just thinking about it made her stomach turn.

The next Sunday morning, someone notified Kaylob that the army had put the finishing touches on bringing him back to life—at least administratively. They had gotten his identity situation taken care of, along with his back pay, promotions and social security card. They also officially notified him of his honorable discharge and let him know there would be an award ceremony to present him with a Purple Heart and a Distinguished Service Cross. Kaylob was one of the few enlisted guys that got out alive from what Beth Ann understood, and she was grateful for that.

Despite all the good news, Kaylob still refused to talk about his time as a POW, and Beth Ann wasn't about to push him. Clearly, something happened when the guys left war. The war might be over, but the battles continued to rage inside them.

Later that morning, Dr. Richardson came into the room, picked up Kaylob's chart and studied it. "Good morning," he said as he pushed his glassed back in place. "Well, Kaylob, how would you like to go home tomorrow?"

Kaylob's face lit up. "Hell, yes!"

It was all Beth Ann could do to keep him from getting out of bed to start packing right then. This was the most excited she had seen him since his return. After the doctor left and things settled down, Beth Ann spent time on the phone calling everyone to let them know that Kaylob was getting out. She also made reservations in the small town of Bodega Bay, sixty-five miles north of San Francisco. It was the sleepy fishing village where *The Birds* had been filmed. After spending an hour searching for accommodations, she found a hotel that featured cottages by the ocean, each with a little yard where they could sit and talk. Providing the weather stayed warm enough.

The next morning finally arrived and they headed to Bodega Bay. Kaylob held the map and navigated while Beth Ann drove. His parents had rented a mid-size car for them since Beth Ann's car was still in Novato and the paparazzi knew what it looked like. Kaylob seemed a little puzzled by the need for a rental car, but hadn't asked many questions—yet. Beth Ann was thrilled to be leaving the hospital but felt her throat tighten at the prospect of what was to come. Maybe she could pretend to have laryngitis and be unable to talk.

Right. As if that would work.

While they drove down Highway 1, Beth Ann clutched the steering wheel so tightly that her fingers began to hurt. The scenery was beautiful, but it was hard to enjoy. The closer they got to the ocean, the more her nerves gnawed at her. Kaylob must have noticed, because she began to feel him staring at her.

"Can we pull over and stretch?" he asked after a while. "I think your hands are going to fall off from gripping the steering wheel so tight."

"I'm just excited," she said unconvincingly. "But I'll stop at the next pullout area we come to. A stretch sounds good."

When she parked and turned off the engine, she saw Kaylob wince as he opened the door and started to get out. It was clear he was still sore, but when Beth Ann tried to help him, he waved her away and wanted to do it himself. She turned and gazed at the birds floating skillfully on the ocean breeze. If only she could feel that relaxed and at peace.

Kaylob strolled over and laced his fingers in hers; she was delighted to see his lips slightly curve up. At least he seemed happy. He led her to the edge of the hillside, and they stood staring at the shore twenty feet below. Golden streaks lit the sky and reflected on the ocean. Waves crashed against the rocks, sometimes sending a salty spray skyward. The sense of peace she'd been wishing for earlier came over her for a moment, but she knew they were merely completing one journey and preparing for an even more challenging one.

As the breeze blew her hair around, Kaylob turned and embraced her, his lips finding hers. The heat that soared through her made her melt. How could he make her world tilt with just one kiss?

After he pulled away, he gazed into her eyes and said softly, "I missed you so bad, sweetheart. It feels so good to hold you again."

He pulled her closer, and she could feel how badly he needed her. His scent and the hardness of his body made her know exactly what he wanted. Couldn't they just forget the past and not talk about it?

"Beth Ann, are you okay?" he asked in the deep, husky tone that only he had.

"Yes, honey," she replied with the best smile she could give. "You're just spinning the same magic spell on me you always have."

"Has anyone else been able to do that to you?"

He held her gaze while he waited for her answer. Her stomach seemed to dive right over the cliff, but she shook her head.

"No. Nobody has ever spun me like you."

He kept looking at her, and she sensed he was summoning the courage to pose the next question. Finally, he said, "I want to talk. I need to know some things."

She could feel her pulse in her throat. Trying to postpone the inevitable a little longer, she said, "Don't you want to get checked into our room first?"

He didn't look away. "No, not until we talk."

She turned again and watched the waves crashing on the jagged rocks below, afraid to speak. This was it—there was no way out.

Kaylob turned her face back around to him. "Please, Beth Ann. Just tell me."

She drew a heavy sigh. "I'm trying to decide where to start."

"Well, how about telling me who gave you that ring," he suggested. "You know? The one you took off. That would be a good start."

Chapter Six

She sighed again. Should she try to break it to him gently or just blurt it all out? She decided to get it over with.

"It was Blake."

Kaylob's jaw clenched, but he said nothing.

When she couldn't bear the silence any longer, she put her hand on his chest and looked up at him with pleading eyes. "Please say something, Kaylob."

After what seemed like an eternity, he said, "Tell me it's another Blake and not Blake Tanner. Why would he be America's most eligible bachelor?" Her face must have registered her shock, because he said, "Yeah, I saw the magazine you tossed away the other day when you thought I was asleep. I fished it out of the garbage can. The cover said you were torn between your childhood love and America's most eligible bachelor, but it only showed a picture of you. A nurse came in before I could read any more, and later it was gone."

He paused a long moment, gazing intently into her eyes.

"Are you *really* torn, Beth Ann?"

She tried to swallow, but her mouth felt as dry as the Mojave Desert. "No, Kaylob. Never—not for a second. I wish I could tell you it wasn't Blake Tanner, but I can't."

He gritted his words through his teeth. "How long have you been with him?"

She reached out and put her hand on top of his. "Kaylob, please, can we stop here and do this later?"

There was an uncomfortable silence, then he turned away and looked out at the ocean. "Okay, but this conversation isn't over."

They walked back to the car and she tried to shake off the horrible feeling that was slithering inside her heart. She started the car and pulled back onto the highway. As they drove, she didn't want the radio on and Kaylob didn't want to talk, so the only sounds were the road noise and the ocean outside the window. Occasionally, she glanced at him, barely taking her eyes off the road in an attempt to decipher his mood. Each time she found him staring out at the landscape.

When they pulled into the hotel parking lot and headed toward the office, Kaylob didn't even look her way. In a million years, she'd never imagine him not opening her door for her.

After they walked into the office, she smelled the inviting aroma of coffee. The coziness of the lobby and the fireplace normally would have put her at ease, but the tsunami of emotions washing over her prevented it. Then when she saw Kaylob pick up a magazine, a warning siren went off in her head. Oh, lord! Just what she needed!

She rushed to his side and tried to take the magazine from his hand. "Honey, please. You shouldn't look at that garbage."

He caught her wrist, his eyes flashing with dark rage. "Stop, Beth Ann. What are you afraid of?"

"Kaylob, please," she protested, knowing the magazine contained pictures of her and Blake with their arms wrapped around each other.

"I guess you don't want me to see you with your boyfriend, huh?" He tossed the magazine into the fireplace. "I don't want to see it either!"

Thank God the lady at the desk was still in the back room talking on the phone. Not only were pieces of the magazine floating around in the air as it burned, but it also made a hissing sound. Kaylob plopped down onto the couch without an apology as Beth Ann watched in shock.

When the desk clerk came out, she said, "Sorry to keep you waiting. I'm Gayle, and you must be Elizabeth Ann Rose." As Kaylob stood and approached her, she added, "And you must be Mr. O'Brien. I'm glad you're here." She smiled at Beth Ann. "I recognize you, Miss Rose. My aunt took me to one of your shows. You were wonderful."

"Thank you." Beth Ann pasted on a smile. "I'm glad you enjoyed it."

Gayle nodded. "Welcome to the Bodega Bay Harbor Inn, Miss Rose." Turning her gaze to Kaylob, she added, "And thank you for serving our country, Mr. O'Brien. You are indeed a hero. My brother-in-law was in the navy."

Kaylob nodded and gave her a polite smile.

"Okay, let's get you checked in."

Beth Ann hoped the woman hadn't noticed the frost between her and Kaylob. At least she didn't say anything about it. When she finished with the paperwork, she held out keys and a map that showed where their cottage was located.

"Thank you, it looks perfect," Beth Ann said.

Kaylob was already out the door before she turned to leave. When she got back to the car, he leaned against it and didn't even glance in her direction as she unlocked the car and they settled inside. A chill filled the inside of the car while she drove to the cottage.

Beth Ann pulled up and right away loved the rustic appearance. The yard had an anchor propped against a large rock that stuck out of the sand. The place appeared weather beaten, but it was truly adorable. Some of the off-white paint was peeling and could have used a little TLC, but Beth Ann couldn't help thinking it was symbolic of herself and Kaylob. They were peeling apart and could also use some tender loving care. She hoped the ambience of the scene would help dispel Kaylob's mood.

Once he opened the trunk and gingerly picked up the suitcases, she said, "Here, let me help, honey."

"I got it," he muttered. "I may not be America's lover boy, but I can carry our luggage."

Trying to be patient, Beth Ann turned and headed toward the house. The key fit perfectly, so she turned the knob and opened the front door. The place was very warm and comfortable—so welcoming after being in the sterile hospital.

One wall had a row of cluttered book shelves adorned with knickknacks and dog-eared paperbacks. The living room had a sleeper couch with two oversized chairs facing a small TV. It was quite cozy. Just what they needed.

While Kaylob unloaded the car, Beth Ann walked into the kitchen off the main living room. A loud thump vibrated the house when he dropped the suitcases; she hoped he hadn't broken the floor. The kitchen was stocked with everything they would need—or at least everything Kaylob would need, since she didn't cook except to make coffee or tea—two things she didn't burn.

Another loud crash came from the living room making her jump. She wondered if Kaylob had kicked one of the suitcases. There was no way with his present mood she'd go in there to find out. Instead, she turned her attention to the beautiful view of the ocean. A few minutes later, she glanced back toward the living room and saw Kaylob observing the books on the shelves and thought it might be safe to go speak to him. But when she went to stand beside him, he turned and pointed at the telephone on an old desk in the corner.

"Need to call anyone?" he asked sarcastically.

Sighing deeply, she stepped closer and put her hand on his chest. "No, I already called everybody and told them we were going to spend some time alone."

"What about Blake? Shouldn't you call him?"

Beth Ann bristled. "No, I'm not *with* Blake anymore. Frankie will be picking up some of my clothes tomorrow, and I'll get my other stuff later."

Kaylob flinched and Beth Ann cursed herself for talking without thinking. He hadn't known she had been living with Blake.

His eyes were vacant, as though he were looking right through her. He didn't say anything for a minute or so, then he said, "Want some coffee?"

That caught her completely off guard. Was he mad or hurt or what?

"Sure, want me to make it?" she replied, turning toward the kitchen.

"No, I think I can handle making coffee," he said, brushing by her and storming toward the kitchen.

Okay, she really didn't know what to think now. She followed him but said nothing when she took a seat at the kitchen table, and Kaylob didn't speak to her either. Amid the sound of the bubbling percolator, the muffled roar of the ocean, and the squawking seagulls, her mind drifted back to the way their life had been before. All the days they'd spent at the beach because Kaylob loved to surf—and he was one of the best.

He interrupted her thoughts when he pulled out a chair and sat on the other side of the table, never even glancing her way. Trying to break the ice, she reached across the table and took his hand.

"I bet you've missed surfing and will be glad to get back to it."

He looked out at the waves and nodded. "Yeah, it's been a long time. Did you do that with Blake?"

"What?"

"Surfing? Did you and Blake do that?"

She sighed. "No, we never went near the water only swimming pools."

He just kept staring out the window. Beth Ann looked at his hand, once so rugged and detailed but now scarred, skeletal, and pale. It was the first time she'd ever had a better tan.

A few seconds later, he pulled his hand away and got up. She tried not to let it hurt, but it did. In the past, they had never shared even one minute of uncomfortable silence. They'd always had a special comfort level, unlike anything she'd ever known. Her mind drifted to the sounds of the ocean again and she tried to relax.

The smell of coffee sweetened the air, so she pointed to the muffins and almonds that had been left on a tray. Kaylob nodded and brought them to the table along with two cups of coffee.

She lifted her cup, blew on it and took a sip. "Thank you. You made my coffee just how I like it."

To her surprise, there was a flicker of warmth when Kaylob reached across the table and touched her cheek. "You're welcome."

Her hopes brightened, although she remained guarded. She didn't know what to expect from one minute to the next. When they finished their coffee and muffins, Kaylob came around behind her chair and rubbed her shoulders, then he bent down, lifted her hair, and gently kissed the back of her neck. Her heart soaring with relief and gratitude, she stood and wrapped her arms around his waist. There was no way she could be mad at him knowing what he'd been through.

All she wanted was to be close to the man she loved, and when their lips met, the desire flared into flames. He guided her to the bedroom, where they fell onto the bed in a tumbling, passionate embrace. With a gentle touch, he unbuttoned her shirt and let it fall open. His eyes heated as he looked at her bare chest. She knew what he wanted, and she wanted it too. His lips covered hers, and his tongue glided gently inside. God, she loved his kisses. His lips were full and tasted like sweet coffee with a hint of brown sugar.

After a few seconds, he rose up, looked deeply into her eyes and sighed. "I love you, Beth Ann."

Feeling his deep voice vibrating against her, she said, "I love you so much, Kaylob." Her hands clutched the back of his neck and pulled him down into a deeper kiss.

While he kissed a line from her breasts to her belly, he whispered, "Oh, baby, I missed you so much."

"Kaylob..." Beth Ann shivered. "I've missed you terribly and I want you too."

She thought everything was going to be okay, then she felt his entire body tense.

"Did Blake make love to you?"

Chapter Seven

The question hit her like a thunderbolt. Her body seized up as though she'd been dropped into a cold winter lake.

"Kaylob, don't. Not now." She moved his hand back on her breast. "Just make love to me. Please, honey."

"Did you let him touch you?" he asked, raising up and looking into her eyes. Beth Ann pulled away and tried to get off the bed, but he held her and wouldn't let her go. "Did you make love to him?"

Searching his face, Beth Ann felt emotion clog her throat. "Kaylob, please…"

"Answer me, damn it! Did you make love with him?"

"Yes, we did."

The pain in his eyes broke her heart, and the anger in them frightened her.

"Did you love him? Do you still love him?" he demanded.

"Yes, I did. And yes I do, but *not* the way I love you," Beth Ann said firmly. "You always had a part of my heart he could never touch."

"But you still love him?"

"Please understand, Kaylob. I thought you were dead!"

"Understand? You want me to understand. You said you knew I was alive."

He got up and kicked a suitcase across the room, then he stood with his back to her in utter silence for a long moment. Finally, he sat down on the bed, his head in his hands. She wasn't sure if the storm was over or if this was just the beginning.

When she looked closer, she saw that he had tears trailing down his beautiful face. She got up, knelt beside him and said softly, "Kaylob, what can I do? I'm so sorry."

"Just answer all my questions—and be honest," he said, swiping away the tears.

Beth Ann pulled herself up and sat on the bed next to him. "I'm in love with you, honey. I've never been *in* love with anyone else." She touched his hand.

"How long did you wait?" he asked. "When did you two start seeing each other? Tell me everything, please. I want to know what happened."

"It was a long time before I even saw him," she began. "I had a nervous breakdown when I got the news that you'd been killed in action. I even cut off all my hair." To show how short her hair had been, she gathered it at the nape of her neck and pulled it up. "I dove into a well of despair. I truly wanted to die and almost did—by starving myself. I got down to ninety-four pounds."

He flinched as though he'd been hit. "Oh, baby…"

"My family stayed with me for two months and kept me alive. I stopped eating, talking and showering. I was in a near-comatose state because the doctor had to drug me since I couldn't stop screaming for you."

She paused for a moment, her lips trembling.

"Finally, my mourning started to lessen a little, but it never fully went away. Things got a little better when I got a lead role and spent every day rehearsing. The show started touring, and I finally began trying to live again. I had something that distracted me. But even though things got better, I still knew I'd never be the same without you."

His expression changed from anguish to anger, and his hands clenched the sheets on the bed. "Blake Tanner is a dead man. He took advantage of you! I'm gonna kill that asshole when I—"

"No, honey, it's not like that." Beth Ann turned and put her hand on his. "The show took six months of rehearsal, and I didn't see him at all until opening night."

"So? That was still too soon for him to make advances, especially after a nervous breakdown."

"It was eight months," she said. "Two months in bed, and over six months with the show rehearsing. Even so, that's not when it started. We kissed on opening night, but that was it." She looked up into his eyes earnestly. "After that, I went on tour and didn't see him for another five months. You'd been gone over a year before we even had a first date."

That first date had been the night she'd seduced Blake, but she decided to leave that part out.

After a few seconds, Kaylob stood and started pacing. "He still took advantage of you. That SOB, I'm gonna kill him!" As he headed for the living room, he added, "I can only imagine how he seduced you. I've already killed, so it won't be that hard."

Beth Ann got up and followed him. "It wasn't like that, Kaylob! Part of me was angry with you for leaving even after I begged you not to go. Blake didn't seduce me." She took a deep breath then said, "I seduced *him*." She tried to touch Kaylob's arm, but he pushed her hand away.

"This is all bullshit, Beth Ann. I'm gonna kill that bastard!"

"Kaylob, you can't kill him. I don't want you to do anything to him. I was lonely and needed a distraction—anything to make me feel alive again."

As her tears began to flow, Kaylob's face softened. She wanted to help him with his mammoth anguish and take away his pain and anger, but she didn't want Blake hurt. She'd hurt him enough already.

"Please calm down, honey," she said. "You need to let go of your anger at Blake."

Kaylob closed his eyes and just stood there a moment. When he opened them, he looked at her from head to toe. "Who should I be angry at, Beth Ann?" He grabbed a beach towel and turned toward the door, bumping against the dresser and sending a vase crashing to the floor. A moment later, the front door slammed, leaving Beth Ann standing, feeling alone and as if her heart was bleeding.

What if being with Blake had really destroyed her relationship with Kaylob? Her legs felt so heavy that she couldn't move. It was as though she were being sucked down by quicksand.

A few moments later, her resolve returned. No, she refused to be pulled down again! She had to believe that it could all be fixed somehow. She loved Kaylob with her entire body and soul, and couldn't imagine what her life would be without him again. She sat down and felt motionless for a good fifteen minutes, listening to the complaining gulls along with the sound of the ocean.

Finally, her decision was made. She got up, fastened her blouse and took a deep breath. She had to go to Kaylob and try to work it out. The vase he had knocked over was scattered all over the floor, so she picked up the pieces and deposited them into a garbage can, staring down at the shards. For some reason, she hated throwing it away. After a few seconds, she retrieved the fragments and decided to glue the vase back together again later. She only wished there was some type of glue for her and Kaylob.

When she finally stepped outside, she found Kaylob lying in the sun that was not as warm as the spring and summer but at least it was sun. She walked over and sat next to him in the sand and felt herself shiver, but wasn't sure if it was from cool breeze or the chill from his mood.

"Kaylob, I love you with all my heart and soul." Her voice wavered. "I'm so sorry you're hurting. How can I make it better?"

Time slowed while she waited for his answer. Finally, he took her hand and pressed his lips to her palm. He had been kissing her hand that way ever since she'd first met him on the railroad tracks in Novato.

Closing his eyes, Kaylob took a deep breath and said, "How long did you live with him?"

"Not very long, we dated for almost a year, but I was on tour and didn't move in with him right away." She struggled to keep her voice steady.

His eyes remained closed. "Sounds like what you had with him was the same thing you had with me."

"No, Kaylob." She touched his chin so he would look at her. "There was a big difference."

He pulled away from her touch. "Let's see. You lived with him, you loved him, and you... did everything with him. You know, you're right. Sounds like just a fling to me! Screw it, I'm done. I want to go back home."

As he stood to leave, Beth Ann pleaded, "No, please don't go!"

She reached up to grab him, but he pulled away. "I can't talk about this anymore."

Without warning, she felt everything begin to spin. Too much sun, too much stress, not enough sleep, the long drive to the beach—it all came crashing down. She didn't see Kaylob turn to look at her when she started to fall, but she was fully aware when he scooped her up into his arms.

Afterwards, the world slowly drifted back into focus, Kaylob said, "Jesus, Beth Ann. Are you okay?"

"I'm losing you all over again," she said. "And there's nothing I can do about it! How do you expect me to feel?" She beat her fists on his bare chest. "Damn it! Why do you keep leaving me? You can't leave me again—I can't take anymore!"

"I'm not leaving you, baby." Kaylob's eyes softened. "I only said I was done with this conversation, and when I said I was going home, I meant back to the cottage." In a weak attempt at humor, he added, "Hell, I guess maybe you *do* still love me."

"I thought you meant you were done with me and wanted to leave me." Her voice was barely a whisper.

"I'm upset, but I'm not leaving you. I'll never leave you again." He lifted her and managed to find the strength to carry her back to the cottage. His arms felt like a safe harbor, the way they always had.

Back in the cottage, he placed her gently on the couch and sat next to her.

"I never should have listened to them," Beth Ann murmured. "I kept telling everyone you weren't dead, but they wouldn't believe me. I kept hearing your voice calling me, and those dreams and visions haunted me day and night."

"I'm so sorry," Kaylob said. "What I put you through was awful and I wish it had never happened, but I can't help being pissed off, and right now I just want to kick Blake's ass."

"No you don't," Beth Ann said.

"Oh, yes I do." He held her gaze. "Believe me, I do."

She knew it was useless to argue, so she tried to change the subject. "I hated that people thought I was crazy. I told you about some of it the first day I saw you, but you don't know a fraction of what happened to me, especially the visions. The ones that showed me you were still alive."

He went to get her a glass of water then sat beside her again. As she took a long sip, he reached over and stroked her hair. "I know you've got to be exhausted. You lost a lot of sleep watching over me in the hospital. Maybe you should take a nap."

"But we need to talk," she insisted, even though her eyelids were heavy.

"We'll talk later," he said, patting his lap. "Put your head here. We'll have plenty of time to talk after you get some rest."

The instant her head touched his lap, she felt like she was home again as Kaylob's fingers gently stroked her hair and calmed her in a way that only he could.

* * * *

Blake stood at the bar in his living room and filled his glass with another shot of scotch. It was the middle of the day, and he was at it again. He'd been at loose ends ever since Beth Ann had left. She'd walked out of their home and hadn't returned. And she'd tried to break up with him over the damn phone! He sure as hell wasn't letting her get away with that. He was tempted to just find her and drag her ass back home again. No way was he letting her end what they had.

Somewhere in the distance, he heard the doorbell ring but ignored it because Dana always answered it. As a matter of fact, lately she had almost flown to the door. What was that all about?

As he took another sip, the doorbell rang again. Where the hell was Dana? He staggered to the front door and swung it open.

"Package for Beth Ann Rose." A smiling deliveryman looked him up and down and frowned.

Blake pulled out his wallet and gave the guy a hundred dollar bill.

"Sorry, sir," the guy said, trying to hand the bill back. "I don't have enough change to break that."

"Just keep it." Blake took the large package and shut the door. While he was wondering what was inside, he heard Dana's voice behind him.

"Blake, I'm sorry about that. I was outside and wasn't able to get to the door."

He studied her face while she looked intently at the package. Why the hell was she so concerned?

"Let me take it," she said, reaching for the parcel. "I'll put it away."

Even though she was his housekeeper, he had practically adopted Dana as his baby sister, and if the truth be known, they sometimes fought like siblings. He pulled the item out of her reach.

"No, I'll take care of it."

"But, Blake, Beth Ann asked me to take all packages and put them away for her."

He arched one of his blond eyebrows. "Is that a fact? When the hell did she tell you that?"

Dana looked like she was ready to cry. "A while ago."

"Well, that's too damn bad," he slurred. "I'm opening it."

"Blake, please don't." Dana tried again to grab it away.

He whipped around and set the package on the bar with Dana right behind him. With his bare hands, he tore it open. It only took a few seconds to see it was from a French boutique and a top designer, Kenzo Takada, whose name was emblazoned on the elegant box. Blake's heart sank as he tried to blink back tears.

It was Beth Ann's wedding dress.

He opened the silk-lined box and pulled it out. It was gorgeous and delicate, just like Beth Ann. He could imagine her wearing it and what their wedding day would have been like. That hurt, but the thought of their honeymoon nearly crushed him.

A sniffling noise from behind made turn to see Dana standing by the bar, biting her lip and wiping away tears. When he glanced at the mirror behind her, he saw how pathetic he looked. Christ, he hadn't shaven in God only knew how long. His twin dimples sure as shit didn't show now. He looked like a bum, and didn't give a flying horse.

"Dana, it's really okay," he lied. "Take this up to the spare room and put it with all the other gifts and wedding stuff."

Dana picked up the box and said softly, "I'm so sorry, Blake."

"No, Dana." He smiled as sincerely as he could. "I'm the one who should be sorry. I've been a real jerk to you lately."

She touched his arm tenderly, confirming what a good person she was. She was sensitive and she had really loved Beth Ann. He'd met Dana when she was working at a home for kids and living in a shelter. He took her in as a housekeeper, got her an apartment and set her up. He had told Beth Ann about it and she had told him how wonderful he was for doing it. He'd never wanted Dana to feel she was a charity case. She had begun taking classes for court reporting and he was proud of her—a lot prouder than he was of himself these days.

What the hell was he supposed to do now with all the love he had for Beth Ann? Screw that. She was coming back home and that was final. At least that's what he kept telling himself. Maybe he could live without her. Couldn't he? He'd had a life before Beth Ann, dated lots of women and had lots of hot, steamy sex. Hell, he'd even had two women at once. Maybe he should try that again. After all, there had been some things Beth Ann wouldn't let him do to her.

His number one rule had always been: *Never fall in love.* The problem was that he was already in love with the little redhead from his hometown. A few years after high school, he'd moved to Texas to go to college, and there had actually been days when he didn't think about her. Then he'd gone to work for a realtor and eventually bought his way into a brokerage firm with the money his parents had left him after they died in a car crash. Just thinking about that depressed him. He hadn't known his parents were *so* rich until they died.

Now he owned properties all over the country but he'd stayed in Texas because he loved the life and the women. The truth was he'd never had any brains where Beth Ann was concerned, going so far as to open a brokerage firm in Palm Springs just because it was only an hour away from Riverside where she lived. At the time, he'd hoped she might get tired of waiting for Mr. Perfect, but that had never happened—until she thought he was dead. Or had she ever really thought that? He had always felt she was waiting for Kaylob to come back. Now that he had, Blake had been dismissed.

He poured himself another scotch, then another, until he finally lost count. The next thing he felt was the floor reaching up and smacking him in the face. He hardly noticed when he felt someone throw him over their shoulder and carry him upstairs. It turned out to be Johnny, his friend and bodyguard.

"Hey, boss, you want me to give you a shower and shave?"

"Hell, no! When I get ready to do that, I'll do it myself," Blake said, then he chuckled. "I always knew you wanted me."

"Sure, boss," Johnny said, laughing too. "You've always turned me on, and you know those dimples are something else. Especially when you're falling-down drunk." He set him down in his bedroom. "Now I'm getting you in the bed."

"At least buy me a drink first," Blake said, putting his arm around Johnny's neck.

"Nah, I can't take advantage of you like that." Johnny shook his head. "You wouldn't respect me in the morning."

Blake noticed Dana in the doorway behind them and saw Johnny wink at her. There was no hiding the crimson that rose from her neck to her face. Damn, they were flirting with each other. He couldn't miss that even while he was drunk.

As he felt the covers being pulled across him, his last thought was that he had to find a way to win Beth Ann back. Maybe he'd kidnap her or hire a detective to follow her. All he knew was that he had to find a way.

"Beth Ann, I love you, darlin! Come hell or high water, I'm gonna get you back," he murmured before he finally passed out.

* * * *

A man's voice entered Beth Ann's dream, but was she awake or asleep? She stretched out her arms and sat up, then she saw Kaylob looking at her.

"Did you just say something?" she asked.

"Not a word, but I was watching TV," he replied. "I had it down low. Sorry if it woke you up."

Beth Ann leaned over and kissed his neck, but he stiffened at her touch.

"I still need some time," he said. "Please try to understand."

She nodded and moved away, trying not to let him see how much it hurt for him to reject her. A few moments later, Kaylob got up, turned off the TV and returned to sit next to her.

"I have one more question," he said, looking at her intently.

"Okay, honey, of course."

"What part of making love with Blake made you happy? Was it better than our seven nights?"

She couldn't believe he was asking her that. She looked into his eyes and said, "My God, Kaylob. Nothing could ever be as good as what we had."

He looked a little relieved, then he ran his fingers through his hair. "Damn it, Beth Ann. Why *him*? I hate feeling like he's had a special part of you, and I hate feeling so much anger."

"Kaylob, you have to believe that nobody has ever had the special part of me that you've had. There were things I wouldn't do with him…things I saved for you. Even if you had never come home, those parts of me were only for you."

He looked at her with curiosity. "What kind of things?"

She felt the heat rising in her cheeks. "You know…those things."

"Can't you just tell me?" he asked. "I need to know."

She shook her head. "You know I don't like to say things like that."

He gave her a look that made it useless for her to try to tell him no.

"You know," she said. "Your special kisses and…stuff. And other things. Remember what I did to you that I learned in that book? You know the book you said you loved so much."

For the first time since they'd arrived, she saw a glint of a smile on Kaylob's face. He nodded with a wink and said, "Oh, okay. I think I understand."

There was a long pause as he sat thinking, as if he were choosing his words carefully.

"Baby, I've thrown a big enough tantrum to last a lifetime. I told you to find love again and you did. I just wish it hadn't been with him. Even so, I'll do my best to stop being pissed off about it all the time. Just make sure he doesn't come around us, because if he does, I'll kill him."

Beth Ann nodded. She didn't want to see Blake hurt, nor did she want them to fight over her. In time, she hoped things would calm down.

* * * *

The next few days were filled with love, though they were still tinged with a certain amount of lingering stress. Beth Ann saw hints of Kaylob's mood swings although he tried to hide them from her, and his night terrors didn't stop. He would wake up screaming, drenched in sweat, his heart pounding. She would try her best to soothe him, but nothing she did made it any better, even the singing had stopped working.

One night, after one of his horrible dreams, he left for a walk and Beth Ann couldn't help but wonder if he was okay. He did it again the next night and the night after that. There was no way she could sleep while he was gone, so she spent hours waiting for his return. Then, one night, she decided to follow him even though he had requested to be alone.

The moon was bright as he walked along the beach, so she had to stay far enough behind so he wouldn't see her. Suddenly, he stopped and she heard his anguished voice carried to her by the ocean breeze.

"Goddamn it!" he yelled to the empty beach as he fell to his knees. "Why do I feel like this? I'm home for Christ's sake!"

"Kaylob!" Beth Ann ran to kneel beside him. "Honey, please let me help. I'm sorry but I couldn't let you go alone again."

He pulled her into his arms as though she were his life raft. The one thing she knew was that she was not going to let him sink.

46

December Road

They held each other until the sun peeked above the horizon and began to dance across the water. Maybe this would be their new beginning. Maybe things were finally going to get better.

Chapter Eight

The next afternoon, when Beth Ann came out of the bedroom, she playfully plopped down next to Kaylob, but just then, the phone rang. He got up and walked over to pick it up. The minute he said hello, his face turned blood red and made Beth Ann's stomach turn.

"Why the fuck are you calling here?" he yelled. "Wait until I get my hands on you, you sonofabitch!"

Beth Ann jumped up and tried to pull the phone from his hands, but he turned away to block her with his shoulder.

"Bring it on, Tanner!" he yelled.

"Kaylob, please give the phone to me," she pleaded, tears running down her face.

He glared at her a few seconds, then he dropped the phone on the floor and walked away. Beth Ann took a deep breath and picked it up.

"Blake, why did you call here? How did you get the number?"

"You should know by now that I can find out anything. I called because you need to come home!"

"I already explained that's not happening." She sighed. "I'll call you later, and please don't call back. This is not the way to handle things."

"Handle things? You call going off with another man while you're engaged to me handling things?"

"I told you we're not engaged anymore and I don't know how many ways I can say it. I'm so sorry but please—"

"She was engaged to me first, cowboy!" Kaylob yelled from behind her. "I'm gonna kick your ass, Tanner!"

"Blake, please," Beth Ann said. "This is upsetting Kaylob. I have to get off the phone."

48

The dial tone told her he'd hung up. She stood there looking at the phone then slowly turned to Kaylob. He was holding a can of beer in his hand, and his face showed pure hate and anger.

"Since we're on the subject of your ex-fiancé, is that one of the outfits you wore for him?" He pointed to her shorts and top. "How many times did you seduce him wearing that?"

She resisted the urge to clobber him. Heat soared through her as she marched into the bedroom and changed clothes, then she left the cottage, slamming the door behind her.

How much more of this could she take? Everything was coming down on her, and nothing she did was right. She was either being cruel to Blake or making Kaylob angry. Maybe she should drink a beer herself.

She walked down to the water's edge, taking in the blue sky that blended together with the ocean. The puffy white clouds cast a shadow across the water while the breeze brought in the aroma of the salty air, reminding her of all the yesterdays with Kaylob.

She whispered to the wind, "I love him. Thank you for bringing him back."

As she lifted her face to the sky tears trailed down her cheeks and fell onto her yellow dress that rustled in the breeze. A noise behind her made her turn around to see Kaylob, tenderness spread across his face. For so many years, he had protected her and been there to dry her tears, and he had never been mean to her, not even once. Now she didn't know what to expect.

"I'm sorry, Beth Ann." He took a long deep breath. "I shouldn't have acted that way." He stepped closer and pulled her into his arms to kiss her, then he gently wiped away her tears. "I see you haven't lost your temper."

She had to smile. "I love you, Kaylob."

"Ah, baby, I love you more."

On their last night there, they watched the waves as they had so many times when they were growing up. She just wanted back the Kaylob the war had stolen from her. Nestled in his arms, Beth Ann said a silent prayer, asking for his full return.

The next morning, they drove to Novato and picked up Beth Ann's car then left the rental with her parents. After a brief visit with their family and friends, saying goodbye to everyone was hard, and seeing Lisa pregnant made her want to stay. Even more so because she was not allowed out of bed, the pregnancy was not going as smoothly as they'd hoped. However, for now, home was at Frankie's house. He'd called and almost begged them to stay at his place while they searched for a new home.

On the drive back, they talked about what Kaylob was going to do now. His parents had surprised him with the news that he'd be receiving some type of inheritance, plus he was getting all his back pay from the military. Beth Ann also had all her earnings from Broadway and teaching, so for the first time, they were financially secure. The inheritance would be deposited directly into their joint bank account as soon as they opened it. Kaylob was touched that his Uncle Martin on his mom's side of the family who had lived in Ireland had done this, especially since Kaylob had never met him. He told Beth Ann that they'd use the money to pay for the wedding. With everything going on Beth Ann silently hoped there would still be one.

When they arrived at Frankie's new place, his new girlfriend Debra was with him. Frankie introduced all of them, and Beth Ann was surprised and felt very short when his girl hugged her. Debra smiled warmly and touched Beth Ann's red hair.

"We match," she said with a laugh.

Beth Ann grinned and felt an instant connection with Debra. "Brown eyes too." Beth Ann pointed.

Frankie helped them get settled and showed them their bedroom, which was surprisingly large and even had its own private bath.

Frankie smiled. "I'm glad you guys are back. I've missed the hell out of you two."

Beth Ann hugged him. "I'm so glad to be home and back in Riverside. I've missed everyone so much."

"She's missed some more than others." Kaylob muttered, then he turned and went into the bathroom.

Frankie lifted an eyebrow as he watched Kaylob walk away and shut the door.

"Life will get back to normal again," Beth Ann said with a half shrug. She prayed every night that it would.

Frankie kissed her forehead. "I'll let you two get settled. If you need anything, give me a yell."

* * * *

The next morning, Frankie and Beth Ann were up first. They sat at his breakfast bar having coffee while Frankie read the newspaper and complained about the news, like he always had.

Beth Ann snagged it from him. "If all you do is get upset, why do you read it?"

He grabbed it back. "Because some of us like to stay informed, brat. Gold in Paris has hit a record high of $188 dollars an ounce. Can you believe that?"

"Wow! I'm so glad to know that." Beth Ann tried not to laugh.

"Okay, fine, Miss Smarty pants." He put down the paper then looked around the room as though he were making sure they were alone. "Debra and I had a little spat last night. Hope we didn't disturb you guys."

"No, we both passed out. That drive was a killer. But what happened? I hope it wasn't because we're here."

"No, of course not." He shook his head. "It's just because I like to look at women's legs."

Beth Ann folded her arms and looked him directly in the eyes. "Do you check out other women when you're with Debra?"

"No. Well, I try not to look, but sometimes my eyes have a mind of their own. It's just... you know me. I have a thing for nice legs." He wiggled his brows. "She gets all pissed off over it."

"Oh, yeah, I do recall you going on and on about legs. But let me tell you, if Kaylob did that, he'd find himself seeing stars."

"Or pillows." Frankie laughed. "I can't help it. It's my weakness." He hung his head and tried to act ashamed but failed miserably.

Beth Ann smacked his arm. "I can't believe you still do that. You need to stop."

"Well, hell, men are only human." He looked away like he was mad, but she could see the smile tugging at his lips.

"Yes, I remember you telling me that once—about being Hu-*man*."

His smile was devilish. "I told you it's my eyes. They won't behave."

Just then, Kaylob walked in and said, "I feel for you, Frankie. Dealing with a jealous female." He winked and moved up behind Beth Ann to kiss her neck.

She turned toward him, arching one brow. "Do you have a weakness, too? What do you find yourself looking at on a woman?"

Backing up with his eyes wide, he lifted his hands in surrender. "Nooo way! I'm not in a mood to die today. Besides, you're my only weakness."

Frankie and Kaylob both laughed, clearly sharing a secret that neither of them were in the mood to disclose. They changed the subject to a pro-bowl game and pizza. Kaylob was excited about eating some, since he hadn't had any in years. The moment reminded Beth Ann of how things used to be. For the second time since Kaylob had come home, she had real hope that things could get back to normal. Maybe *this* was really their new beginning.

Later, while the guys watched the game on TV, Beth Ann decided to go down to the pool because of all the yelling and shouting, not to mention she didn't want any part of the greasy pizza. For a January day in Riverside, the temperature in the seventies was nice but not surprising. Besides, it would give her time to read her new book.

A few minutes later,- she stretched out beside the pool and engrossed herself in *The Valley of the Dolls*. Just when she got into an awesome scene a noise pulled her away, then she looked up to see Debra standing over her.

"Jeepers, those guys are yelling at the TV and saying words I won't repeat. I had to get out of there. I hope I'm not interrupting."

"No, not at all," Beth Ann lied. "I don't blame you. Someone made a homerun on the NFL side—that's why they were yelling when I left."

Debra bent over, laughing. "It's called a touchdown, and both teams are in the NFL. Usually it's pretty boring. I think they're just excited to watch football together."

"I think you're right." Beth Ann smiled as Debra slid into the lounge chair next to her.

Debra rubbed her temples. "I'll never understand all that yelling at a TV, although, yesterday I wanted to do some yelling myself."

"Why?" Beth asked a little warily.

"Oh, it's this chick with big boobs who keeps coming on to Frankie. Yesterday, when Frankie showed Kaylob the pool, I came down to ask what they wanted for lunch and she was standing way too close to Frankie and was looking at Kaylob like he was her next meal."

Beth Ann felt her temperature rising, and it didn't have anything to do with the sun. She did her best to act mature. "Does she live here?"

"Yes, and I'd like to kick that blonde broad's butt to the curb." Debra lifted her foot to demonstrate.

Beth Ann couldn't help cracking up. "If she gets near Kaylob, I'll help."

"Don't worry," Debra said. "Kaylob was behaving like a gentleman and kept his distance."

"What's her name?" Beth Ann asked.

"I don't know. I just call her Floozy Bell." Debra grumbled. "She lives around the corner near the lobby. You pass it on the way upstairs." She pointed. "One time she walked up behind Frankie and put her hands across his eyes and said *guess who*? He told me later that she had her entire chest pressed into his back."

"You're kidding." Beth Ann scowled. "What did he say to her?"

"He told her she must be the grim reaper, because if I came out and saw her that close to him, they were both dead." She paused to laugh. "He said she's really pushy, but she's clueless too. You know Frankie's not a chest guy. It's all about long sexy legs for him."

Beth Ann nodded, then she grabbed a bottle of tanning lotion and put some on her arms. "How did you find out Frankie's a leg man? Did he tell you?"

"Oh, I've always known that. But you know guys with their big mouths and bigger libidos. Before I came down here, I walked into the living room and heard Frankie going on and on about some girl to Kaylob, then he said, 'Oh that's right. You're a big boob guy.'"

Beth Ann glanced down at her chest. "Great. I never knew that about Kaylob. He sure kept it a secret."

"Kaylob didn't agree or disagree. Frankie was probably just giving him a hard time about liking big boobs. It's probably not even true." Debra took a sip of her drink and leaned back in her chair. They didn't talk for a minute or so, then she said, "Frankie told me about Kaylob's nightmares. Is everything getting better with those?"

"Not really," Beth Ann said with a sigh. "He slept on the floor in the bedroom last night. He's afraid of hurting me because he gets a little wild." She looked at the pool and felt tears well up. "And we're still working through the whole Blake thing. I just wish I knew how to fix things. Kaylob sends me like nobody else ever could, and I love him with all my heart, but I'm really sorry about hurting Blake."

Debra nodded. "I bet that's hard. After all, Blake is one fine specimen. God almighty, those dimples are something else, along with that blond hair. But I've also heard he's a nice guy and he seemed really polite and everything. I'm sure he'll find someone else soon."

Beth Ann looked surprised. "I didn't know you knew him. Yes, he is a nice guy. And well… anyone can see he's very good looking."

"I met him at a party a few years ago," Debra said. "Women were all over him. Wow, just think—you were engaged to America's most eligible bachelor. Sexy as hell and rich too. From what I've heard, he's really good at… everything."

"You knew someone he dated?" Beth Ann asked.

"Besides you, I knew a couple of ladies he went out with."

"Yes, he's really a great guy. I've known him since I was in grammar school, so I've always known he was attractive, but I didn't find out he was rich and famous until we dated. He's always been good at many things, but—"

"Ahem."

Both girls turned to find Frankie and Kaylob standing at the gate directly behind them. Frankie was shaking his head with his eyebrows furrowed. Beth Ann looked from him to Kaylob and there was no mistaking that he glared at her for a few seconds before doing an about face and storming up the stairs.

"How much did he hear?" Beth Ann asked Frankie when she stood up and gathered her things.

"Oh, not much. Just a few sentences about how you always knew Blake was attractive way back in grammar school. No big deal. Oh, and a little something about how good he was at many things. And let's not forget how sexy and rich he is. Yeah, that about covers it," Frankie said sarcastically.

"Oh, my God," Beth Ann said.

"Those aren't the kind of things he needed to hear," Frankie said, frowning at her.

Debra looked up at him, shading the sun from her eyes. "We thought you guys were watching football."

"Halftime," he snapped.

"Wait, Beth Ann." Debra held on to her arm. "Let me go talk to him. This is my fault."

"Your fault?" Frankie said. "Why?"

Debra got up and looked uneasily from Frankie to Beth Ann. "I asked Beth Ann about him and wanted details."

"Why the hell would you do that?" Frankie asked.

Debra looked at the ground. "I was just wondering that's all. It's what girls do. Don't you start with me. You're the man who cried when the short shorts craze died out."

He glowered at her a few more seconds then walked away to the little café and bar beside the pool.

Debra watched him with a coy smile. "This is the first time he's been jealous."

"I'm sorry he's mad at you," Beth Ann said, "but I have to get upstairs to Kaylob."

"No, don't be sorry. I think I like him being jealous." Debra's grin was big. "Now I know he cares. This will be our first jealousy fight ever. Maybe we can have some fun making up." She sat back down and took a sip of her drink. "I think I'll let him stew for a few."

Beth Ann knew she was facing a much more daunting challenge. With her stomach churning like Gram churned butter, she trudged up the stairs to find Kaylob. It had been an accident, but she'd hurt him with a most devastating weapon—Blake.

She found him on the couch in the townhouse, staring at the TV with the sound turned down. She sat down next to him, but he ignored her.

"Kaylob, honey—"

"Don't say a word to me about anything. I don't want to hear a damn thing about it."

"But, honey—"

"No but anything! Drop it now, I mean it!"

Chapter Nine

"But you didn't hear the whole thing before you got down there. I had just told Debra you're the best in the world. You're my love, you know that."

"Leave me the hell alone!" He got up and walked over to the window.

She stood up, feeling defeated. "Fine, Kaylob. You win."

She shuffled down the hall and closed the bedroom door. The sound of the muffled TV came into the room. She didn't know what to think or do, so she picked up her book and read for hours. Much later, she made herself a sandwich and offered Kaylob one. When he didn't answer, she returned to the bedroom and ate alone.

He didn't come to bed that night, choosing instead to sleep on the couch. The circumstances were doubly uncomfortable since they were Frankie's guests. He and Debra returned later, and there was no missing the sounds of passionate rumblings coming from their room. It made for an unusual mix, with tense silence in the other camp. She and Kaylob had never gone an entire evening being angry with each other.

The next morning, she woke up early and got ready to return to her job working with the children. Kaylob was still asleep on the couch, and her eyes filled with tears as she looked down at him. How had they gotten to this place? Right now, it felt like a place of no return.

Maybe this was their new beginning but of the end.

All day at work, Beth Ann thought about Kaylob and how bad she'd hurt him. If only she could find a way to make it better. By early afternoon, it was clear that the stress at home and work did not mix. She was unable to concentrate on the children's performances, so she put in for a leave of absence.

On her way out, she ran into a man with brown hair who looked familiar. He smiled and held out his hand.

"Hello there, Beth Ann. It's been a long time."

55

She shook his hand and said, "Hello." Shoot, where had she met him?

He must've been able to tell she was struggling to remember because he laughed. "I'm Peter Steel. We met a while back in Chicago. You were out with Blake Tanner. I'm one of his agents."

"Oh, of course I remember you." She grinned. "How are you?"

"I'm good, just picking up my little girl. She wants to be a singer and dancer. I didn't know you were still training here."

"No, I'm one of the teachers." She smiled even though she just wanted to leave and get home. "Who's your daughter?"

"Cathy. Tiny little brunette." He smiled. "She's the light of my life."

"Oh, Cathy, she's so talented. I'm glad to have her for a student." Beth Ann took a step closer to the door. "I'm sorry, but I have to get going. It was so nice to see you again, Peter."

She shook his hand and was surprised when he brought it up to his lips and kissed it, then arched a brow.

"Thank you," he said. "I'm happy to hear my baby is doing well."

Beth Ann nodded, then turned and almost ran out the door. God, she felt so rude. The man just wanted to talk about his little girl, and she'd practically run away. She'd been afraid he might ask about Blake, and she sure as heck didn't want to talk about that, especially right now. That made it even clearer that she wasn't fit to teach with everything she had going on in her life.

On the drive home, she decided she would do whatever she could to make things right with Kaylob. When she opened the front door, Debra was in the kitchen putting ice in a glass.

"Hi, Debra. Have you seen Kaylob?"

She frowned and lowered her voice. "Yes, but be careful what you say to him. He's been drinking all day." She looked around. "Listen, last night after Frankie and I left for dinner, we ran into Blake. He looks like death warmed over. He was unshaven and had lost a lot weight, and he was pissed as hell. He threatened to come get you at school and drag your ass back to his house. Frankie almost got into it with him."

Beth Ann let the words sink in and wondered what the heck she could do about it. He had always been so particular about his appearance. Well, there wasn't much she could do since she had Kaylob to worry about right here and now.

"I'll go see Blake soon and call him later." Beth Ann felt like the world was on her shoulders and was getting fed up with it. She'd never asked for any of this. When was it going to be her time to let it all out?

"The hell you will," Kaylob slurred as he walked into the kitchen. His eyes seethed as he walked over to the fridge and pulled out a beer. "Not unless I go with you and kick his ass."

"I think I'll go for a swim." Debra grabbed a towel hanging beside the sink and rushed out the door. Beth Ann didn't tell her it was the kitchen towel.

"I thought you'd be okay with me going to get my stuff," she said.

"On what planet would you think that's okay?" Kaylob chugged his beer, some of it spilling down his chest. "You're not that naive. You're not going over there alone to see Mr. Eligible butt wipe."

"I have to go sometime." She took a paper towel and tried to dry off his chest, but he pushed her hand away.

"What the hell, Beth Ann? You think it's okay for you to go to your old boyfriend's—oh excuse me—old *fiancé's* house without me?"

She returned his drunken gaze evenly. "I have to go talk to him sooner or later and give back his ring."

Kaylob drained his beer, then opened the refrigerator and grabbed another. He tossed the empty one into the sink with a metallic rattle.

"Sure, it couldn't be because he's sooooo good, so handsome and oh, you've liked him since grammar school. Now at least I know the real truth. I'm fed up with it! I'm here having a major meltdown, and you're worried about the man you were swinging from the frickin' chandeliers with."

His words pelted her and left her speechless. She decided she had to get away from his anger. She turned and took two steps when he grabbed her arm.

"If you walk away," he said, "then don't expect me to sit around here thinking about what you're doing. I'll find something to take my mind off you. Something you're not gonna like one bit."

She turned back toward him, feeling like her gasket was about to blow. "What's that supposed to mean?"

He didn't take the time to explain. Instead, he brushed past her into the bedroom and came back a couple of minutes later wearing his swim trunks. He walked by her without a word and left. She tried to collect her thoughts, but all she did was pick up the empty can he'd dropped on his way out and threw it in the trash.

"Shit!" She kicked the wastebasket twice. "I need a punching bag!"

The emotionally charged outburst enveloped her like a suit of armor. She had to find some relief. Maybe she would take a swim and keep an eye on Kaylob before he got hurt or hurt someone else. The phone rang just as she turned to go put on her bathing suit.

She picked up the receiver. "Hello."

"Hi there, stranger," Lisa said. It was her best friend in the whole world.

Beth Ann tried her best to sound normal. "Lisa, I'm sorry I haven't called. How are you and the baby? Are you still staying in bed?"

"Really good and yes still in bed. It won't be long now, or so I hope. I also hope you and Kaylob are still coming down to be with us when the baby comes."

"Of course we'll be there," Beth Ann said. "My best friend's having a baby."

"Is everything okay?" Lisa asked. "You sound funny."

Beth Ann felt tears sting her eyes. She should've known she couldn't fool Lisa, but she tried to play things down. "I'm fine. You know he's still having the nightmares, but things will get better."

She wanted to tell her the truth, but Lisa was Kaylob's best friend too, and she was also pregnant. The last thing Beth Ann wanted was to stress her out, especially after all the time it took for her and her husband Terry to get pregnant.

"Are you sure that's all?" Lisa asked.

"I'm sure. Don't worry."

"Okay, Beth Ann. But you better be telling me the truth."

"Hey, guess what?" Beth Ann tried her best to sound excited. "We're close to finding our own place, and we're buying instead of renting."

"Really? That's so exciting. I want pictures." Lisa laughed and went along with the subject change.

A few minutes after she hung up, Beth Ann sat at the kitchen bar and wondered if she should go down and check on Kaylob. Debra was down there with him, or so she thought until the living room door opened and Debra walked in.

"I think Kaylob needs to get back up here and go to bed," she said, putting the dishtowel back.

"Why?"

"He's drinking with that blonde, the one I told you about." Debra snarled. "You better get down there. She's moving in for the thrill."

Beth Ann put on her swimsuit and was out the door in five minutes, barely touching the stairs on her way down. No way in hell did she want him flirting with some other woman, and especially not when he was mad at her and smashed.

She saw him sitting with the woman at a table as soon as she walked into the pool area. He was laughing and seemed oblivious to the fact that the bimbo wanted to make him her next meal. Luckily, he didn't see Beth Ann, giving her time to take a deep breath and calm down. She walked over to him and noticed just how gigantic the woman's chest was.

"Kaylob, want to go swimming with me?"

"Oh, hello, sweetheart. Meet my new friend here…Mary. No—Maria. Yeah, Ma-*ree*-a. She's been telling me about her home based business. She shells Amway—I mean, she sells it. She said she could train me. Wouldn't that be nice?"

Good Lord, he was plastered.

"I'm going swimming," she said, purposely not looking at or acknowledging the woman at all. "Come join me, Kaylob."

"Maybe later," he said. "I'm not done talking yet."

Beth Ann stared at him then walked toward the pool, determined not to let the hussy see her upset. Half of her wanted to throw anything not tied down straight at that harlot, but the other half didn't know how to handle this, because Kaylob had never acted this way before.

She picked a spot on the side of the pool where she could keep an eye on them and sat down to put her feet in the water. When he whispered in the woman's ear and touched her leg, it took everything Beth Ann had not to make a major scene. Kaylob glanced over at her and—what an ass—he actually smiled as though he were enjoying her jealousy. Ms. Boobs-For-Brains got up and handed Kaylob what looked like some kind of brochure, then left.

Kaylob staggered his way over and sat down next to Beth Ann. After a few seconds of silence, he put his feet in the pool, then picked up his drink and chugged it again.

"I'll see you upstairs in a little while," he said. "I'm gonna go pick up some stuff of hersss, then I'll be up."

"Better not be the clap," Beth Ann muttered.

He laughed and tried to give her a kiss, but she turned away, letting him catch her cheek. He smelled like a flooded brewery.

"Would you like me to come with you?" she asked.

"No, I think I can handle it by myshelf—I mean my*self.* You know, like you can handle things alone without me." He chuckled at his drunken wittiness.

She glared at him and shook her head. "Okay, well, I think I'll read for a bit and be up later."

He pulled his feet out of the pool and shot her a nasty look just before he staggered away. At least he left his drink behind. Beth Ann picked up the beer can and got up to throw it away. She was mad at him for drinking so much, but she wasn't worried about what he was going to do. She figured he would pick up the information from the woman, then go sleep it off. She knew Kaylob would never cheat, not even when he was falling-down drunk.

She still needed to escape for a while, so she engrossed herself in reading *Valley of the Dolls.* It was a great book about the fall of a young actress and singer. The story was wonderful, but she still couldn't get her mind off Kaylob. She didn't see any way around it—she'd have to agree not to see Blake alone, even though he deserved better. In truth, right now, she could really use his friendship, but that wouldn't be fair to anyone. So she put a lid on that thought.

After about twenty minutes of trying to read, she decided to go up and talk to Kaylob. She grabbed her towel, then headed upstairs. She went directly to the bedroom, but Kaylob wasn't there, so she went out to the living room where Debra was painting her toenails, large cotton balls were stuck between all her toes.

"Debra, have you seen Kaylob?"

"He's not at the pool? I thought you guys were swimming together." Debra looked up at her with a frown. "I hoped you two might be making up."

Beth Ann's stomach knotted. "I have to go find him."

Kaylob had never left when he was mad even though he'd threatened to. Beth Ann headed downstairs and checked the bar area, but he wasn't there. Her next stop was the pool, but it was deserted. Thoughts of him wandering alone in his drunken stupor made her fear for his safety.

She turned to rush up to Frankie's and get Debra to help her look for him, but stopped dead in her tracks when she saw Kaylob coming out of an apartment near the lobby. His shorts were all twisted, and he was wet and had lipstick smeared on his face. He turned back toward the open door when a towel flew out and hit him in the head. Guess the floozy got all she wanted from him and was done. Kaylob was fixing his shorts when he turned to leave and saw Beth Ann standing there.

"Beth Ann, baybeee…" He smiled stupidly at her. "I was looking for you!"

"You're a complete asshole!" she yelled, running by him toward the elevator.

"Wait, where you going?"

"As far away from you as I can get, you cheating bastard!"

Inside the elevator, her battered heart beat so fast she was afraid it might explode. Kaylob was heading toward the elevator, barely able to walk, so she smashed the buttons and the door closed right before he reached it. Damn him! How could he hurt her like that? Kaylob had always been the man she trusted with her life. Never could she imagine him cheating until now.

When she got off the elevator, her legs couldn't move fast enough. She ran into Frankie's apartment and dashed to her bedroom. She was throwing clothes into an overnight bag and sobbing uncontrollably when Debra came to the door.

"Beth Ann, my God. What's wrong?" Debra asked cotton balls still between her toes.

"He slept with her! I'm leaving him." Beth Ann grabbed her makeup bag with trembling hands.

Debra tried to say something, but Beth Ann swept by her.

"I'll call you later. I just can't see him."

She decided to take the stairs hoping she wouldn't run into Kaylob. He was probably still trying to figure out how to work the elevator with his drunken brain. Tears pelted down her face, and the clomping of her footsteps reverberated in the stairwell. When she got to her car, she took a deep breath and tried to steady her broken heart.

A few minutes later, she found herself driving around in a daze and knew she had to stop before she wrecked the car and killed herself. She spotted a hotel and pulled into the parking lot. The place appeared safe since the rooms were on the inside.

After she checked in and got settled, she knew she should call Frankie so he wouldn't worry, but she couldn't face talking to anyone yet. Right now she needed to cry and mourn a loss—a loss of trust and the innocence of their childhood love that was now gone. Her heart would never be the same.

Chapter Ten

A few days later, Frankie hung up the phone with Beth Ann, relieved that she had finally called to tell him where she was. He had been worried sick for the past three days even though she'd left a message at his job saying she would call later. He'd had to promise her that he wouldn't tell Kaylob before she would agree to give him her phone number and hotel room.

When Frankie entered the living room, Kaylob was sitting on the couch looking like he'd lost his whole world. His eyes were bloodshot, his face pale, and his shoulders were slumped in a way Frankie had never seen. Kaylob had never even checked out other women, so he knew he was telling the truth. The only thing he'd ever done eons ago was admit he'd had a thing for big boobs, and that was only after Frankie had hounded him to death. It just wasn't in Kaylob's nature to cheat.

He sure as shit isn't like me. He's like the anti-Frankie.

"She won't listen to me," Frankie said, sitting on the couch next to Kaylob. "She thinks you cheated."

Kaylob shook his head. "I didn't, I swear. I was just trying to make her jealous, and I was drunk as hell. The woman came on to me and I don't remember everything clearly, but I know I didn't cheat."

Frankie stared at his hands a few seconds. "Kaylob, I need to talk to you about something." He shifted in his seat and felt his stomach flip, but he had to say it.

"Go ahead," Kaylob said.

Frankie took a deep breath and pulled up his courage. "You need to stop being so hard on Beth Ann. You told her to go on with her life, and you made her promise she would."

"I know I did, but I sure as hell didn't know it would be with Blake Tanner."

"Did you give her a list of who she could date in the event of your death?"

Kaylob looked at him, his eyes wide.

"You know, Kaylob, she almost died." Frankie ran his fingers through his hair. "I was there. I saw her fall apart and witnessed what she did to herself. Do you know how goddamn scary it was when we found her in the bathroom holding a pair of scissors with blood all over the place and vomit in the shower?"

Kaylob winced. "Good God, are you serious?"

"As Watergate. She hadn't spoken or eaten much of anything for at least two months. Jesus, Kaylob, she took a long time to get back to anything close to normal. And even then she wasn't her old normal."

"I had no clue it was that bad." Kaylob hung his head. "She left that part out when she told me about it. My poor baby. I wouldn't blame her if she never looked my way again." He looked up at Frankie. "By the way, what's Watergate?"

"Never mind, I'll explain later. Right now you need to seriously rethink how badly you've been treating her."

Frankie was pretty darn sure that shame swept across his friend's face. After a few minutes of unrelenting silence, he thought he saw a light flash in Kaylob's eyes.

"You're right, Frankie. I've been a goddamn idiot."

Frankie nodded. "Idiot or not, you need to find a way to convince her you didn't cheat, because she's mad as hell at you right now."

"I was sauced and don't remember everything, but I know damn well I didn't sleep with that woman or anyone else." He looked like he was deep in thought. "Beth Ann has always been the only woman I've ever wanted."

Frankie put a hand on his shoulder. "I don't know what to say, buddy. Maybe you'll think of some way to make this up to her and make her believe you. What do you remember?"

"I know my shorts were twisted and the woman had been pawing at me. I think I got sick and remember being in the bathroom. She started yelling at me, and the next thing I knew I was all wet. I don't have a clue how that happened, so don't ask."

A noise made them both look up. Debra was standing in the doorway with Beth Ann's suitcase. "Are you ready, honey?"

Frankie patted Kaylob's shoulder as he stood. "I'll tell her how sorry you are. But like I said, she isn't listening to me right now."

"Thanks buddy. I appreciate that."

Frankie picked up the suitcase and left. He felt horrible about the whole thing.

* * * *

Beth Ann was deep in thought as she sat on the couch in her hotel room. How could being a POW for two years change someone so much? Blake had warned her that Kaylob might be different. She hated to think of him as a two-timing jerk, but right now, that's what he was. Every once in a while she would get a glimpse of the old Kaylob, but for the most part, he seemed to be still missing in action.

She thought about calling Blake and meeting with him, but she knew this wasn't the time. It might give him false hope, and she wouldn't do that. The first three nights she had eaten alone and slept with the TV on for company. For over two years, she had dreamed about Kaylob being alive, but never had those dreams included him screwing a blonde home wrecker with boobs for brains.

Anger nibbled at her gut. She wanted to punch something or someone. The bimbo had known Kaylob had a girlfriend and knew he was drunk, but she'd seduced him anyway. Before she started foaming at the mouth like some crazed mad woman, she decided to order room service.

A tap at the door startled her, but a quick glance out the peek hole confirmed it was Frankie and Debra. She blinked back the tears as she opened the door and motioned for them to come in. When they both hugged her, she almost lost it.

Frankie put his hands on her shoulders and kissed her forehead. "How are you holding up, sweetheart?"

"I've been better, Frankie." She tried to hold back the tears, but when his arms went around her she bawled without mercy.

Debra stepped back toward the door. "I'm going downstairs and let you two talk. Beth Ann, if you need anything, call me, okay?"

Beth Ann nodded. "Thank you so much for packing my stuff."

"No problem." Debra smiled at Frankie before she left.

After she was gone, he said, "I'm so sorry you're going through this."

"He's an asshole, Frankie. I'm done with him." Beth Ann swiped angrily at the tears.

Frankie touched her cheek. "You know I don't believe he cheated. He swore he didn't, and he's not a liar."

"Screw him. I saw what happened."

Frankie tilted his head. "You saw them having sex?"

"No. If I had, you'd be bailing me out of jail."

"Well, just so you know, he hasn't eaten or slept since you left. Remember how you felt when he was gone? He looks almost as bad as you did."

"I don't care," she said but didn't sound convincing.

Frankie put his hands on her shoulders again. "Kaylob's a good man, but he's been through a lot more than any of us can imagine. None of us can even guess the pain and torture he went through. My dad said it's beyond what we think we know about hell."

Beth Ann couldn't deny that, so she just looked away and didn't say anything.

Frankie gave her another big hug. "Listen, if you need me or Debra to come and stay with you we will. Do you want one of us here with you?"

"No. Honestly, I need the time alone. I'll call Kaylob in a few days, I promise."

"Well, okay." Frankie hugged her one last time and walked out the door.

A few minutes later, she sat on the couch again and turned on the TV, determined to get her mind off everything. Her stomach growled, reminding her that she needed to eat, so she picked up the food menu just as another knock sounded at the door.

"What did you forget?" she asked when she opened it.

"Baby, can I please come in?" Kaylob pleaded.

She stared at him a few seconds then said, "How did you find me?"

"I followed Frankie and Debra. I had to see you and tell you that it's not what you think."

She motioned for him to come in and couldn't remember the last time she'd seen him unshaven, with red eyes and looking so pale, except for when she'd first seen him in the hospital. It was hard to see him in so much pain. But he had cheated on her, and he couldn't deny it.

"Don't expect to come in here all lovey dovey," she said, keeping her distance from him.

He nodded as he shuffled over to the chair and plopped down. Beth Ann sat on the couch with her back arched facing him.

"Beth Ann, I'm so very sorry. I wanted you to be jealous, but what I did is unforgivable." He paused and stared at his shoes, then he continued. "My behavior's been appalling. I'll do whatever you want me to do." He looked up at her again. "You decide. I'm in no condition to make decisions. Nothing happened between me and that woman, but even if it had, it would have meant nothing."

"Oh, is that how you think you can defend yourself, by saying it was meaningless?" Beth Ann bolted up out of the chair. All she heard was her boyfriend admitting infidelity. She glared down at him with unadulterated anger. "How could you do that to me? You go and have sex with a stranger, yet you've been unwilling to touch me because of Blake! What a hypocrite you are!"

He stood up and moved closer, pleading with his eyes. "I swear I didn't cheat, Beth Ann."

He reached out for her, but she took a giant step back and pointed a trembling finger at him. "Don't you dare touch me!"

"I'd rather be dead than hurt you," he said, his voice barely audible.

"Really, Kaylob? I'm happy you're not dead like everyone thought, so why the hell do you keep hurting me? If you wanted to punish me, you did a really good job!"

Tears streamed down her cheeks. When he tried to touch her again, the intense emotions overwhelmed her and she felt as if she were losing her mind.

She raised her hand to hit him, but he caught her wrist and looked into her eyes while he shook his head.

"I don't blame you for being angry. What I did was wrong, but I won't let you hit me. I've had my share of being hit, kicked, beaten and humiliated. Enough to last me several lifetimes. " He dropped her wrist.

Oh, God. What had she done? How could she even think of hitting him? She looked down at her hand in shame, unable to speak for a moment.

He turned toward the door. "I'll go away now and give you your space. I just wanted you to know that I love you with all my heart. I'll be in Novato at my parent's house when you want to talk to me."

Wait, did he really just say he was leaving her again? He was always leaving her! If he left this time, she wanted it to be for good. There was no way she could take him walking out now. The last time she had almost died.

"I can't believe you're leaving me again."

He turned to look at her. "Beth Ann, I'm no good to you or anyone the way I am now, and you won't believe me. I feel like I'm broken. I don't know myself anymore. I hurt the one person in this world I have loved all my life. How do I get you to ever forgive me, when I can't even forgive myself?" His eyes showed true pain as he held her gaze.

He opened the door to go but she ran over and slammed it.

"Stop trying to leave me all the time! Do you want to work this out or run away from me? Do you really think that leaving is the answer?" He opened his mouth to respond but she cut him off. "Shut up—just shut the hell up! Yes, you hurt me deeply, but if you leave me again, I won't take you back. You left me before and it almost killed me." She placed her hand over her heart and felt it breaking. "I won't gamble with my life again. If you walk out that door, you say goodbye to me for good and don't come back—ever!"

"What are you saying, Beth Ann?" He lifted his hands in surrender. "You know I can't do that. I love you, I'll do whatever you want me to do. We're both trying to reach the same goal." He took both of her hands in his. "I don't want to lose you. I want to spend my life with you, always. I didn't cheat on you. Please believe me."

She looked up into his face. "I want to, Kaylob, but I know what I saw. I'm sorry for attempting to slap you though. I don't know what you went through over there, but I would never want to be the cause for making you relive it."

"It's okay," he said with a half-hearted shrug. "You didn't slap my face, but you did slap my heart."

Chapter Eleven

A week later, they had resolved things enough to check out of one hotel and into a larger one. This one had a kitchenette and living room, and since they still weren't sleeping together, it also had a pullout sofa. Neither wanted to go back to Frankie's because they knew they needed to be alone to work out their problems. And Beth Ann had no desire to see *that* woman with whom Kaylob had cheated. Even if it turned out that he was telling the truth and hadn't slept with her, had they kissed? Had he fondled her? He'd had lipstick on his face, hadn't he? The whole thing had crucified Beth Ann's heart, and she didn't trust what she might do if she saw that strumpet.

The next week or so was tough. Kaylob was walking on eggshells, and Beth Ann's unexpected moodiness was something new to both of them. If she dropped something or her hair didn't do the right thing, she got upset. More than once, she had to bite her tongue to keep from blurting out his grievous mistake. Kaylob must have sensed her moods, because he tried to make her feel better by always telling her how beautiful, special and talented she was.

The best part of their days was when they were hunting for a new home. Finally, after weeks of shopping, they found the perfect place. It would be the first time either of them had owned a home, and this one happened to be a very nice townhouse. They both had great credit and were able to make a nice down payment, so everything went smoothly enough for them to close thirty days later.

On their last morning at the hotel, Beth Ann stepped outside to a beautiful crisp day. She walked over to a bench and sat down near the lawn. A faint breeze scented the air, which whispered the hope of spring. The blades of grass were sparkling as the sun shined its golden light across the lawn.

"Hey, beautiful," Kaylob said when he came out to join her. "What're you doing out here all by yourself?"

She turned and saw him regarding her in a way that made her heart flutter. He was one sexy man even when she was mad at him.

"Just taking in the morning," she said, trying to sound cheerful.

"Baby…" He came over slowly to sit beside her. "Are you okay?"

She turned away and sighed. "Not really, but I'm trying to be."

"I'm sorry, Beth Ann. Do you want to talk about it?"

"No!" she said too sharply. His face dropped making her regret her tone, and then she tried to force a smile. "I'm sorry for snapping. Are you ready to go to our new home? Jack and Lenard said they were able to get inside and drop off some of our old things"

"That's great. Let's go, beautiful." He stood and held out his hand. "Let's blow this dive."

When they arrived at the townhouse, she couldn't help but feel joy even though the shadow of distrust still lurked in her heart. She opened all the windows to let the cool breeze inside that made her dream once again of spring. It had been awhile since she'd cared about the different seasons, mainly because of all the memories she and Kaylob had shared throughout the years. Spring and fall were her favorite times and summer was Kaylob's because he loved to surf. One of the first things they'd always done to mark the end of winter was have a picnic in Novato at Stafford Lake. Those memories were the golden thread that held them together

That evening, a knock at the door interrupted them while they were unpacking. Beth Ann was sure it was Frankie and ran to fling it open.

"Hey there, kid!" Mitch said with a big grin. He'd been the producer of her first and only Broadway show, and she hadn't seen him since the tour had ended. He still had a tiny mustache that matched his thin body. "You're looking fine as always." Mitch winked.

"Mitch!" Beth Ann laughed. "What a great surprise. Please come in." She gave him a big hug.

He hugged her back then nodded to Kaylob as he entered. "Nobody knew how to find you, so I called Frankie." He held up what appeared to be a telegram and handed it to Beth Ann.

She opened it and the shock made her do a double take. "Oh, Mitch, is this true?"

"Yes, kid. I'm not surprised at all. I think you're going to win."

She looked up at Kaylob, her eyes wide. "I've been nominated for a Tony. It's not just a rumor."

He swept her up in his arms and spun her around. "Ah, baby, I'm so proud of you!" He turned to Mitch and stuck out his hand. "Nice to meet you, and thanks for bringing us such good news. I've heard a lot about you."

"You don't even know how glad I am to meet you." Mitch grinned as he shook Kaylob's hand. "This little girl went through a lot while you were gone." He shot Beth Ann a wide grin.

She stared at the telegram while a wave of emotions washed over her. "Thank you, Mitch. This means the world to me." She chewed her lip, trying not to lose it.

Mitch cleared his throat. "Well, listen, I won't stay and bother you two. I just wanted to stop by and give you this. We're both invited, and of course you can bring Kaylob."

"We'll be there." Beth Ann glanced at Kaylob and saw him nodding with certainty. "Can't you stay for a cup of coffee or a glass of wine, Mitch?"

"Okay, sure. I'll take some coffee if you have it. But don't go to any trouble."

"It's no trouble," Kaylob said. "Let Beth Ann show you around while I put on a pot of coffee. I was getting ready to make some anyway."

Beth Ann smiled at Kaylob and took Mitch's hand. "Let me give you the grand tour."

And she did think their place was grand. Even though she'd lived with Blake in his gigantic home, she absolutely loved their new townhouse, all eighteen hundred square feet of it. As they entered the living room, she smiled at Mitch and pointed to the white brick fireplace and the large picture windows overlooking the garden area.

"This is going to be a great place to read." Excitement filled her heart because she loved books and had plenty of bookcase room.

"It's very nice." He nodded and took her arm.

She led him down the hall to the bedrooms that were set at the rear of the house.

"We love the bedrooms on the other end of the house. Not any traffic noise." Emotion flowed through her and almost brought tears to her eyes. Maybe because after all they'd been through, she had finally found home.

Mitch smiled when they were done and said, "You have a lovely home, Beth Ann."

"Thank you, Mitch. You saw the kitchen—that's Kaylob's department. He loves the island with the pots and pans hanging above it. He's a great cook and always wanted to be a chef. You'll have to come over for dinner some night."

As they headed back down the hall, Mitch said, "So, you guys set a date yet?"

"Not yet, but we will. I'll let you know." She didn't want to tell Mitch about their problems.

"You'd better invite me." He laughed.

"Of course." She tried to look happier than she felt.

Thank goodness someone had left bar stools for them to sit on and have coffee. Kaylob handed them their cups when they entered the kitchen.

Beth Ann thanked Kaylob for the coffee and turned to Mitch. "Have you heard from any of the other cast members?"

"Most of them have gone on to do other shows." He took a sip of his coffee. "A few have asked about you and when you're going back to work."

"Right now I'm just enjoying some time off from everything," Beth Ann said.

"That's understandable. Been quite a year for you."

"Yes, it has." She glanced at Kaylob.

They talked about the funny things that had happened on the tour while they drank their coffee. It was a nice visit, and Beth Ann could tell that Mitch was happy for her. He had always been good to her while they traveled, always comforting her after the nightmares about Kaylob. She had grown to love him as a friend as well as a boss.

After Mitch left, she was unpacking boxes when she felt Kaylob staring at her. "What is it, honey?"

"Do you want to do another show, Beth Ann? Please don't let me stop you from living your dream."

She shook her head. "Not right now. It's hard work—harder than I ever dreamed. Besides, we're unpacking and getting our home set up. I have other priorities right now."

"Okay, baby. If you're sure."

She nodded and continued unpacking. Someday she'd like to do another show, but right now, she had to fix their life. And being on the road again just didn't appeal to her.

She was glad Jack and Lenard had put a lot of her belongings into storage. She'd had no idea they'd stored the furniture and so much stuff. Thank goodness, they had dropped it off, or they wouldn't be having coffee right now.

The next few days were filled with furniture deliveries that gave them a chance to see what else they needed, and they needed plenty. So, that Friday she decided to go shopping while Kaylob was putting up her new bed that eventually would be their bed. They needed new towels and "bed sheets" as Kaylob called them. She had never understood why he called them that. What other kinds of sheets go on a bed?

After she was done shopping, she headed out to her car and felt an odd feeling rush through her—a familiar sensation of icy tingles down her spine. Someone was watching her, she was sure of it. As she walked to her car, she glanced around but didn't notice anything that stood out. While she put her purchases in the trunk, she still couldn't shake the feeling. Then, out of the corner of her eye, she noticed a dark car with tinted windows driving by too slowly.

Not this again. Is that the stupid paparazzi?

The blood-sucking gnats raced out of the parking lot. Funny, they had never done that before. Usually she was the one running from them. Maybe it wasn't them after all and was just some weirdo. She climbed in her car and shook off the incident before she headed home.

She carried all the bags inside and put her keys in the basket. *Holy mashed potatoes,* Kaylob had cooked her favorite food in the world. The aroma jostled memories of happier times from her childhood. Gram had sent them her recipe for fried chicken and her one-of-a-kind mashed potatoes and gravy.

She moved into the kitchen and stuck her nose in the air. "Honey, that smells great." She stood on her tiptoes and kissed Kaylob's cheek while he stirred the gravy.

"Thanks. Did you find our bed sheets and everything?"

"Yes, Kaylob. I found our *bed sheets.* I almost bought music sheets but then I remembered you'd said bed sheets. Good thing you put the *bed* in there."

"Ha-ha-ha." He playfully smacked her behind with a dishtowel.

After what seemed like a century, dinner was finally served. It was every bit as good as her Gram's if not better, but she'd make sure not to mention that, at least not to Gram.

When they finished eating, they went into the kitchen and started on the cleanup. Beth Ann stopped Kaylob as he was loading dishes in the dishwasher.

"Thank you, honey. That was so good." She rubbed her tummy.

He pulled her into his arms and tried to kiss her on the lips, but she shifted away. "I'm sorry, I still can't."

The happy sheen faded from his eyes, making her wrestle with her conflicting emotions. He never said a word to push her, but his eyes spoke volumes. She yearned to kiss him again, embrace him like they had done a million times. But just thinking of his lips on that tramp caused her to recoil. She would work through it, but on her own time frame. Actually, it was possible he hadn't slept with that woman because he was so slow and easy. Holy crap, she couldn't think about him with another woman or she'd lose it. Now, she understood what Kaylob had felt, but what she did was *not* cheating.

When the kitchen was all cleaned, Kaylob guided her toward the living room and pointed to the couch. "Sweetheart, please sit down with me."

Out of habit, he tried to pull her on his lap, but she refused and sat beside him.

He lifted her hand to his lips and placed a sweet kiss on her palm. "My heart belongs to you and only you, even if you never kiss me or make love with me again." He pushed a strand of hair behind her ear. "I just wanted you to know I'll wait as long as it takes. You're the love of my life, and my life is with you."

Beth Ann felt his words etch into her heart and put her head on his chest. She knew he meant every word of it. The thumping of his heart stirred her longing for him, bruised and buried though it was. They sat that way for over an hour and fell asleep in each other's arms.

The shrill ring of the phone jarred her awake the next morning. She *had* to remember to turn down that stupid thing. When she jumped up to answer the insistent object, she accidentally bumped Kaylob and startled him. His hands went up like he was ready to fight, but he quickly stopped when he saw it was her. Thank goodness for that. Getting punched was not her idea of how to start a good day.

"Hey, are you guys coming?" Frankie said when she answered the phone. "We're cooking that breakfast we promised!"

"Holy cow, I forgot." She turned to look at Kaylob and pressed the phone to her chest. "Do you want to go over to Frankie and Deb's? They're cooking us breakfast, remember?"

"No, not this time." Kaylob sighed, rubbing his neck. "I think I aggravated something sleeping on the couch. I'll have to take a rain check. Tell them thanks though."

"Kaylob isn't feeling well, but I'll be there soon," she said to Frankie.

"Okay," he said. "Tell Kaylob we hope he feels better. See ya in a few."

She hung up the phone and stood over Kaylob, stretched out on the couch. "Come on, honey. Go with me, please." She gave him a cute pout and pulled on his arm.

His forehead wrinkled and he shook his head. "I'm just not up for it today. I'll go next time, I promise."

"Okay, but I promised them I'd come." She let go of his arm and gave him a tender smile.

"That's fine. You go ahead. I'm just not ready to go back there yet."

She didn't push him because she had an idea why he was avoiding the place. She ran into the bathroom and threw herself together. On her way out, she stopped to give Kaylob a tiny kiss goodbye.

* * * *

Kaylob kept up his façade until the door closed. He was with her, but he was afraid he would never have her back again. Why the hell had he done

73

something so stupid as going into that woman's apartment? He stood and kicked the sofa, which only served to make his ankle hurt along with his heart. But that was okay because he deserved it.

"Shit! I just tried to make her jealous, and now I'm paying the price."

He hobbled his way to the medicine cabinet to take a couple of aspirins, the harshest drug he would take. He knew he needed to eat something, so he went into the kitchen and took out some bacon and started frying it in the cast iron skillet. Maybe he should fry up his own ass in a pan for being such an idiot.

Trying to make her jealous had been the stupidest thing he could do. He'd known her since childhood and knew what it was like when she was pissed. That had always been lethal. Nothing like a redhead shooting fireworks at you to make you run for cover.

It was just those things she'd said about Blake had made him see red. Just thinking about Blake touching her made him want to put his fist through the damn wall.

His drinking had been a great way to mask the multileveled pain of the horrors of Vietnam combined with his distorted belief of his fiancée's betrayal. His therapist had pointed out that his way of thinking was totally out of line. Beth Ann had not betrayed him because she'd thought he was dead. When he'd pointed out that Beth Ann hadn't really believed he was dead, his therapist had told him that the facts were he was gone and had told her to go on with her life. In fact, he'd told her to find love again. Frankie had pointed that out to him too, and they were both right. He didn't need anyone to tell him he'd been a jealous, self-centered shithead. He already knew it.

There had only been one time when he was fourteen that he'd been with another girl, and that had been before he was Beth Ann's guy. And why did that happen? Because he'd seen Beth Ann give Blake a kiss on the cheek. He'd allowed that jealousy to push him into spending the summer with Dusty, an older girl who had given him many lessons in carnal knowledge. He had been fully aware back then that Blake had a thing for Beth Ann, and he'd always suspected she had a crush on him too. Obviously, he was right.

This was the second time he'd let his stupid jealousy of Blake Tanner cause him to do something to make Beth Ann mad at him. He had to find a way to make her believe that he would never cheat on her, but how? He yearned for things to be right again. He longed for all of her—heart and soul. All he wanted was to get married and grow old with her. He'd love to have children too, but he wasn't sure she'd ever go for that. No matter how long it took, he would keep working on it until he made things right. Beth Ann was worth it. They were worth it. Their love was worth it.

He pulled some eggs out of the fridge to go with his bacon. Maybe today, when she got home, they could talk about marriage. She had pretty much avoided the conversation since he'd screwed up. Just then, the phone rang and he walked over to pick it up.

"Hello." He paused, waiting for someone to speak. "Hello? Is someone there?"

Click.

That was the fourth time this week. It was like they were just listening to his voice. Probably that asshole Blake. Maybe he should march over to his place and tell him if he didn't stop calling and hanging up, he was going to kick his ass.

Yeah, that would win him some brownie points with Beth Ann. He went back to cooking his bacon and wondered if there would ever be a day when he didn't want to beat the shit out of Blake Tanner.

* * * *

Frankie's place was filled with its normal hustle and bustle that always got crazier over the weekend. Beth Ann walked through the lobby and headed for the bank of elevators, but she stopped when she saw the strumpet who had seduced Kaylob over by the mailboxes. Beth Ann felt flames scorch her cheeks, and her heart pounded like warrior drums. She steadied her breath and marched directly toward the woman.

"Excuse me," Beth Ann said, "do you remember me?" *You floozy* she added silently.

The woman turned and cocked her head. "No, why should I?"

The woman's figure was even more outrageous up close. Her breasts were like melons, and she wasn't wearing a bra. Imagining Kaylob's hands on them made Beth Ann want to play kickball with the woman's head.

The wench noticed Beth Ann staring at her chest and said, "Uh, sorry, you're not my type." She turned away and looked down at the mail in her hand.

Beth Ann took a step closer and lowered her voice. "How could you let some drunk guy who was obviously in pain have sex with you? Do you have any idea what it's done to us?"

"You're gonna have to be more specific, honey." She shot Beth Ann a harsh look. "I'm not a virgin."

Beth Ann wanted to smack her but kept her cool. "I think everyone from here to Timbuktu knows that. I'm speaking of Kaylob O'Brien—big blond guy, beautiful blue eyes, and a dimple in his chin. He was staying here with Frankie Russo, the tall dark handsome guy. You know the other guy you tried to get in bed."

75

"Oh yeah, that Italian hunk!" She nodded then frowned at Beth Ann. "Wait a minute…look, Red. I didn't have sex with that blond. He was way too wasted, plus he kept going on about some Beth Ann chick and how pissed he was at her. Beth Ann this and Beth Ann that. Then the asshole throws up on my new shag. Sonofabitch! I threw water on him to sober him up, and you know what he does next? The idiot went into my bathroom and pissed in my sink! That's when I threw him out the door."

Beth Ann could only gawk at her for a moment as she processed what she'd said. The woman looked Beth Ann up and down before a smirk crossed her face.

"Wait a minute, now I remember seeing you at the pool with him. You must be Beth Ann." She shook her head with a huff. "You can have that loser."

That brought back Beth Ann's voice. "Don't you *dare* call him a loser! He's got everything a woman could want. He fought for this country so hussies like you can be free to sleep with any Tom, Hank, Larry or Jerry and the entire maintenance crew!"

The chick's face grew red and her mouth twisted into a scowl. "Screw you and your drunken war hero boyfriend too." The woman turned and stormed off since she'd apparently left her broomstick at home.

Beth Ann's insides were doing cartwheels. Kaylob hadn't cheated! He'd been telling her the truth all along. She squealed and jumped for joy, heedless of the odd looks she got from the other people in the lobby.

When she got upstairs to Frankie's, she sailed through the door. Frankie was reading the paper at the kitchen bar while Debra cooked. They both stopped what they were doing when Beth Ann ran over and hugged Frankie.

"He never had sex with her! He was too drunk and besides, all he did was talk about me!"

A wide grin spread across Frankie's face. "I tried to tell you, silly."

"You know what else he did? He used her bathroom sink as a toilet and threw up on her shag rug. That's why she threw water on him before she kicked him out."

"I knew it." Frankie held his stomach and howled. He raised his hands as if he were the one who'd been vindicated. "See, you should always listen to me."

"Yeah, well, someone should have listened to me when I said he wasn't dead."

Frankie nodded and hugged her back. "You're right."

Debra stepped over and made it a group hug. "I'm so glad for you, honey."

Beth Ann pulled away and looked at both of them. "Would you mind if I took a rain check on breakfast? I have to get home."

"Go on home to your man," Debra said.

Frankie pointed to the plate of pancakes. "Take some of those with you or they'll end up around my waist."

Deb shook her head. "Yeah right, Mr. Fatty, the man who eats organic everything." She laughed as she put some pancakes in a container and handed it to Beth Ann.

"Love you guys," Beth Ann said, just before she flew out the door. "Thanks for the pancakes!"

Chapter Twelve

The drive back home moved at a snail's pace. It seemed as if every slow driver was on the road. When Beth Ann burst through the front door, she startled Kaylob.

"Why are you back so soon? Did they burn the pancakes?" he asked while he relaxed on the couch.

Beth Ann didn't respond. All she could do was stare at him and remind herself of how lucky she was to have him, and how much she loved him.

"What's going on, baby?" he asked. "Is my fly open?" He glanced down at his zipper.com

Beth Ann laughed and flipped off the TV then sat on the coffee table and watched him squirm, his passionate blue eyes full of questions.

"We need to talk," she said, trying to sound resolute and hide her elation.

His smile dropped. "Okay, what about?"

"Guess who I ran into at Frankie's house?"

"Santa Claus?"

"Of course, Kaylob. I came back home all excited because I saw Santa at Frankie's." She folded her arms. "C'mon, be serious."

"Well, then who did you run into that made you so happy?"

"I ran into that slut." She narrowed her eyes. "You know the floozy with the big boobs. I almost pulled off her head. I wanted to break her fingers, and I—"

"Whoa, wait a sec," he said. "*The* slut floozy with the big boobs? I take it you held back on all the ninja stuff since I didn't hear any sirens."

"Very funny, Mr. O'Brien. Yes, she's still in one slutty piece. She was there checking her mail, so I confronted her about what happened."

"Oh." Kaylob fidgeted nervously.

"Now let's try this one more time, okay?" Beth Ann put a hand on his chest and pushed him backwards. "I want you on your back while I ask the questions." Now, she was turning the tables.

"Okay, Beth Ann, go ahead." He folded his hands behind his head. "I'll answer anything."

"First, are you sure you didn't have sex with her?" She looked deep into his eyes.

"Honest to God, I didn't. When I touched her leg, I was only trying to make you jealous. I promise I'll never do that again."

"That's a very good idea," she said firmly.

"If she said we had sex, she's lying." He tried to sit up again, but Beth Ann pushed him back down and moved closer. She put her arms around his neck and gave him a kiss that would have short-circuited Hoover Dam.

Kaylob looked surprised but happy. Tracing his fingers around her neck, he said, "Does that mean you believe me now?"

Beth Ann nodded. "Yes, I do. I'm sorry for not trusting what you told me."

She moved on top of him and gave him another kiss, then she said, "I love you so much, Mr. O'Brien."

"I love you too, Elizabeth Ann Rose, and I understand why you didn't believe me."

"Hush! I should have believed you." She put her fingers over his lips then gave him a wry smile. "Although I can't believe you *peed* in her sink and threw up on her carpet. She's still really pissed at you, by the way. But that's the end of the story."

"Oh, man." His eyes rolled back and he groaned. "I don't remember peeing in the sink. Is that what she told you?"

"Yep." Beth Ann smiled and gave him another quick kiss before getting up and heading towards the kitchen.

Kaylob followed and moved behind her as she stood at the kitchen sink. When he pressed his body against hers, desire rushed through her like a wildfire. The man's hands were magic and reminded her of what he had done during their seven nights together.

"Can we make love now?" His lips touched her ear and sent another wave of desire flowing through her.

"Kaylob, I know it's what we both want but—" She turned to face him. "I want to wait until our honeymoon."

"You still don't want me?" His face drooped in dejection.

"Of course I want you—more than you'll ever know. But I think we should wait until we're married. We can handle it, can't we?" She gave him a playful smile.

His face brightened a little. "Does this mean the wedding's back on? You're going to marry me?"

"Yes, sir." She smiled broadly. "That's exactly what it means. What would you think about a June wedding in Hawaii?"

He enfolded her in a joyous embrace. "I think that would be perfect!" He looked into her eyes and said, "So tell me again why we can't make love right now?"

She cupped his face. "We're going to save that for our honeymoon." She took his hand and led him back to the living room.

"But that's so many months away." He stopped and clutched his heart, swaying as if he were about to collapse. "I could die from lackocoitus disease before then."

"Lackocoitus, huh?" Beth Ann laughed. "I'll have to look that one up."

"And I thought I was the old-fashioned one." He sat on the couch and pulled her onto his lap, making her wonder if he might really die from that dreaded disease.

"You usually are, but I think waiting will make our honeymoon all that more special," she said.

He nodded in resignation. "Okay, we'll wait. But if I start to die, you better know CPR."

He picked up a pillow and smacked her with it. Beth Ann retaliated, and they were soon running through the house play-fighting just like old times. Suddenly, he pulled her to the floor and began tickling her just above the knees—a secret spot only he knew about.

"Okay," he said, "who's the boss?"

"I'm the boss!" Beth Ann squealed through her laughter.

In a signature move, he pulled up her shirt and gave her a raspberry, bringing back heartwarming memories of their adolescence.

"Who's the boss?" he asked again.

"Okay, okay!" She gave up the struggle. "Kaylob Shawn O'Brien is the boss."

He picked her up and carried her back to the couch. When he kissed her deeply, the kiss was filled with more than desire, but also with unconditional love.

When he saw the tears in her eyes, he said, "Baby, what's wrong?"

"Nothing," she said, wiping her cheek. "Everything is finally perfect."

* * * *

They spent a lot of time alone over the next few days. It was important to become whole again, even though there was still one issue that caused tension between them—Blake. Whenever Beth Ann brought up going to get her stuff, a dark cloud would fill the room. Kaylob's therapy was helping, but he was still like a jigsaw puzzle with some pieces missing. The war had stolen them, but she had real hope now.

A week or so later, Kaylob began leaving mysteriously to work on some type of surprise he said he had planned for their wedding. Beth Ann desperately wanted to know what it was—she'd never been good at waiting—but he wouldn't even give her a hint.

One Friday morning, a lady called from the bank to say the money from Kaylob's inheritance had been deposited. The bank lady wanted to know if they could come down to talk about what kind of accounts they intended to set up, which was confusing since they'd just opened a joint checking and savings account. But maybe it was red tape, since it was an inheritance.

After Beth Ann finished her shower, she walked into the bedroom wearing only her lacy underwear. Kaylob was lying on the bed, and when he saw her, his eyes slid over every inch of her body, from her head down to her toes.

"Kaylob, what are you doing?" Beth Ann asked, hiding her breasts.

"Brain surgery," he said with a wide smile, rolling off the bed.

He got up and was moving toward her when the doorbell rang. Saved by the bell! Seeing Kaylob look at her that way sent butterflies through her entire body. A moment later, he returned to the bedroom carrying the largest bouquet of long-stemmed red roses she'd ever seen.

She finished tying her silky robe. "Kaylob, how sweet!" Beth Ann squealed with delight. "Thank you, honey." Then she saw the look on his face.

"They're not from me."

"Oh." She took a card from the bouquet and read it.

I love you and miss you. Please come home. Your fiancé, Blake.

Kaylob held out his hand to see the card, so she handed it to him. His jaw tightened and his eyes darkened to a stormy blue. Beth Ann took the card back and threw it in the trashcan, then she took the roses into the guest bedroom. When she returned, she found Kaylob sitting on the edge of the bed, his jaw still clenched and his hands gripping the comforter.

She sat next to him and touched his arm gently. "I'm sorry, Kaylob. I don't know what to say."

He looked at her, his expression a mixture of pain and anger. "Do you miss him?"

"No," Beth Ann said firmly, even though she did miss their friendship. "And I wish he'd stop doing things like this." That part was true.

Her words seemed to help a little, and Kaylob sighed. "Okay, let's not let him ruin our day."

He rose, pulled Beth Ann into his arms and gave her a tender kiss. She wanted to push him back down on the bed and make passionate love to him, but she managed to resist the heat building in the pit of her stomach.

"Let's get ready to go to the bank," she said breathlessly.

He sighed and touched her silky robe. "I love you and I'll sure be happy when we get married."

"I love you, too." She gave him a tender smile before she turned and sauntered away.

The bank was packed when they arrived, but they finally made it to the front of the line. Kaylob cleared his throat and smiled at the teller.

"Hello, I'm Kaylob O'Brien. Someone called and asked us to come down to talk about checking accounts."

The teller's face flushed and she stammered, "Could you wait for one minute, please?" She walked over almost tripping to talk to an older lady sitting behind a large desk who picked up her phone as she stared at them. In the next instant an older gentlemen walked out and led them to over to the silver-haired lady.

"Thank you both for coming in." He shook Kaylob's hand and then Beth Ann's. "Have a seat and Francis will help you with everything."

Francis was typing when Kaylob whispered, "I wonder what's going on."

"Aside from you making young ladies blush and almost fall, I don't know. But it does seem strange," Beth Ann replied.

When the woman finished typing a wide grin was spread across her face. "My name is Frances Morgan and I'll be helping you today." She looked at them over the top of her glasses. "You really need a financial advisor, but I'll try to get you started. Have you thought about what kind of accounts you'd like to set up?"

Kaylob nodded. "Just a separate checking account for now. We're going to use it for our wedding and our honeymoon." He took Beth Ann's hand and smiled at her.

Frances pulled her glasses to the ridge of her nose then turned her attention to the computer monitor. "Do you have any idea how much money we're talking about?"

Beth Ann and Kaylob exchanged a glance, then Kaylob shrugged and looked at Frances again. "Not exactly. How much are we talking about?"

"Mr. O'Brien, we're talking about slightly more than one million dollars. And the other half will be released in two years."

Chapter Thirteen

"What?" Kaylob gasped. "You're kidding?"

Beth Ann couldn't get her voice to work at all. Until that moment, she'd thought her savings was a big deal, but this was unreal. The room started spinning, and she felt herself sliding down the chair.

Kaylob reached out to her. "Are you okay, sweetheart?"

"I will be in a minute. I need some water." She exhaled as the air clogged her throat and sat back up in the chair.

"Just take a deep breath," Kaylob said, rubbing her back.

Frances waved to someone and asked them to get Beth Ann some water. The girl came back and handed a paper cup to Beth Ann. She drank it down in one giant gulp.

Kaylob looked at Frances and said, "Look, are you sure about this? I didn't even *know* my Uncle Martin."

Frances smiled again and pushed a file across the desktop for Kaylob to examine. "It's all here in the paperwork, Mr. O'Brien. You'll get copies of everything before you leave."

Kaylob thumbed through the papers, shaking his head like a man in a trance. Frances led them through the paperwork of setting up another savings account for now, then she gave them the number of an attorney who specialized in helping people invest their money.

When they left the bank and had recovered from their shock, Kaylob and Beth Ann went shopping and purchased a top-of-the-line camera to capture their wedding and honeymoon. Then they drove to three homeless shelters and wrote them each a check for $10,000 dollars. Beth Ann was so excited she could hardly think straight. Walking into the shelters and handing money to the directors was her idea of a really *good* day.

The phone was ringing when they got home, so Beth Ann hurried in to answer it. "Hello."

"I want you and I need you. I could make you so happy." A dark voice vibrated through the phone.

"Who is this?" Beth Ann said just above a whisper, but all she got in return was the dial tone. The voice had almost sounded familiar. Could Blake be disguising his voice?

Kaylob walked up beside her. "Another hang up?"

"No. Well, yes. He hung up after he said ..." She didn't want to finish.

"Said what?" Kaylob frowned.

Beth Ann sighed. "He wanted and needed me. And he could make me happy."

Kaylob's face reddened and he frowned. "Damn that Tanner! I swear I'm gonna—"

"No, it wasn't Blake," she said even though she wasn't sure.

"That sonofabitch!" Kaylob's eyes darkened. "I should go knock on his door right now. First you get flowers, now you're getting phone calls."

"Kaylob, it wasn't him!" Beth Ann insisted. "Don't you think I'd know if it was?"

"Okay, all right." He reached for her hand. "I don't want to argue about him and spoil our happy day."

"Me either." She went into his arms and laid her head on his chest. "Let's just forget that phone call."

"Okay. I believe you if you say it's not Tanner."

She looked up at him. "The paparazzi followed me the other day when I went shopping. Maybe it's them taunting me."

Kaylob's expression changed to concern. "Why didn't you tell me about that?"

"I didn't think it was a big deal. I still don't. They're just ignorant parasites."

"They better not let me see them," Kaylob growled. "Maybe we should change our number."

"Let's just wait and see. I really don't think it's anything to worry about." She put her head back on his chest and hoped she was right.

When Beth Ann's stomach growled, they both laughed.

"Let's order pizza," Kaylob suggested.

Beth Ann couldn't help but grin at her fiancé. He loved his pizza. "Okay. We definitely can afford it now."

Kaylob leaned back on the couch after he ordered and shook his head. "I'm still in shock about the money, sweetheart. Why would my Uncle Martin do that for me?"

She leaned on his shoulder. "Because you're so wonderful."

Kaylob stood up suddenly, his eyes wide with a grin the size of Crater Lake. "Jesus, holy mother of God! We're millionaires!" He picked her up in his arms and swung her around. "I'm gonna buy you the world!"

"You already did. With you, I have the world." She kissed him while they both tumbled backward on the couch, exploring how sensual lips can be. It wasn't long before they forgot all about the money. They touched, kissed and made out until their pizza arrived which forced them to stop. When Kaylob paid for the pizza, she saw him tip the guy a hundred dollars. The smile on the kid's face was priceless. He must have thanked Kaylob twenty times.

Yep, that was her man. Kind, generous and one of a kind.

* * * *

Sunday morning, the phone rang so loud that it jarred Beth Ann out of her much needed sleep. Why hadn't she turned down that darn phone? She glanced at the clock and saw it was 4:14 then turned on the lamp? She heard Kaylob picking up the phone in the other room, so she lay back down for a few more minutes of blissful sleep. She didn't like him sleeping in the guest room, but it was getting hard for them to keep their resolution if they slept together.

A few seconds later, her eyes opened again when she heard Kaylob's voice getting louder, but she couldn't make out what he was saying. What in the world was going on? Maybe it was that person saying bad things to him. She started to get out of bed, then she heard him hang up and a second later, he flew into the room like a windstorm. What the heck was going on?

"Kaylob, what's wrong?" she asked. "Who was on the phone?" A knot formed in her stomach when she saw how panicked he looked. She had never seen his eyes so wide or his face so pale. "Kaylob, hello! Was it that creep calling again?"

"No it wasn't him." He rushed by her like the house was on fire. One second he was in the bathroom tossing lotion into her makeup case, the next he was dropping his shaving kit into her suitcase. Clothes were launched in several directions and hastily stuffed into two random suitcases, an overnight bag and her purse.

Getting up on her knees, she waved her hands at him. "Kaylob, stop! You're scaring me. What's the matter?"

"No time …. Lisa … the baby." He paused briefly to look at her. "The baby's coming!" He grabbed a pair of Beth Ann's shoes she'd had since 1965 and put them on the bed next to her. "Here, put these on. You want socks? I'll wear this—hurry!"

She did a double take when she realized he was trying to pack her housecleaning shirt—the one she wore to clean the bathrooms and was god-awful ugly.

"Honey, please calm the heck down."

"We have to hurry!" He feebly attempted to shove three weeks of clothes into one overnight bag.

"Kaylob, slow down and talk to me. Is something wrong with Lisa or the baby?"

"No, but we have to go! The baby's coming!" He darted into the closet for the sixth time. "Wait, I need—"

CRACK! *Thump.*

"Kaylob!"

Oh Lord, he had knocked himself out. Beth Ann crawled across the bed and looked over the side to see her fiancé sprawled out on the bedroom floor, one of her fuzzy pink slippers in his right hand.

"Holy Bunny slipper, it finally got him." That bunny slipper had been trying to get him since his first trip home from Vietnam.

She knew she shouldn't laugh when she didn't even know if he was really hurt or not, but he looked so funny lying flat on his back with that deadly slipper in his hand. While she was still giggling, he put his other hand on his forehead and groaned. At least she knew he wasn't unconscious.

It appeared that every shred of clothing they owned was spread out in every direction, and her curling iron was lying in the middle of the floor. It looked like something from a silent film or a robbery gone wild. She couldn't believe her strong, ex-military fiancé had just freaked out over a baby. This was a man who had been in a war, made it through a POW camp and used to have a Zen-like approach to conflict. She glanced around the room again and shook her head.

"Breathe, Kaylob. Just take a deep breath." She went down on her knees and cupped his head in her hands. His eyes were vacant as she leaned down and gave him a kiss on the forehead. Gently, she took the slipper from his hand and scolded it. "See what you finally did, you bad bunny." She dropped the slipper and fell on the floor, laughing and holding her stomach. "Where's the camera? We have to mark this moment."

It was several minutes before she could stop laughing. Every time she looked at him, she got the giggles again. What was even worse was that he had toothpaste covering one of his big toes from when he'd dropped it and stepped on it. That officially pushed her over into the laughter hall of fame.

He sat up and frowned at her, but after a few seconds of her unrelenting laughter, he cleared his throat and slanted his lips. "Beth Ann, what is so damn funny?"

She pointed at the bunny slipper and his big toe covered in toothpaste. "Do you want me to get a toothbrush? Does your toe have bad breath?" She started to get up but started laughing again. "Do you want to floss?" The look on his face almost made her lose it all over again, but she finally managed to be serious. "Well, I know who not to call when somebody's having a baby."

A partial curve of his lips let her know he wasn't mad. "And I know who to call when you need a spanking."

"Really? Isn't it hard to spank someone when you're running into walls and knocking yourself out?"

He sat up and pulled her into his arms. "Maybe we'll have to find out!"

She smiled while letting the laughter slowly subside. For a few minutes, they sat just holding each other, a giggle escaping every now and then. Finally, Beth Ann sighed. "Honey, I guess we should go now that you've finished the best comedy show I've ever seen."

He snickered. "I'm so glad I could entertain you."

She stood and picked up her cleaning shirt from the floor where he'd dropped it. "You were trying to pack my ugly shirt."

"I happen to love this shirt." He got up and took it out of her hand. "You might even say I get excited and entertained when you put it on."

Exasperation filled her. "Why? Tell me you're kidding. Nobody could get excited over this shirt. It's the one I clean house in. It's awful."

"Yeah, I know it's your housecleaning shirt. I also know I get a day off from cleaning when you put it on. That excites me."

She tugged it out of his hands and slapped him with it. "Funny, Mr. O'Brien."

He tried not to laugh. "Come on, brat. Let's get ready to go."

After they cleaned up the mess and got everything ready, they were out the door before 5:30 AM. Lisa's mom had said she was probably going to be in labor for over 24 hours, so despite Kaylob's comical meltdown, they had plenty of time.

While they drove to Novato, Beth Ann found an oldie station on the radio. She and Kaylob sang along with their favorite songs. Just from leaning her head on his shoulder, she could feel the love move through her like a shooting star. Those moments sitting beside Kaylob confirmed what she had always suspected—she and Blake had been missing something. She had never been in love with him, not like this and not even close. With Kaylob, just one touch melted her into a sea of emotion, a sensation she'd never once felt with Blake.

It just wasn't the whole cigar, and now she knew that for sure. Or was it the whole taco?

After driving for several hours, Beth Ann needed to stretch her legs and asked Kaylob to pull over at the next exit. They pulled into an old truck stop and practically had the place to themselves. Beth Ann wanted to take some time to walk, hold hands and talk without interruptions, but Kaylob pulled her down under a big old shade tree nearby and sat facing her.

"Beth Ann, I need to know something," he said, "and please try to understand the reason I'm asking. I know when we get back home you need to go see Blake, and you need to do it alone. I'm trying very hard to let go of my jealousy, and I think I'm doing an okay job." He tucked a strand of her hair behind her ear. "Are you still in love with him?"

She cupped his face. "I've come to realize something since you got home. I was never *in* love with Blake the way I should have been. What I understand now is that it was more ... " She looked up at the leaves on the tree. "Well ... other things that kept me with him."

He tilted her face back down to look in her eyes. "Would those other things be sex?"

She shrugged. "Not really. He was good to me and I was so lonely. I liked him as a person and loved him in another way, but I was not *in* love with him. I think what I meant was that I just felt safe with him. Not the same way I do with you though."

"You can tell me the truth, Beth Ann. Was the sex better? You guys had more time to explore."

She looked deep into his eyes and felt tears well up. "It was never better with Blake, not for one minute. What we had filled a void. I hope that makes sense."

She could see the relief in his eyes. "In some strange way, I do understand. I'm sorry you went through so much. Frankie told me you almost died when you got the news about me, and he gave me the details you didn't."

"I was so lost without you." A tear pushed its way down her cheek.

"I'm so, so sorry, baby." He pulled her into his arms and leaned into her neck. "If anything happened to you, I would've wanted to die myself." He lifted his head and took his hands parting the front of her hair.

"Oh, my god, you still have the scars." His eyes filled with tears as he whispered. "I wouldn't have wanted to be here if you weren't."

"That's how I felt. I honestly didn't know how to live without you. I had to learn how to move forward, and it took months and months—almost a year—before I was back to normal, and even that was a new normal. I didn't laugh or smile as much. Jack said my twinkle had faded."

He wrapped his arms around her tighter. "Beth Ann, I'll never leave you again, I promise. You're stuck with me for a lifetime."

"That's all I've ever dreamed about," she said.

Something shifted that afternoon under the big shade tree. Maybe it was more of an understanding and a bond forged even deeper. It made it hard to get up and leave, but Beth Ann knew that baby wouldn't wait for them. If it was anything like its mama, he or she would come into the world when it was ready and not a minute sooner.

"I hate to leave, but we probably need to go, Kaylob."

He nodded and smiled. "Yeah, I guess so."

As they walked back to the car, Beth Ann noticed a black car drive by.

"What's the matter?" Kaylob asked when she stopped walking.

"That car." She pointed. "Someone was inside taking pictures of us I think."

Kaylob whipped around to look, but the car squealed its tires and drove out of the parking lot. "What the hell?" He dropped her hand as though he was thinking of running after them, but she grabbed it again.

"Just ignore them, honey. It could've just been someone traveling and taking pictures."

Kaylob scowled. "Right—of a truck stop. And why would they peel off like that then?" He turned to stare in the direction the car had gone.

"I have no idea. Let's just go." She pulled him toward the car.

After the eight-hour drive, they arrived in their hometown and headed straight to Novato General Hospital. Beth Ann was amazed at how empty the place was. When they walked in and approached the counter a lady typing behind the desk looked up at them.

"We're here to see Lisa and Terry Lane," Beth Ann informed her.

The lady picked up a clipboard and stood up. "You must be Kaylob and Beth Ann?"

"We are." Beth Ann said.

"Follow me please." The lady pointed.

As they followed her, the unmistakable sounds of a woman in labor echoed down the hall.

"This is bullshit! It hurts, make it stop!"

There was no doubt it was Lisa.

The lady stopped at a labor room doorway. "Enter at your own risk."

Beth Ann stepped into the room to find her best friend looking like Linda Blair in The Exorcist. When she glanced back at Kaylob, he had attached himself to the doorframe and didn't look as if he planned to budge. Beth Ann motioned for him to come inside, but he took a giant step backward, as though he were offering Beth Ann to an Alien Queen in order to save his own life.

"I think I'll wait right here." He swallowed and looked more than a little pale.

"Beth Ann, I'm so glad you're here!" Lisa's voice interrupted before Beth Ann had a chance to drag Kaylob's butt inside the room.

Beth Ann had no choice but to step over and take Lisa's hand while she lay in bed. "Of course I'm here. I love you, Lisa."

Lisa's parents, Betty and Gary, made a hasty retreat out of the room as if they'd been waiting for a chance to escape. At least Lisa's husband stayed and tried to look cheerful but failed miserably.

"*Ahhhhh* ... Damn, shit!" Lisa yelled. "Terry, why did we want this again?" She was bent over in pain but managed to look up enough to glare at her poor husband, who seemed to be doing his best to comfort and soothe her.

The things Beth Ann witnessed in the next hour made her want to run down the hall and ask a doctor to spay or neuter her. The nurse was sticking her hand in places Beth Ann didn't want to think about, and Lisa's yelling got louder as the pains increased. Beth Ann decided she would never, ever have children. Forget those visions she'd had of that little girl. Kaylob could just forget it.

Finally, the nurse yelled, "TIME! Call the doctor!"

Other nurses scrambled and Terry followed as they wheeled Lisa's bed into another room. Beth Ann trailed behind trying to keep up, shooting her chicken boyfriend a look as she ran by. When she entered the delivery room, Terry was hovering around Lisa's head while he continued to tell her he loved her.

"I hate you, Terry!" Lisa smacked his hands away, but he put them right back.

Soon they were telling Lisa to push. Beth Ann was on one side holding her hand while Terry held the other. He kept rubbing her head, kissing her and encouraging her to push.

"Come on, Lisa, you can do it," the nurse said. "Push! Give it your all! Come on, Lisa, push harder! Okay, breathe, now PUSH, PUSH, PUSH!"

Lisa rose up and glared at the nurse. "I can't push any harder! Why don't you jump inside and push it out yourself!"

Beth Ann looked around to see everyone in the room trying not to laugh. The nurse, whose nametag read Georgia, looked at Beth Ann's face and chuckled.

"Is this your first time seeing someone in labor?" Her Southern drawl was as thick as her mother's was.

Beth Ann nodded. "Yes it is."

Georgia laughed again. "You wouldn't believe the things we hear wives tell their husbands during labor. *I'm cutting your thing off* and *I hate you! Don't you ever touch me again!* Along with plenty of choice language. I have to admit, though, I've never been asked to jump inside and push a baby out myself. That's a first." She turned back to Lisa. "Now, honey, you don't really hate your husband. Right now you're just very pissed off and in pain. When this baby comes, you'll fall in love with him all over again. You just wait and see."

Finally, after one last gut-wrenching scream followed, the doctor shouted, "That's it, we got him!" A few seconds later, he lifted a beautiful baby for everyone in the room to see. The baby's response was a fitful cry. "Congratulations, you have a perfect baby boy."

All the fear, pain and anger disappeared instantly from Lisa's face. She went from looking like a goblin to the most stunningly radiant woman Beth Ann had ever seen. Both new parents had tears in their eyes as they looked at their little miracle. Beth Ann almost cried, too, but forced herself to stop. Why was she suddenly feeling so emotional over a baby?

She beamed at her friend and gave her a hug. "You did it, Lisa. I'm so proud of you."

With drill-like precision, the medical staff cleaned up the little guy and swaddled him in a blue blanket, then they handed him to Lisa. While she held him, Terry leaned down and kissed the top of his little head. It was sweet joy to see their little family together, and Beth Ann couldn't help but feel a bit envious as she watched.

"Look at him, Beth Ann, he's perfect." Lisa held the baby up so she could see his little face.

"Yes he is." Beth Ann nodded and felt another tug at her heart.

After Lisa and Terry had both held and marveled over their son, Lisa held him out to Beth Ann. "Here, you can hold him, he won't bite. Benji, meet your new Auntie Beth Ann."

"No, Lisa, I can't—"

"Take him, Beth Ann," Lisa said. "I know you want to hold him. Don't force me to turn into the devil woman again."

Beth Ann moved closer and hesitantly took the baby from Lisa's arms. As she cradled him, she watched the little guy conform to her arms as if he were meant to be there. A strange feeling came over her, as though she were holding onto joy and innocence personified. He was absolutely adorable. She kissed the top of his head and welcomed him into the world.

"I'm your Auntie Beth Ann," she whispered, her voice breaking with emotion. "Welcome, little one."

She could see Lisa and Terry watching her talk to the infant and reacting to her admission of his beauty. That day, March 10, 1974 in Novato General Hospital, Beth Ann fell in love with Benjamin Riley Lane, all 8 pounds and 21 inches of him. Kaylob held him too, and it was absolutely love at first sight.

Chapter Fourteen

When they left the hospital, they drove across town to Beth Ann's childhood home. Jean and Stanley were thrilled to see them and smiled when they walked in the door. As they all sat down on the couch in the living room, Beth Ann's parents had tons of questions about the labor and birth. Of course, Beth Ann had to be the one who filled them in since Kaylob had chickened out and missed everything. She told them in full detail about how Kaylob had handled hearing that Lisa was in labor, including how he had almost knocked himself out running into walls. The room echoed with laughter when Beth Ann told them about the toothpaste on his toe. Kaylob of course tried to give her a dirty look, but he couldn't help but chuckle along with them.

"By the way," Jean said after catching her breath from laughing, "Gram called twice and wants to talk to you, honey."

"Is everything okay?" Beth Ann asked.

Jean smiled. "I think she just misses you, that's all."

"I'll go call her now." Beth Ann got up, dialed Gram's number and waited for her to answer. "Hi, Gram"

"Hello, my sweetness. How are you?"

"We're doing okay. A little tired after the trip and our visit to Lisa and her new baby boy. His name is Benji, and he's just plain adorable."

"Well, I'm so happy to hear you describe a baby without a hint of disgust. Maybe now you'll reconsider making me a great-grandma."

"Don't think it will be me, Gram."

"I guess we'll see," she replied, sounding skeptical. "Will you and Kaylob have time to come up and see me?"

"I'd love to see you. Let me ask Kaylob." Beth Ann held the phone to her chest, and Kaylob was already nodding yes. He told her he wanted to take a day or two at the coast before they went up, and he also said he needed to make some phone calls regarding the surprise he was working on for their wedding. Beth Ann wondered again what he was up to.

"Gram, how about if we start heading up that way today? I think we'll make a little road trip out of it. Does that sound good?"

"That would be wonderful. Thank you, Beth Ann. You've warmed my heart. You two be careful driving now."

"We'll be careful, I promise. Love you, Gram." The minute Beth Ann hung up the phone, it rang again and she picked it up. "What did you forget?"

"What the hell are you doing in Novato? I've tried contacting you everywhere. I was worried?" Blake's voice was so loud that Kaylob heard him through the phone, and it made his face redden with anger.

"Lisa had her baby," Beth Ann said, "and I asked you not to call anymore, Blake. How did you know I was here?"

"You said for me to stop calling you at Kaylob's place, so I'm calling you at your parents' house. I couldn't find you anywhere else. I want your ass home, Beth Ann!"

There was no doubt in her mind that he'd been drinking again. She turned to speak into the phone, lowering her voice. "Kaylob's place is my place too, Blake. We're back together for good. I'm sorry, but you need to stop this." Kaylob tried to take the phone from her but she shook her head and whispered, "Please, not at my parents' house."

"You still have my goddamn ring," Blake slurred. "And you're still my fiancée. I'm coming to get you!"

Jean walked over and held out her hand for the phone. Beth Ann gladly gave it to her.

After listening for a couple of seconds, Jean spoke to Blake in her soothing Southern accent. "My dear boy, you need to calm down and get someone to fix you a nice big cup of coffee." She paused to listen then said, "No, you can't make a decision to come here when you're drunker than a sailor." She waved Beth Ann and Kaylob away before speaking into the phone again. "Blake, you listen to me. Lisa just had her baby. How do you think she would feel if you came here and acted like a wild man from Borneo? You know how long it took them to even get pregnant with this child."

That was the last thing Beth Ann heard before she and Kaylob stepped outside. What the heck was she going to do about him? She needed to give him back his ring even though she'd told him it was over more than once.

"I'm gonna kill that asshole if he doesn't leave us the hell alone," Kaylob muttered when they got outside.

Beth Ann reached up to cup his face. "Honey, he was drunk and he's hurting." She tiptoed to kiss him but he backed away from her.

"Oh, boo hoo. That Texas cowpie better get over it and knock this shit off. We've always been in love forever and he knows that."

Beth Ann pulled him back close again. "You're right. Everybody knows that, Kaylob." He let her kiss him this time, and she could feel the tension in his body start to relax.

"Speaking of that," he said, "I want to stop by my parents' and get your ring back." He put his arms around her and brushed his sweet lips over hers again. "I want it on your finger where it belongs."

"Okay. I want it there, too." She felt a pang of guilt because she wished she'd already given Blake his ring back. She'd have to take care of that as soon as they got back home.

Jean told them everything was fine and not to worry when they went back inside. They said their goodbyes and tried to forget about the phone call from Blake, but it wasn't easy. Their visit to Kaylob's parents was short, and Beth Ann could tell they were glad to see him. Jackie was thrilled to hear the wedding was back on, and she happily handed the ring to Kaylob. Instead of putting it on Beth Ann's finger, he stuck it in his pocket.

When they left, Kaylob took a different route than Beth Ann expected. "Where are you going, Kaylob? You missed the turnoff."

"We have somewhere else to stop first," he replied with a mischievous smile. "Somewhere special."

"What are you planning, Mr. O'Brien?"

"You'll see."

They continued into town in such a roundabout way that Beth Ann said, "Kaylob, are you going around in circles?"

"Yes I am," he said.

"Why?"

"Just wait and see."

Finally, he stopped the car in front of the train station, and Beth Ann realized what he was up to when she saw both sets of their parents there waiting on them.

Kaylob took her hand and gave her a tender smile. "I asked them to be here. I hope you don't mind."

Her eyes filled with happy tears. "No, I'm touched that you invited them."

Their families watched as they both got out of the car and walked over to the spot where they'd first met a dozen lifetimes ago. Jean looked so lovely in her yellow dress and her oversized hat, with her dark hair hanging to her shoulders and her brown eyes lit up with joy. Beth Ann was so glad to see her mom looking happy and relaxed after what she'd put her through a few years ago. Jean had stayed with Beth Ann for two months after they thought Kaylob had been killed. Even though he wasn't her biological father, Stanley had stayed by her side too and now his green eyes sparkled with happiness. She had two dads and loved them both. Stanley was tall and very handsome with dark hair and olive skin. Nothing like her birth daddy who was blonde with fair skin.

Once she came away from her thoughts she witnessed Kaylob get down on one knee and look up into her eyes. "Elizabeth Ann Rose, I know you already agreed to this once, but I wanted to ask you again when I put this ring back on your finger. Would you make me the happiest man alive and marry me? I promise to do my best to make you the happiest woman in the universe." He slipped the ring on her finger and placed a gentle kiss on her hand.

The ring was so beautiful, and she treasured every inch of it. One diamond cut in the shape of a rose with diamond petals all around. Just touching it made her heart swell with joy. She pushed away the memories of the day she took it off and kissed the band of gold goodbye.

"Yes, Kaylob Shawn O'Brien, I'll let you make me the happiest woman in the world, now and forever."

Both sets of parents clapped with joy. A few cars driving by beeped their horns in what must have been approval. Most of the people in town knew their story since *The Novato Advance* had shared much of Beth Ann and Kaylob's history. And many of the townspeople had seen them together since they were kids.

That first day when Beth Ann arrived had been one of the best days of her life. It was the summer of 1963 when she first stepped off that Greyhound bus in a little town called Novato, California. Her mom had remarried, and Beth Ann was on her way to meet her step-dad for the first time. A new school, a new home, and a brand new life.

As she stepped off the bus, the smell of eucalyptus had filled the air. Beth Ann had a feeling that Novato held the secret to her future. It was a feeling she'd never experienced in all her travels with her mom, dad and two brothers.

Boy, had that feeling been right on. That was the very day she'd met Kaylob.

She'd put on a brave façade even though she was only eleven at the time. As soon as their eyes met for the first time, Kaylob had winked while she sat in the car. That caused her mom to think she had a fever. Later when she ran into him, he had flirted as he told her his name and asked for hers. But when he touched her hand, his eyes had widened and he almost fell backward, as if he were scared of her. That had made her feel brave for real, even though she'd been blushing furiously the entire time.

"Sorry if I scared you, Kaylob O'Brien," she said, then she'd giggled and turned to head home.

The next thing she knew, Kaylob had stepped in front of her, his blue eyes sparkling and his grin something out of this world. "You didn't scare me, Beth Ann." He moved closer and lifted her chin with his finger, then he'd said something that had made her heart melt like an ice cream cone on a hot sunny day. "It's just not every day that you meet the girl you're gonna marry." Then he'd raised her hand to his lips and kissed her palm.

Now here they were in that same place so many years later.

"Baby—hello?" Kaylob waved his hand in front of her face. "Did I lose you?"

Beth Ann smiled up at him. "No, I was just remembering the time you told me it wasn't every day that you meet the girl you're going to marry. Guess you were right."

Kaylob threw his head back and laughed. "Oh yes. I remember that day very well."

Their parents gathered around them and wanted to hear the story, so Kaylob told them about how they'd met and known from the start that something special had taken place.

Beth Ann smiled at her mom. "Do you remember the day you picked me up from the bus stop?"

"Like it was yesterday," Jean drawled.

"You reached over and touched my head while we were waiting for the train because I was blushing so badly that you thought I had a fever."

Jean laughed. "Yes, I do remember thinking you had a fever." She looked at Kaylob and arched an eyebrow.

Beth Ann pointed at Kaylob. "He was my fever. He winked twice and that's all it took." Everyone laughed.

Later, after both sets of parents hugged and kissed them goodbye, Kaylob and Beth Ann got back in the car, and he sat for a minute with his hand on the key. "Ready to head out to the redwoods? I was thinking we could spend the night at Patrick's Point."

"I'd love to, honey," she said with delight as her heart overflowed with joy.

It was a beautiful drive and just as she expected, the dose of nature's majesty lifted their spirits even higher as they drove up Highway 101 listening to the radio. When they finally arrived, the redwoods were breathtaking and a true paradise. The trees appeared as gentle giants blocking out the sun. Their trunks were surrounded by wispy ferns, like slippers on absent feet. All the brilliant foliage covered the ground around them. Little butterflies sailed through the air, gliding near the fallen giants called nursing trees where new life blossomed. It was a spectacular sight, and the aroma was heavenly. Several times, they pulled over to the side of the road to take pictures and touch the serene columns of life.

After taking in the beauty of the forest, Kaylob headed north toward the small ocean town of Trinidad, California, a place where the redwoods meet the ocean. The views often made people wonder if they had been transported to another planet, by the way it uplifted the spirit. As Kaylob drove down through the tiny town, Beth Ann spotted a small lighthouse.

"Kaylob, can we stop here?"

"Of course." He turned into a little parking area and shut off the car, then he got out and came around to open Beth Ann's door. He'd always done that for her even though she could do it herself. But the truth was, he was just trying to be a gentleman, a very slow one.

It seemed like an hour later when they finally got out of the car and walked hand in hand to the lighthouse. When they stopped to read the sign, they were amazed that it had been built back in the 1940s and was dedicated to the ones lost at sea. From where they stood, they could see the ocean and little rocks that poked their heads out of the water. Some of the bigger rocks had trees growing out of them. The place was amazing and the smell of the salty air filled her with joy of the new memories they were making.

The town itself was quaint as they headed down to the ocean and treated themselves to delectable seafood. After lunch, they strolled down a very long dock watching the seagulls fly around singing their feed me song.

"This place is enchanting," she said just above a whisper. "Listen to the sea lions." Beth Ann felt Kaylob watching her and turned to smile at him. "What is it?"

"I love it here." He leaned closer. "Ready to go find a place to spend the night?" he asked.

"Yes." She nodded, feeling a sudden warmth wrap around her heart as she glanced down at her engagement ring. Her dreams were really coming true, and this place was their somewhere over the rainbow.

Just up the road, they found a rustic lodge with cottages that sat up on a hill overlooking the ocean. It was peaceful and very quiet. While they sat on the porch swing after they checked in, Beth Ann spied some clouds that looked like something familiar.

"Look, Kaylob. Two people running in the sand." She pointed upwards.

He glanced up and grinned. "Look, they laid down in the sand and he's taking off her clothes."

"Kaylob!" She smacked his arm but giggled.

That evening they left the windows open and fell asleep to the sound of the waves, with Kaylob's arms around her and his heart beating comfortingly next to her ear, she felt like everything was going to be okay. She would give back the ring to Blake and she and Kaylob would have the wedding they had dreamed about since childhood.

Then, sometime in the middle of the night, she found herself being hurled across the room and woke to Kaylob's infuriated shouts.

"Get away from me, you goddamn pigs!"

Beth Ann touched her head and felt blood. Ignoring the pain, she scrambled to her feet and hurried back to the bed so she could try to wake him, being careful not to get too close until he was fully awake.

"Kaylob, honey, wake up."

"Aaaaahhh! Get me outta here!"

God, what did those bastards do to him?

"Honey, it's me—Beth Ann. You're back home and safe now." She took her chances and moved closer so she could touch his face. "Kaylob, please wake up!"

He grabbed her wrist and she thought for a second he was going to hit her, then he slowly opened his eyes.

"Shit ... what's going on?"

"You were having a nightmare." Without thinking, her hand went to her forehead and she winced.

"Oh, my God, baby, I did that to you?" He touched her head.

"It was an accident." She went into the bathroom to get a washcloth and he followed.

"We need to take you to a hospital." He took it from her and gently wiped at the gash on her forehead.

She shook her head. "No, I'm fine. It's just a little cut."

"Goddamn it, Beth Ann! How can you stand me? I thought I was getting better."

She turned and took the rag from him then kissed his neck. "I love you, and you *are* getting better."

He scooped her up and carried her back to bed. "I'm so sorry, baby. I'd rather cut off my hands than hurt you."

"I know that, Kaylob. It's getting better, really. The counseling has helped a lot, but it's going to take time. Let's just move past this, okay?"

He nodded and held her as they drifted off to sleep.

The next morning, Beth Ann awoke to the sounds of the ocean. She felt her head and was relieved to find that it was barely sore at all. While she lay there looking at Kaylob's beautiful face as he slept, the far-off sound of a foghorn made its way into the room. Very quietly, she got out of bed, went to the window and pulled back the blue linen curtains. The ocean was amazing the way it stretched out for miles while the misty fog rolled away from the shore. She smiled and began softly singing one of her and Kaylob's favorite songs.

"*Hark, now hear the sailors cry. Smell the sea and feel the sky. Let your soul and spirit fly into the mystic.*" Sung by, Van Morrison, one of her favorites.

A moment later, she felt strong arms go around her, caressing not only her heart but her soul. She turned to look up at Kaylob's face and kept singing. Tears pooled in his eyes, and by the time she finished the song, he was crying. Kaylob Shawn O'Brien was such an amazing man. He could fight a war to protect the country, yet here he was showing his deep emotions.

They ended up staying two nights and left that Wednesday morning, promising each other they would return again soon. The magical forest with towering redwood trees and the ocean were as much a part of them as their eternal love for each other.

They hadn't been driving long when they spotted a trail right outside Patrick's Point. They decided to stop and get in one last walk through the spectacular area before heading to Gram's. After they'd been walking for ten minutes or so, they came across a sitting area. It was surrounded by the thriving forest. Beth Ann thought about all she'd learned on the reservation as a child, and understood that the forest was a treasure, but one had to be aware of their surroundings and watch out for creatures and hidden dangers. The sun filtered through the giant trees causing highlights to shimmer over the plants. Sitting there on a shaded bench with Kaylob, Beth Ann felt as if they were the only two people on Earth.

Kaylob must've felt it too, and she could tell he wanted to talk about something. He looked around the lush forest as if he were contemplating what to say. She hoped it wasn't about what had happened the other night. She knew he felt horrible about it. Kaylob cleared his throat and turned to take her hands in his. "I need to talk to you about something, sweetheart."

"What is it, honey?"

He took a deep breath as if he were trying to brace himself. "I wanted to spare you all this, but I feel like I need to explain why I do things like I did the other night. When I was in the POW camp, they beat me daily. Sometimes they'd do things to me that no human should ever go through. Words can't begin to explain what it was like."

"You don't have to talk about it if you don't want to, but you can tell me if you need to," Beth Ann said softly.

"I'd like to share what I can. You deserve to know why I keep acting so crazy."

Chapter Fifteen

She covered his hand with hers. "Okay, take your time. You know I'm here for you."

He took another deep breath. "When they captured me, I was trying to save Patterson and some of the other guys. I got hit twice by gunfire before I blacked out." His voice trembled when he went on. "After they beat me, they would bury me alive with just my nose sticking out of the dirt. Sometimes they'd pinch my nose so I couldn't breathe. Other times my mouth was up enough to get air, but they'd put rats and spiders near my lips or drop them on my head."

Beth Ann tried not to let him see how badly he was horrifying her because she knew he needed to talk about what had happened. She made it through hearing how they'd beaten and tortured him, but when he shared how he had to crawl across the ground with his arms tied behind his back to eat food that was riddled with maggots, she started to tremble. The tears fell and there was nothing she could do to stop them, so they cried together.

No wonder, just no wonder. She knew it had been bad for him over there, but her poor Kaylob had endured more than she could ever have imagined. She looked up at him and put her hands on his face.

"Kaylob Shawn O'Brien, you know I've loved you my entire life, but I want you to know right now how brave I think you are and how incredibly proud of you I am. Don't you *ever* apologize for anything you do because of what you went through over there. I just thank God every single day that you came home to me."

He closed his eyes with tears streaming down his cheeks. "I love you, Beth Ann. You're the only reason I survived."

She put her arms around him and held on tight. "We'll get through this, honey. We can get through anything as long as we have each other."

* * * *

When they pulled into Salem, rolling hillsides, silver skies and lush greenery greeted them. As usual, the sun only whispered through the Douglas firs that lined the streets. Beth Ann thought about all the waterfalls and walking trails, and her insides jumped for joy.

Life was a different pace here much like it was in Novato, the complete opposite of Riverside. As they drove down Gram's tree-lined street with its historical elegance, she couldn't help but wonder what it had looked like back in the olden days. Gram had lived in this neighborhood since Beth Ann was a little girl, and everything appeared to be frozen in time. Many of the homes had wraparound porches like Gram's, which Beth Ann had always adored.

When Kaylob pulled in front of Gram's Victorian house, she was sitting on a wicker chair on the white wooden porch, snapping green beans. The minute she looked up and saw them, she put down her pot and waved with a beaming smile. Beth Ann couldn't get out of the car fast enough. She ran down the sidewalk and bounded up the front porch steps to embrace her Gram.

"Oh, my sweetness, I've missed you so much," Gram said.

"I've missed you too." Beth Ann pushed her tears away when she gazed into Gram's smiling blue eyes that had always made her feel loved. There was an old saying that said, eyes were the mirrors to the soul, and Gram's soul was beautiful.

Beth Ann could feel Kaylob watching them, so she stepped back and motioned for him to come up the stairs.

Gram turned toward him and smiled. "My Lord, it's good to see you, and you're still as handsome as ever. Come give me a hug."

Kaylob did as he was told. "It's good to see you, too, and I can't believe how much Beth Ann looks like you."

Gram nodded then waved them both inside. "I made up Beth Ann's old bedroom and put a bigger bed in there. Well, James did." She led them down the hall. "Since you two are engaged and living together I figured it was okay." Beth Ann nodded and said, "Thank you Gram."

Beth Ann hadn't seen her birth Dad since he'd visited her at one of her shows in Colorado when she was on tour. His visit had touched her deeply because it had been on the one-year anniversary of when Kaylob was declared Missing in Action and Presumed Dead. Her dad and Gram hadn't seen Kaylob since he was nineteen when they'd come for a visit to Novato.

Later that evening, they all sat on the front porch watching the stars and listening to the crickets. Kaylob sat next to Beth Ann on the porch swing while Gram told stories about Beth Ann's childhood. It was plain to see how he enjoyed hearing all Gram's old Southern sayings.

"Well, young man, it looks like you love my granddaughter. You know she's the apple of my eye."

Kaylob gave Gram a wide smile and nodded. "I can see that, and I know how much she loves you too."

Gram picked up her glass of tea and took a long sip. "Her childhood was harder than it had to be. Her daddy wanted to travel the world and become famous."

Beth Ann held Gram's gaze. "There was still a lot I loved about my childhood. Look how much time I got to spend with you. I loved my summers here." She looked around and took in the beauty of the night with a little shiver. "It's a little cool tonight though. Do you need a sweater, Gram?"

"I am a bit chilled. I'll go fetch it." Gram started to stand but Kaylob stopped her.

"Let me get them," he said. "I know Beth Ann's is on the coat rack. Is yours there too?"

Gram nodded. "Just grab me the old white thing. It's wool and keeps me plenty warm."

Kaylob bent down and kissed Beth Ann's head. "I'll grab them right after I make a quick pit stop."

Beth Ann watched him go inside then lowered her voice. "I love him so much. After the time we just spent together alone, I know more about what he's gone through, and it's worse than I ever thought." She lifted her hand and stared at the ring. "I'm so glad I get to spend my whole life with him."

Gram reached over and took her hand. "I can only imagine, honey. You know the kind of love you and Kaylob have, doesn't come around every day. God has blessed your life, and this ring is breathtaking."

Beth Ann lifted her hand to kiss the ring. "I love it so much. I was so mad at God for a long time when I thought he took Kaylob away. I'm not sure He'll ever forgive me."

Gram looked at her a few seconds then said, "God expects us to get mad at him, but He forgave you for it as soon as it happened, and it proves that you believe in Him, because you can't be mad at someone you don't believe in. He knew you were just upset. God never gives up on us. Remember our song?"

Beth Ann paused for a second. "Yes, I remember."

Gram smiled and started humming their favorite hymn, then they sang together. Sweet tones blossomed outward to the otherwise still night.

"It is no secret what God can do. What He's done for others, He'll do for you. With arms wide open, He'll pardon you."

Beth Ann looked up to see Kaylob standing behind the screen watching them. He waited until they finished then clapped.

"That was beautiful," he said as he stepped out and handed them their sweaters.

They spent the rest of the evening listening to Gram share stories of long ago days when she was growing up. Although Kaylob seemed to enjoy it as much as Beth Ann did, later when they were in bed, she could tell he had something on his mind.

"What is it, honey? Is something bothering you?" She propped her head on her hand so she could see his face.

He hesitated. "No, not at all... I was just thinking about tonight. I was touched hearing you and Gram sing together."

Beth Ann smiled. "Thank you, I'm glad you liked it." She let her fingers brush his chest lightly. "You're so wonderful, Mr. O'Brien. I hope you know that. Not to mention sexy, handsome, thoughtful and sexy. Oh, and did I mention sexy?"

He laughed and pulled her closer. "Want to show me how sexy you think I am?" His hand moved to her nipple and it hardened. "Baby, come on, please. Gram's all the way upstairs. We could do something. We don't have to go all the way. Remember how good we got at that when we moved in together?"

"No, I don't trust myself to stop, Kaylob."

He groaned and closed his eyes. "All right, fine, but it's torturing me."

She scowled at him. "Don't forget I'm in this, too."

"Well, maybe we both better learn CPR." He pulled her on top of him and growled like an old bear, making her giggle too loud.

"I need to ask you something else, sweetheart," he said. "Do you believe the words in that song you were singing about God, or were you only singing it for Gram?"

Beth Ann moved beside him and thought for a moment before she answered. "Yes, I do believe it."

"I'm not sure what I believe," he said. "I'm not even sure I believe anything."

Beth Ann tried to explain what God meant to her and didn't push him to agree or disagree. They drifted off to sleep in each other's arms, and Beth Ann dreamed happy dreams of her childhood times spent with Gram.

The morning light filtered through the lacy curtains and woke Beth Ann. They were the same ones that had hung there forever. She couldn't believe Gram had kept every finger painting, Popsicle stick figure and paper plate drawing she had ever made. A quick whiff made her stomach roar to life. Gram was making potatoes, homemade biscuits, and what smelled like the steak she always substituted for bacon. She knew Beth Ann wouldn't eat pork because of the time she'd spent on her auntie's farm as a child and had fallen in love with a pig named Herbert. One day when she'd headed out to play with him, he was gone, and she'd found out later that he'd been turned into pork chops. That had been the end of eating pork for Beth Ann.

"Hey, beautiful," Kaylob said beside her, "Whatcha thinking about?"

She turned and smiled at him. "Did I wake you?"

"I thought maybe I had died and gone to Heaven."

"No more bad dreams?" Beth Ann looked concerned.

"No, but something is tickling my nose, and now my stomach is yelling." He chuckled. "Gram must be cooking, and it smells great." He threw the covers aside and got up, looking around the room. "Beth Ann, this is amazing. She kept all your art stuff. I love it. I didn't notice all this when we got here."

Beth Ann climbed out of bed and stood next to him. "I've never been a very good artist."

"You wrote little notes on most of them. That's priceless." He pointed to one and read it aloud. "*To Gram. God gave me a specail gift when he gave me my Gram I luv you. Your grandaughter, Elizabeth Ann.* I don't know which is cuter—your art or your spelling."

Beth Ann laughed as she sat on the bed and watched Kaylob chuckling as he read all the little notes. When he was done, he lifted his nose in the air.

"Wow, we're not in Kansas anymore. I bet you loved waking up to smells like this as a child."

"Yes, and I'm not sure I'll ever outgrow loving it. Waking up to Gram's cooking, seeing her smiling face whenever she looks at me." She didn't know why tears were filling her eyes. Maybe it was because her life was changing, and being there in her old childhood room reminded her that someday Gram wouldn't be there. She bent over her suitcase and said, "I need to get dressed."

"And it's my duty to watch." Kaylob gave her a mischievous look.

She giggled then found her blue jeans and her favorite pink sweater that buttoned down the front and had a little butterfly over her heart.

Kaylob watched and made little wolf whistles. "Baby, that could most definitely get you in trouble. You're killing me here."

With a saucy smile, she turned around and slipped up her blue jeans.

"You little minx." He stood and took a step toward her. "Maybe we should rethink this agreement."

Before he could reach her, she sidestepped him and turned on her old yellow radio that still sat on the antique dresser, then she sang along with "California Girls."

"*I wish they all could be California girls. The west coast has the sunshine and the girls all get so tanned.*"

Kaylob grabbed her hand and began to dance and sing with her. His voice had a uniquely deep tone that harmonized magnificently with hers. When the song ended and applause rang out, Beth Ann realized they had an audience. Gram and her daddy had been watching from the doorway. Beth Ann went to her dad and hugged him, then Kaylob came over to shake his hand.

"Breakfast will be ready soon," Gram said. "Did you two sleep okay?"

They both nodded and Kaylob said, "Until I smelled that aroma from Heaven."

"That's my alarm clock." Gram chuckled and headed down the hall.

"Now that kind of alarm clock I love." Kaylob moved over to his suitcase and grabbed some clothes. He was still in his pajamas, which he only wore when people were around. "I hope you two will excuse me. It's time to get dressed and ready to eat."

Before Kaylob stepped out of the room, James placed his hand on Kaylob's shoulder. "I'm glad you're home, son. I wanted to tell you how proud I am of you."

Kaylob looked surprised. "Thank you for saying that, sir."

"No, thank you for doing what you did for our country," James said.

Beth Ann felt proud of her dad for expressing those feelings. Her dad was so handsome and so tall. Just then, he reached over and pulled her into warm hug.

"Beth Ann, it's been too long." She hugged him back and saw his blue eyes get misty.

"I missed you too, Daddy," she whispered as Kaylob left the room.

It was a precious moment between her and her father. When he finally left the bedroom, she had to push back the tears.

On the way to the kitchen, Beth Ann and Kaylob heard Gram and her dad bickering good-naturedly, so Beth Ann called out, "Do you need any help, Gram?"

"No, sweetness. Go enjoy the morning. I will be done in about twenty minutes. James, get your hands off that right now before I jerk you through a knot."

They tried their best not to laugh as they headed outside to take in early morning scenery. A sparkling, sunny day hovered patiently just above a fine foggy mist. Salem didn't have a lot of sunny days, but when it did, the whole area showed the vibrant green beauty.

The porch swing was dry enough for both of them to sit and let the gentle momentum carry them to and fro. Morning sounds from the neighborhood rolled in, accompanied by a jingling bell attached to a red miniature dachshund. Beth Ann watched as the dog lifted his leg, did his business, then growled and scraped his back legs in the dirt. Beth Ann wondered why dogs did that, as though the previous dog had left them a bad message. She shared her theory with Kaylob and they both laughed.

"I have to go pet him," she said. "You know how much I love Dachshunds."

"I know." He gave her an amused smile. "Go on."

She got up and hurried down the steps. "Hi," she said to the dog's owner, a nice-looking man with blond hair and blue eyes who was wearing a brown fedora and light leather jacket. "I love wiener dogs. What's this little guy's name?" She bent down to get a closer look.

"His name's TJ. He's a meanie wienie sometimes, but he seems to like you. Let him get a sniff of you before you pet him though. He could get grumpy."

"Hello, TJ, you're so cute. My name is Beth Ann." She reached down, started petting the puppy and got a burst of tail wagging in return.

The man looked surprised. "He acts like he knows you. Maybe it's your red hair. His mom's a redhead too."

Kaylob stepped up beside Beth Ann and nodded at the guy. "Uh-oh, another redhead."

The man arched an eyebrow. "Yeah, keeps you on your toes, huh?"

They both laughed as if they shared some inside secret about redheads. Beth Ann thought about asking what was so funny but changed her mind. She was still petting TJ as if the two were long lost friends when she noticed a lady with red hair approaching. She had an open, inviting smile, and her hair was just a lamb's breath difference from the color of Beth Ann's. There was something very familiar about her, but Beth Ann couldn't put her finger on it.

The lady came and stood next to her husband. "I leave you for five minutes and you end up with another redhead?" She chuckled. "Should I beat you again?"

"Not today, baby doll. I just finished healing up from the last time." He turned to Beth Ann and pretended to lift up his jacket. "You want to see the scars?"

"That's enough, show off," the woman said. "You know I don't leave scars."

"My name's Robert and this is my wife Louise. This is Beth Ann and ..." He looked at Kaylob. "I didn't catch your name."

"It's Kaylob."

Louise tilted her head toward Beth Ann. "Do I know you?"

Beth Ann laughed. "Funny, I was thinking the same thing."

They looked at each other as if they were trying to recall when they met last. It was a strange sensation for Beth Ann. She felt as if she knew this lady and the little red wiener dog.

Louise turned her attention to Kaylob. "You're a very handsome gentleman. You make sure you take very good care of your soon-to-be wife, okay?" She punctuated her request with a flirtatious wink.

Kaylob smiled then winked back, causing her cheeks to flush.

After saying goodbye, the older couple left but Louise turned once more to dispense a bit of wisdom to Kaylob and Beth Ann.

"Have a wonderful life and enjoy your youth. Don't waste one minute of it. Finally, never lose each other."

Beth Ann watched as they turned the corner and disappeared into the mist.

"You think you might know her?" Kaylob asked.

Beth Ann shrugged. She did feel as if she knew the woman but couldn't explain why. "Did you mention we were getting married?" Beth Ann questioned.

"No, I never said a word."

"Strange." Beth Ann glanced down at her hand. "Oh, she must've noticed my ring."

Beth Ann stared down at her ring perplexed, as Kaylob headed away. Just when she started to turn, she saw a black vehicle speed by. "Kaylob!" she shot over her shoulder but the-car was gone by the time he got back out to her.

"What, Beth Ann?"

"Never mind," she said. "It's nothing." After all, there were a lot of black cars in the world. That didn't have to be the one that had been following her, right?

Chapter Sixteen

They went back to the porch and were about to sit down when Gram's voice summoned them. "Beth Ann, Kaylob! Breakfast!"

They pushed each other playfully as they scrambled to get through the door and were laughing when they entered the kitchen, but their laughter died when they saw the table. Gram had gone all out—biscuits, potatoes, eggs and steak with gravy. In the middle of the table was a large bowl of fruit. The presentation looked like something out of a Southern cooking magazine.

When they were all seated, Gram looked around the table and everyone held hands while she bowed her head to pray.

"Dear Lord, thank you for this time to spend with family. Thank you for bringing Kaylob back to Beth Ann and to all of us. By the way, Beth Ann is not mad at you anymore, although she might still be mad about her red hair." Everyone chuckled. "Lord, help all those dear soldiers still over there fighting, and keep them safe in your arms. With love, we give thanks on this day for the life you have given us, and the love we've been able to share with each other. Amen."

"Amen," they all said in unison.

The minute Beth Ann picked up her fork to take a bite the phone rang. "I'll get it." She jumped up and ran to the phone.

"Hello." She paused and could hear breathing. "Hello. Is anybody there?" A dial tone told her they had hung up. A creepy feeling washed over her. It could have been someone calling the wrong number. Once she sat back down, she smiled and said, "It must have been someone calling the wrong number."

Gram nodded and took the cloth napkin from the table, opened it and placed it on her lap. "Tell me, Kaylob, what church did your family go to?"

He sighed and looked nervous. "I've never been to church in my life. It's just something we didn't do with Dad gone all the time and Mom..." A suggestion of the sad memory finished the sentence.

Gram shook her head. "Don't worry. We'll fix that on Sunday."

She picked up the eggs and passed them around the table. James grabbed the biscuits and gravy, plopping a large amount on his already overflowing plate.

"Mother, not everyone goes to church. Hell, I don't go to church."

"James Joseph Rose, hush up now. You're getting too big for your britches."

"I'm a grown man, Mother. My britches fit me just fine."

"Well, that just dills my pickle," Gram said. "I would have never dreamed you would grow up."

Kaylob looked at Beth Ann and they both tried in vain to hold back their laughter. Gram grinned at them then glared at James. Ever since Beth Ann could remember, her father had always been on the wrong side of Gram's wrath, but there were sweet moments between them too.

The breakfast was yummy and Beth Ann could see by the way her dad and Kaylob ate that they agreed. When they were done, everyone helped clear off the table and sat down to finish talking and drinking coffee. Kaylob thanked Gram over and over for the scrumptious food and asked for a few recipe details for future breakfasts. Unfortunately, the topic of cooking sparked Gram to ask the dreaded question.

"How's your cooking coming along, Beth Ann?"

Kaylob tried to stuff back a laugh but did a horrible job. Beth Ann gave him her best mean look along with a gentle kick on the leg as he continued to chuckle.

"Oh, it's going all right," Beth Ann replied, purposely being vague. "I'm sure it will get even better. I'll catch on soon."

"The only thing likely to catch is our house on fire," Kaylob whispered loud enough for everyone to hear. He picked up his napkin to wipe his mouth and winked at Beth Ann.

Gram looked at Kaylob then back at Beth Ann. "You need to learn how to cook. Someday when you have children, you'll need to cook for them."

Kaylob nodded with his famous smartass grin. "Yes, sweetheart, when we have children, you might want to make them breakfast without inviting the fire department."

Beth Ann's lips puckered as she lifted her left eyebrow. "Keep laughing, smarty pants. You've just volunteered to be my food guinea pig forever."

"At least I'll die a happy man," he replied with feigned reverence. "The tombstone will read: *Was it something I ate?*"

"You're such a funny man, Mr. O'Brien." Beth Ann stuck out her tongue at him. "Maybe your tombstone should read *I died laughing from cracking myself up.*" Everyone chuckled as they finished drinking their coffee.

They all headed out to the front porch to catch the now beautiful day. Gram and James both told stories of Beth Ann's childhood, and they also shared the story Beth Ann had heard about a hundred times about Gram giving birth to James in the kitchen and how he had come so fast that his head bounced off the kitchen floor.

Gram laughed and said, "See what happens when you hit your head on the kitchen floor being born. You end up like James."

He rolled his eyes as Kaylob and Beth Ann chuckled. Gram got up to go inside but came back to the screen door a moment later.

"James, for Heaven's sake. Get in here and take out this garbage. You're about as useful as a pogo stick in quicksand."

"It's not even full yet, Mother," he said.

"It's got food in it that will draw flies. Don't be contrary, just take it out."

"Yes, Mother."

As he went inside, Beth Ann heard him mumble something about how the flies would stay away in fear they would be yelled at. A second later she and Kaylob heard Gram scolding him again.

"James, were you raised in a barn? Close that door, you're letting in the flies!"

"Your Gram is a trip," Kaylob said, laughing. "I love her funny sayings."

"It's always been that way. I think she's been mad at him since the day he was born. But mostly it's because he caused my mom to leave with all the traveling. My mom got tired of it."

Kaylob took her hand. "I love Gram. She's a feisty lady and reminds me of someone else I know."

"I know, but I worry about her." Beth Ann sighed. "She's almost sixty five and so alone. But she does take good care of herself. She won't eat anything from a box and walks daily. She always says *Old Arthur will catch up to you if you don't walk.*"

Kaylob smiled and put his arm around her. "Gram's a very smart lady, just like her granddaughter."

Beth Ann put her head on his shoulder while he sang his version of the song he'd first serenaded her with out at Tom Sawyer's Pond when they were kids. That had been the same day he'd told her he was going to open his own restaurant, and she would be his wife when he did. The sound of his voice vibrated a deep, sexy tone.

> *Hey, hey, Beth Ann, I wanna marry you*
> *Hey, hey, Beth Ann, no one else could ever do*
> *I've waited so long for school to be through*
> *Baby, I can't wait no more for you*
> *My love, my love*

Just as Kaylob finished the last verse, James came back out to join them and told them Gram was still puttering around in the kitchen getting ready to make her famous chocolate chip cookies.

"What do you have planned now that you're out of the military?" James asked, tilting his head.

"I'm still thinking over a couple of trades," Kaylob replied.

"What kind?"

Kaylob gave him a grin. "I've got time to think it over and make some choices, thanks to the inheritance I got. I still can't believe an uncle I never met left me all that money. It's kind of confusing."

Beth Ann squeezed Kaylob's hand. "I'm sure he wanted you to have it because he was proud of you like everyone else is, honey."

"Speaking of that, I need to make a quick phone call," Kaylob said. "I'll be back in a few minutes."

After Kaylob left, Beth Ann recognized the look on her dad's face and knew what was coming.

"How is she?" he said softly. "Is she happy?"

"Yes, she's very happy." Beth Ann watched the smile vanish from his face and his eyes turn glassy. "I'm sorry, Daddy. I don't want to make you sad, but Mom's doing great."

"She was my first love you know." James seemed to drift away, as if in deep thought.

Beth Ann's parents had met at a dance when they were both seventeen. Jean said it was love at first sight. After they dated for less than a year, they were married at City Hall. They traipsed from one end of the country to the other, following gigs. Jean had always supported James's desire to be a star, but he'd promised to settle down when they had children. After their first child arrived, James kept making excuses why he had to stay on the road. By the time Beth Ann arrived, Jean surrendered and figured he'd get tired of it sooner or later, but he didn't. Beth Ann was eleven years old when they split up. It hadn't really come as a surprise to any of them. Unfortunately, James had been oblivious and too busy having a good old time to see that he was losing his family.

Beth Ann had seen her mom place the Dear John letter on his pillow. Her dad was devastated when he'd called and pleaded with Jean to take him back, but she told him she was through living a vagabond life behind the wheel of a car. James frequently stayed gone for days or weeks, and on one of those nights, Jean had met someone else—Stanley.

James cleared his throat trying to get Beth Ann's attention. "You look a thousand miles away, sweetie. Are you sure your mom's okay?"

"She's doing well, Dad." Beth Ann put the tear-stained memories back in their box. "She loves Novato, and she's made so many friends."

James looked down at his left hand, and for the first time Beth Ann realized he still wore his wedding band. How could she not have paid more attention and noticed that before?

A fragile smile touched his face. "I'm glad to hear she's happy." He touched his wedding band, picked up the newspaper and pretended to read but Beth Ann could see he was trying to hide his eyes.

"Dad, don't you have a new girlfriend?"

James nodded and looked away. "Yes, her name is Vera."

Kaylob came out and sat down beside Beth Ann just as James answered her question. He started to get up again, but she held his arm and made him sit back down.

"Well, Dad, maybe it's time for you to take off that wedding ring. How does that make Vera feel?"

James looked at his hand then back at Beth Ann. "I'll take it off soon. I know I should."

Beth Ann couldn't help but think about another ring that she needed to return. But she shook off the thoughts and met her dads gaze. "I'm sorry if you're still hurting. Mom will always hold a special place in her heart for you."

A wistful smile crossed his lips. "I always wanted her to be happy. I just wish it could have been me doing that instead of someone else. I was too damn busy chasing my own dreams. Nobody's gonna ever take your mama's place in my heart. She was—and will always be—the love of my life. I reckon that's why I can't settle down."

Beth Ann started to say something when Gram's voice came from the kitchen.

"Anybody want more coffee?"

Kaylob looked up. "I'll take a cup. Any cookies ready yet?"

Beth Ann turned and frowned at him. "No cookies, Mr. O'Brien. We just ate, for crying out loud."

"Okay, no cookies." Kaylob gave her a pout.

Gram came out a few minutes later with a cup of coffee for Kaylob. After she handed it to him, she walked by James and touched his shoulder. When he looked up at her, she leaned down and kissed his cheek before she sat down. Beth Ann knew she must have overheard and knew her son was hurting.

James looked at Kaylob. "So it sounds like you have a lot of choices now that you've got all that money. Maybe you could open your own restaurant."

Kaylob shrugged as he sipped his coffee. "That's definitely possible now. It's more money than we could spend in our lifetime, especially considering we've always been so frugal."

"Gram," Beth Ann said, "do you have any bills you need us to pay off?"

Gram picked up her knitting. "No, for Heaven's sake. I'm not taking your money."

"Dad, how about you? Do you need anything?"

"No, no, I'm doing fine. I have no bills," he said with a firm tone.

Kaylob looked at Beth Ann and winked. They had already talked it over and knew what they were going to do for both of them. And they wouldn't take no for an answer.

Beth Ann smiled at the thought, but just as she did she saw a black car drive by. Someone was taking pictures. She did her best to ignore it since her Gram and Dad were there, and Kaylob had his head leaned back with his eyes closed. So why worry them? But she couldn't help but wish whoever it was, would go away.

Later that day, they were all back out on the front porch while Gram continued to work on her blanket. Beth Ann found herself staring at each car as they drove by.

"I'm playing this evening at a club downtown," James said. "Would you guys like to come have some fun? It's a nice night club."

Gram was already shaking her head. "Good Lord, James. Beth Ann doesn't go to bars."

"Gram, actually I would love to go hear Dad play." Beth Ann smiled and gave him a wink.

"Well, okay, but I'm not going tonight," Gram said, going back to her knitting. "I'm not in the mood to sit around and watch people get drunk on a Friday night."

Beth Ann was surprised at the word *tonight*. "Gram, have you been before?"

"Yes, I went to hear your daddy play a few times. He sure knows how to play that guitar. I'm very proud of him."

Beth Ann saw Gram look at James and exchange a smile. He went over to kiss his mother on the forehead, and Beth Ann gave Kaylob a knowing look. Even though Gram never approved of her son's traveling and playing in bars, she went down to hear him play his music. Her love for her son was clear.

"I really like Vera," Gram said. "Will she be there tonight, James?"

"Of course," he said. "Beth Ann and Kaylob will get to meet her."

"Oh, good," Beth Ann said.

"At least Vera is more mature than your father's other girlfriends," Gram said.

"Other girl friends?" Kaylob looked back and forth between Gram and James.

"Yes, I'm afraid James is a runaround." Gram gave him a disapproving look. "He's never sown all his wild oats."

James stood up with a sigh. "I'm going to cut the grass and do some weeding it's getting thick around here."

Beth Ann turned to Gram. "What do wild oats have to do with girls?"

Gram glanced up from her sewing and stifled a laugh. "Oh, my beautiful granddaughter. You are a funny child."

Kaylob stood up and tried to escape, but Beth Ann pulled on his hand.

"Kaylob, what do wild oats have to do with girls?"

He laughed and shook his head. "Nothing you have to worry about with me. I think I'll go help your dad." He winked and went down the porch steps.

Beth Ann sat there for a while thinking about wild oats, then her thoughts drifted to Gram's marriage to her Grandpa. He'd passed away so young—when Beth Ann was just a baby—but Gram had never remarried.

"Gram, you must have loved Grandpa the same way I love Kaylob."

"I cared deeply for your grandpa. He was a dear man and a good friend. But if truth be known, I only had one love of my life, and we never got to be married."

Chapter Seventeen

Beth Ann's eyes widened. "Why, what happened?" She folded her legs under her in anticipation of Gram's story.

"My family didn't want me to be with him because they thought he wasn't good enough for me. He was a poor farmer and in the military." Gram paused and looked off in the distance. "My parents wanted me to marry someone who could give me a better life than they had. The ironic thing is that your grandpa ended up losing all his money one year after we were married." Gram looked down at the sewing in her hands. "But I never loved anyone like I did Nicky."

"Nicky? Who was he?" Beth Ann asked.

"Well, his name was Nickolas, but I always called him Nicky." Gram's entire face lit up when she said his name. Beth Ann had never seen that happen before.

"I'm sorry, Gram. That must have been sad for you." Beth Ann looked down at her ring and thought how awful it would be to have to marry someone just to please your family.

"It was hard, sweetie, but I learned to love your grandpa as a friend and companion. Albert James died so young." Gram picked up her knitting and started with her stitches again.

"What ever happened to the other fella, Gram?"

"My parents made me write him a letter before the wedding. It was a very hard letter to write, but they stood over me to make sure I said what they wanted." Gram's blue eyes filled with tears. "I told him I didn't love him anymore and had met someone new." Gram put down her knitting again and looked away. "I broke his heart."

Beth Ann moved over to the chair next to Gram. "Where did he live?"

"Just up in Woodburn. Last I heard from a friend, he was engaged and taking care of his parents' farm."

Beth Ann touched Gram's arm. "What's his full name?"

"Nickolas Jon Ballas."

"We should go see if he's listed." Beth Ann stood.

"Oh, sweetie, we don't want to open up a can of old worms. Besides, he wouldn't recognize me. I'm an old woman now, not the young girl he fell in love with. Besides, I'm sure he was angry when he got that letter. He never came after me and probably never wanted to see me again." She put down her knitting and stood up. "Come on, let me show you something."

Beth Ann followed her into the house and upstairs to her bedroom. Nothing had changed since the last time Beth Ann had seen it. Even the handmade patchwork quilt was still on Gram's bed.

"Gram, are those stairs getting hard on you?" Beth Ann asked.

"No. I like those stairs. They keep me limber."

She opened her closet door and pulled out a box filled with letters, but she waved her hand after she looked inside. "Not this one. These are from your Great Grandma Ann. Someday you'll get all these letters and trinkets. A lot of history inside this box." She put it aside. "I'm going to read them someday, but I just haven't done it yet."

She reached back into the closet and found a beautiful cedar box that she carried to the bed. She sat down and pointed to the spot beside the chest for Beth Ann to sit. Inside the box were dozens of letters neatly bundled, as if they were priceless artifacts. Gram touched the top of the letters with a look of deep regret on her face.

"These are all Nicky's letters from our childhood and when he was in the military."

Beth Ann lifted one of the letters. "May I open it?"

"Sure, honey."

Beth Ann read the letter aloud.

> *"Dear Maggie,*
>
> > *I am missing you with all my heart. I cannot wait to get out of the service and rush home to your arms. I envision your beautiful blue eyes and your radiant smile, and they give me the strength to hold on. My love for you is eternal as is the light in my heart and soul. I hope things are going well with your piano lessons. I eagerly await the day when I can hear you play again. I cannot wait to be in your arms and to kiss those tender, sweet lips.*

I can't wait until we are married so I can have
all of you every day for our entire life. I guess I
can't wait for a lot of things.
Love you forever,
Your Nicky"

"After he sent this next one, my parents made me write him a letter saying I wasn't in love with him anymore." Her voice broke as she handed it to Beth Ann. "This was the last letter he ever wrote to me."

Beth Ann pulled the note from the aging envelope.

> *"Dear Maggie,*
>
> *Please don't do this. Don't marry another man. You are the only woman I will ever love. There is no other for me. I am heartbroken about this and I know you are too, because I know you love me as much as I love you. You can never be completely happy without me, just like I will never be completely happy without you. Our love is like the moon with its everlasting radiance.*
>
> *If I truly thought this man was your choice, I would be able to turn away and move forward knowing your happiness was secure, but I know you don't love him. You love me, and I'm the one you hold in your heart. I will be waiting forever until you come back into my arms. We've loved each other since we were ten, and we both know that will never change. Not now, not ever. You were the first girl I ever kissed, and I was your first guy. Please rethink this. We need to be together.*
>
> *I will be waiting with my love always,*
> *Your one and only Nicky*

Beth Ann looked up to see Gram wiping away long-dormant tears. She had given up true love to make her family happy, a sacrifice no one should ever have to make. Beth Ann slipped one of the envelopes into her pocket, knowing there must be something she could do to make things right again.

She gave Gram a big hug and whispered, "I'm so sorry, Gram. You must still love him."

Gram stood up and stiffened her shoulders, trying to act brave. "Let's head back down."

As they were going down the stairs, the phone rang.

"Would you mind answering that?" Gram said. "If it's Margaret, tell her I'll call her back later."

Beth Ann nodded and ran to pick it up, but there was no reply when she said hello.

"Who is this? Who's there?"

"You can't hide from me." The male voice sent shivers into her stomach. "I want you and you're going to be mine. I'm the man you should be with."

Before she could say anything, she heard the dial tone. It was that same voice that called her townhouse, and now she knew it wasn't Blake. But who the heck was it? She didn't want to worry Gram, so she turned and forced a smile. "Wrong number I guess."

Gram looked surprised. "That doesn't happen often especially twice in one day."

They went back to the porch and watched the guys do yard work. Beth Ann tried to put the creepy phone calls out of her mind, but she couldn't help wondering who was calling and why the voice sounded so familiar. Maybe it was her imagination and just a creepy paparazzi. However, right now she was going to push it out of her mind so she could enjoy her visit.

After lunch, Beth Ann and Kaylob decided they would go to the park once they went to the power company and took care of Gram and James's bill for the next year. They also stopped at the grocery store and set up an account to ensure that Gram could buy all the food she wanted. They left instructions to everyone at the store that if Gram was hesitant, they should encourage her to use her savings to help others in the community.

The drive to the park was like going back in time. Nothing at all had changed. When they arrived, Beth Ann took in the beauty of the plants and trees surrounding the area. She loved the early 20th century carousel where squealing children pretended they were riding magnificent horses, ferocious bears and springing lions. Mom-and-pop storefronts offered everything from pulled taffy to cotton candy.

Beth Ann guided Kaylob to a secluded park bench where she relayed Gram's heartbreaking story, and she could tell it touched Kaylob's heart as well. The decision was easy for them—they were going to find Nicky. Woodburn was only thirty minutes away, so what could it hurt? They went to a pay phone, found his address and bought a map.

On the drive north to Woodburn, they could tell it was still a farming community surrounded by the snow-peaked Cascade Mountains off in the distance. When they entered the city limits, the map directed them to head east to Marion Lane. More pastoral farmlands and rustic houses speckled the countryside. Clotheslines ran across back yards with sheets and towels blowing gently in the wind. The fields held orchards and grazing cows. A green tractor sat by stacks of hay, waiting to be driven. One farm had several Paint horses that seemed to be excited as they watched a boy running with a kite. Beth Ann took in all the sights and placed her hand across her heart.

"Kaylob, I love this. The horses and all this land. It's so beautiful."

"Not as beautiful as you, sweetheart." He took her hand and kissed it, then he slowed down so they could watch more of the show.

When they finally arrived at the farmstead on Wheat Lane, they were both mesmerized. Norman Rockwell would have been envious of such a captivating scene. Surrounded by oak trees was a majestic ivory-white house with a spectacular wraparound porch, adorned with an American flag hanging proudly from its mount. The windows on the second floor were open to reveal curtains that played peek-a-boo with the breeze outside.

The side of the house was graced with apple orchards and other fruit trees. The backdrop was the magnificent Cascade Mountains that stood as though they were protecting the land. It certainly didn't appear to be a home of a poor farmer. Beth Ann wondered if Nicky had sold it and the new owner had updated it to its present condition.

She got out, looked at the name on the mailbox and was excited to see it read BALLAS 2109. She motioned for Kaylob to come over.

"Look, honey, it has the name Ballas."

"It could be a relative or one of his children," Kaylob said.

They got back in the car and drove down the driveway, gravel crunching under their tires. When they got close to the house, Beth Ann spotted a man who had stopped fixing his tractor and was watching them approach. She almost jumped out of the car before Kaylob came to a stop, and she most definitely didn't wait for him to open the car door.

"Sorry, honey," she said when he grumbled about it. "I'm anxious you know!"

He took her hand with a laugh and they walked towards the man. The Italian looking older gentleman was about six feet tall and very handsome. He had olive skin, black-and-silver hair with dark green eyes. Beth Ann felt excited because he fit Gram's description.

The man put down his rag. "Can I help you folks? Are you lost?"

Kaylob shook his head. "We're not lost. We're looking for a Nickolas Ballas."

"That's me, but if you're selling something, I'm not interested."

Beth Ann walked over and handed him a letter. "Did you write this?"

He opened it, and his eyes widened. "Yes, I wrote it many years ago to Maggie. Where'd you get this?"

"You wrote that to my grandmother," she said with a smile.

"Has she passed away?" His eyes appeared fearful. "I knew Maggie very well."

"Oh no, Gram's healthy and walks every day. She still wears the same size she wore when she was sixteen. She's an amazing woman with tons of energy."

He picked up his rag and started working on the tractor again. "And her husband?"

"He's been dead for many, many years," Beth Ann said.

He turned and Beth Ann saw a mixture of emotions on his face. "I'm sorry to hear that. Tell me, how can I help the two of you?"

"Well, I thought...we thought"—she pointed to herself then Kaylob—"that maybe you'd like to visit Gram."

He threw down his rag and shuffled his feet in the dirt. "Visit her? Why would I do that? She never tried to contact me, even after her husband died."

Beth Ann's voice quivered. "Because she still loves you, number one. And number two, because she was afraid you hated her. And threely..." She paused and scowled at Kaylob for snickering. "Okay, so there's no threely."

Nickolas's lips curved in the corners as he watched Beth Ann. He looked at her thoughtfully for a moment, then he seemed to brace himself. "Yes, we did love each other at one time, and I suppose I did hate her for a while. Maybe I still do. She hurt me bad. Now I'm not sure how I feel."

"But she only married my grandpa because her parents made her," Beth Ann said, and felt grateful when Kaylob took her hand and squeezed it tight.

"She was an adult," Nickolas snapped. "How could they make her?"

"She didn't feel she had a choice. Her family controlled her back then, but that's the past. She still loves you. Surely, your wife would let you visit an old friend."

"Maggie was more than a mere friend, young lady. She was the love of my life. I never married after she broke my heart. I never trusted anyone after that. I came close once but backed out."

Kaylob pulled on her hand, trying to lead her away.

"Kaylob, stop! I'm not leaving!" She yanked her hand back and felt tears escaping. "Mr. Ballas, please think about it. Please... I watched her cry for the first time today. I used to see Gram looking sad sometimes when I was little and wondered why. I thought it was because of my grandpa, but now I know it wasn't. It was always you. She will die loving you."

She could see that took him by surprise, but he only turned to look out at his trees with a deep sigh. Kaylob nodded toward the car again and looked at her sternly, but she ignored him.

After a few seconds, Nickolas turned back to her. "I can tell you're related to Maggie." He glanced at Kaylob and raised an eyebrow. "She was stubborn too."

"You don't know the half of it." Kaylob shook his head and got an elbow from Beth Ann.

"I want to show you something," Nickolas said. "Would you two like to come in the house for some iced tea?"

"Yes, we'd love some ice tea." Beth Ann ignored Kaylob's scolding look and pulled him toward the house.

Up close, Beth Ann could see it was even more of a picturesque farmhouse than it appeared from the front. They stepped through the screen door that opened into the dated kitchen with light yellow walls accented with antique white crown molding. On the aged lacquer, white stove sat a percolator coffeepot. It was lovely, but Beth Ann noticed there wasn't the simple elegance of a woman's touch.

At the table against the far wall next to a window, Nickolas pulled out a chair for Beth Ann and waved for Kaylob to sit too. Kaylob nodded politely but remained silent. After Nickolas got them each a glass of iced tea, he excused himself and left the room.

"I hope we haven't caused him any more pain," Kaylob said when they were alone. "We should've left when I said so."

Beth Ann rolled her eyes. "Everything's going to be fine. Stop acting like you can boss me around, Mr. Bossy O'Brien."

He narrowed his eyes. "We'll discuss this later in detail, Elizabeth Ann Rose. Ever heard of a compromise?"

Beth Ann was just about to say something when Nickolas returned, carrying an old shoebox that he placed on the table and removed the top. Beth Ann could see it held old letters and notes and could tell they were from Gram. He had kept them all just like she had. His calloused hands rummaged through the yellowed letters before he pulled out one in particular that he handed to Beth Ann.

"Here, you might want to read this," he said, his tone void of emotion.

Beth Ann took the letter and read it silently.

Dear Nickolas,

I am so sorry, but I can't marry you or be with you anymore. You have to believe that. I know my last letter must have shocked you. But I have met someone else and my family wants me to marry him. I know this is sudden. You must think I couldn't love him as much as you after so little time, but you're wrong. I do love him.

Please just go on with your life. I am very happy and we are getting married next month. Enclosed you will find the ring you gave me. I'm sorry I couldn't meet with you, but my future husband did not like the idea. Please try not to be hurt because I do want you to be happy and have a wonderful life. That is so important to me. You will always be important to me.

Thank you for being my boyfriend all these years. I hope you find someone who can make you happy. I hope someday you will forgive me.
Love always,
Maggie Ann Benins

Beth Ann handed the letter back to Nickolas. "Gram's parents made her write that letter to you so you would leave her alone. Didn't you see the underlying message there? You were important to her, and she wanted you to be happy. It was killing her to write that."

"How do you know all this?" He scratched his head and pulled up a chair to sit down. "And if that's true, why didn't she contact me after her husband died?"

"She thought you hated her. And she didn't know if you had a wife."

"We know what it's like to have that kind of love," Kaylob said. "That's why we're here."

Nickolas was staring at Beth Ann. "Now that I look closer, I can see how much you look like Maggie. She was a blonde, but the resemblance takes my breath away. It makes me remember how much I loved her, but it also makes me remember the pain." He turned away as his voice broke. "I'm so old now that she wouldn't even know me. I used to be handsome. That's the man she remembers."

123

Beth Ann reached out to touch his arm. "Funny, Gram said the same thing about how she looks. Age happens, but Gram is still beautiful. She still has beautiful blue eyes, and her smile is one of a kind. You would know her as soon as you saw her, just like she would know you. That kind of love will always hold a key to your heart."

Nickolas looked at her again and touched her cheek "Thank you for coming, but I need time to think about all this. Can I keep the letter you brought that I wrote to her?"

"Yes, but please think about it fast. Gram is sixty-five years old and could live to be a hundred, but…" Beth Ann swallowed back tears. "Think of the years you two could spend together and not let any of them go to waste."

They sipped their tea a few moments longer, then Kaylob stood and looked down at his fiancée. "It's time for us to leave and let Nickolas get back to what he was doing. Not to mention Gram will be wondering where we are."

Beth Ann stood and took his hand. "Okay, Mr. O'Brien. You can have your way as usual."

Nickolas gave Kaylob a knowing smile. "Yes, the apple doesn't fall far from the tree." He stood and walked them to the front door. "Thank you both for coming to see me and letting me know about Maggie. I know it took courage."

Beth Ann hesitated a second them boldly let go of Kaylob's hand and embraced Nickolas. "I hope to see you again soon." She looked up into his dark green eyes and saw that they were a bit too shiny. *Yep, he still loves Gram.* She opened her purse and pulled out a pen and paper. "Here's Gram's contact information, just in case."

"Thank you."

He took it from her and was still staring at it intently when she looked back as she and Kaylob walked to the car. She didn't know if Nickolas would come to visit Gram or not, but at least now he knew she had always loved him.

Before they'd driven even a quarter mile down the road, Kaylob parked the car in a pull-out area. He turned to Beth Ann and embraced her. "We are so lucky. We could have been them, you know. That could have been us."

"What do you mean? My family has always loved you."

"I came from a poor family, too. There were a lot of guys in town who were much better off."

"My mom didn't care about that," Beth Ann said. "She only wanted my happiness. And you know it would never have worked anyway if they'd tried to split us up. I'm a lot pushier and more stubborn than Gram. Besides, things were different back when Gram was growing up."

"Thank goodness for that. But I don't know that things are so different. A guy in my platoon told me he couldn't marry the girl he loved because her family didn't like that he was just some enlisted guy. It broke his heart."

"That's so sad," Beth Ann said. "But nothing could keep me from marrying you. Not even a war."

Kaylob smiled, then he raised his eyebrows. "Now about my trying to boss you around. Sometimes you need to listen to me."

"Oh, don't be silly. I do listen to you—if you're right." She kissed his cheek and giggled. "But since that doesn't happen very often, it must feel like I never listen."

"Elizabeth Ann Rose, you're a brat. The cutest one I know, but still a brat. Don't make me have to spank you for real."

"Yeah right. You and what army?" She grabbed his arm and laughed. "Get it? What army?"

Chapter Eighteen

He flexed his muscle and winked at her. "I think my army could handle it just fine. It's your bottom that might not be able to handle it, even as fine as it is." He pulled her closer and nibbled on her neck. "Wanna find a private road?"

"Kaylob Shawn O'Brien!"

"What?" He grinned.

She slapped his hand that was trying to crawl under her blouse, then she pointed at the ignition. "Gram's waiting on us, remember? Let's go."

He gave her a pouty look as he started the car. While they drove, Beth Ann wondered how in the world she was going to keep resisting him until their honeymoon.

When they pulled up at Gram's, she was sitting on the front porch knitting again. Looking at her from the car window, Beth Ann studied Gram's hair in the bun and wondered if she could talk her into changing it. She started to open her own door but stopped when Kaylob cleared his throat. Man, she really needed to get him up with the times. Guys didn't always have to open a woman's door anymore. Still, she needed to let him have his way some of the time, so she sat there and waited for him to come around and open her door.

"Holy slowpoke," she said, rolling her eyes. He chuckled as he took her hand and they walked up the steps.

Gram looked up from her knitting and smiled. "Did you have a nice afternoon and walk off all that food?"

Kaylob put a hand on his stomach. "Sure did. Now I need those cookies. Do you mind, Gram?"

"Not at all. Go help yourself. Take as many as you want."

Beth Ann gave him a look and held up three fingers before he dashed off inside. She sat down beside Gram and touched her hair. "I was wondering about something."

"What might that be, sweetness?"

"Would you be willing to cut your hair, maybe get a new style? You need to get rid of that bun."

Gram shook her head. "Now, why would I go and do that? I've had this bun since you were three."

Beth Ann got an idea and said, "For my wedding pictures. I want to get a professional photo taken of all the family members." She touched the bun again. "Your hair's so thick and pretty, but I never get to see it down. A little makeover might be a good idea. Please, Gram?"

"Well…" She paused from her knitting and looked up at her granddaughter. "I guess I could do that, for the wedding and all. It *is* getting hard for me to brush it and keep it up. Shorter might be good."

"Wonderful! Thanks, Gram."

Beth Ann kissed her on the cheek then ran in the house to tell Kaylob. She almost collided with him on his way out the door, six cookies in his hands. She grabbed three and scowled at him.

"Trouble counting, Mr. O'Brien?"

He grinned at her. "What? I thought you meant three for each hand."

After she put three of the cookies back, she called a few salons and found one that had an opening in thirty minutes, so she hurried back out on the porch to tell Gram.

"We can get in right away at the salon!"

Gram put down her knitting and shook her head with a sigh. "Like I say, when Beth Ann gets ants in her pants, nothing can stop her."

Kaylob chuckled. "Tell me about it."

When Beth Ann and Gram were ready to leave, Kaylob was standing with her dad in the living room.

"We're gonna go play some pool." Kaylob said as James picked up his jacket and slipped it on.

Beth Ann tiptoed to kiss Kaylob and whispered, "Behave yourself. No flirting and no more cookies."

"Do I look crazy?" he said. "Why would I flirt when I have you?"

James laughed. "Don't worry. I'll do all the flirting for both of us."

"Good Lord, James," Gram said with a frown. "Behave yourself."

Beth Ann and Gram drove downtown to the salon right off the main road. The Beauty Arcade was a cozy place that she guessed was the center for local gossip—hair dryers lined up in the back, sinks on the far right and pictures of the latest hairstyles on every wall, beckoning those who weren't sure what they wanted. Gram glanced nervously around at the styles in the pictures, as if she had stepped into a monster movie makeup room.

"When was the last time you were in a salon?" Beth Ann asked.

"I was about five. I went with my momma."

"Five years old?"

"Yes, Momma was getting her hair trimmed because Sissy stuck gum in it."

Beth Ann shook her head. "So you've never had your hair done?"

"No. I took care of my own hair when I was young. I only trimmed the ends."

An older lady approached them and asked, "How can I help you ladies?"

Beth Ann smiled. "We're here to see Ashley Daniels. She's cutting my grandmother's hair."

"Oh, yes. She's almost ready for you. She's in the back and will be right out. Please have a seat."

They sat down and picked up two of the hairstyle magazines. Gram flipped through hers then leaned over to whisper to Beth Ann.

"Reading those letters today made me miss Nicky all over again. Not that I ever stopped, of course. Hearing one of our songs always made me miss him even more."

Beth Ann looked surprised. "You guys had a song?"

"Oh, Heavens yes. We were together for over ten years and had several songs. Our favorite was 'Moonlight, Hawaii and You.' You know, I remember every word of that song." Gram got a far-off look in her eyes. "He was stationed in Hawaii, and it was our dream to have our wedding and honeymoon there."

Beth Ann put her hand in Gram's. "We were keeping this a surprise, but that's where Kaylob and I are getting married and having our honeymoon."

Gram squeezed her hand. "I'm so happy for you, sweetness."

"We'll be buying everyone's tickets and making arrangements for lodging," Beth Ann said. "I can't wait for that day and you being there..." Beth Ann felt a lump but swallowed it. "Makes my future wedding even more perfect."

Gram's eyes got misty. "I can't think of anything I would love more than to see my granddaughter married in Hawaii."

After a few seconds of silence, Beth Ann had to ask. "Gram, did you and Nicky ever ..." Beth Ann lowered her gaze. "Well, did you guys..."

Gram chuckled. "Yes, of course we did. We were in love. We tried for a very long time to hold back and wait, but we just couldn't do it." Gram looked lost in memories again. "As soon as I turned eighteen we went out to the lake and—"

"Hi, I'm Ashley." A lady with jet-black hair that highlighted her blue eyes walked up to them. "Sorry for the delay. I was cleaning up my mess from my last haircut and spilled a whole bunch of stuff in the back room."

Beth Ann breathed a sigh of relief, grateful for the interruption before Gram could tell her more than she wanted to know.

"Oh it's fine," Gram said to Ashley. "We were enjoying ourselves."

"Gram has never had a professional haircut." Beth Ann reached over to touch Gram's hair. "Could you give her something with a little more style? We're having professional photos done."

Ashley looked at Gram and nodded. "Certainly. Would you like some color too?"

"Oh, no," Gram said. "I'll go with a younger style, but I'm used to my white hair."

Ashley led Gram to her chair then draped a black cape around her shoulders. "I'm going to make you look twenty years younger. You're already beautiful, but let's just spice you up." She glanced at Beth Ann and winked.

Gram took a deep breath. "Okay, let's do this."

Ashley was right about Gram being beautiful. Her dark blue eyes and peaches-and-cream complexion made her stunning, although the way she dressed hid her figure. Beth Ann made a mental note to help her pick out a dress for the wedding. Maybe she could talk her into a whole new wardrobe. She went back to the lobby and sat down to read a magazine when she had a brilliant idea and got up again. Gram was just heading to the shampoo chair when Beth Ann pointed to the pay phone outside.

She slipped inside the phone booth and was dialing just as she noticed a black car parked across the street. The hairs on the back of her neck stood up when she saw the tinted window roll down to reveal a male hand holding a camera. It looked like the same car that she'd been seeing everywhere. Who was it and why were they following her? This was getting serious. They'd called at Gram's, and now they were stalking her around Salem taking pictures. Why would the paparazzi take that kind of interest in her?

She turned her back to the car and stood there for a minute, trying to shake off the creepy crawlers. After a few seconds, she heard them speed off and glanced over her shoulder. She regained her composure then called information to get Nickolas's number. It rang five times before he finally picked up.

"Hello, is this Nickolas?"

"Yes, this is he."

"Hi, Nickolas. This Beth Ann, Maggie's granddaughter."

"Hi, Beth Ann. My goodness, you sound like Maggie on the phone."

"I do?"

"Yes, just how I remember her. What can I help you with?"

"Well, I'm downtown with Gram getting her hair done, and she doesn't know I'm calling you and as a matter of fact she has no clue we came to see you."

"I see," he said. "And why are you calling me?"

Beth Ann took a deep breath. "Gram just told me about the song you two had together. The one about Hawaii."

Nothing but silence for a few seconds, then he said, "Yes, I remember our song."

"Well, I was wondering … would you like to come to our wedding and surprise Gram? Kaylob and I are getting married in Hawaii, and we'd love for you to come."

"Well, I don't know ..." he said. "How do we know Maggie would like that idea?"

"She will, I promise. She just told me about the dream you two had about Hawaii."

"Yes we did, but I don't know … it's been a very long time."

"Oh, please come, Nickolas. It's in June so you have plenty of time. And we would pay for everything."

"I'm not a poor farm boy anymore." He sounded offended. "I don't need help. I can pay my own way."

Beth Ann winced. "I didn't mean to imply anything. We're paying for tickets and hotels for everyone." Her voice broke with emotion. "Please, Nickolas. Gram still loves you, and I think you love her too."

After a long pause, he said, "My goodness, Beth Ann. You're hard to refuse, just like Maggie. Tell me, young lady, how do you know she still loves me? Fond memories are not the same as love."

"She told me she would always love you."

"She said that?" The hope in his voice was clear. "Did she really?"

"Yes, that's why I'm calling."

He sighed. "Okay, I'll be there, but I hope this isn't a mistake. I can't wait to see her again."

Beth Ann squealed with joy. "Thank you, Nickolas! If you were here right now I'd kiss you."

He chuckled. "Well, I'll get that kiss from you on your wedding day."

She told him they would be mailing his tickets and all the information soon and that she would make sure he and Gram got a room next to each other. She knew she was taking a risk, but what a great surprise for Gram.

After she hung up with Nickolas, she knew she had to make one more phone call. When he answered, she said, "Hi, Blake. It's me."

The uncomfortable silence that followed felt like the anxiety that follows a delicate china cup in mid drop.

So, you finally decided to call me again. "Do you think it's fair to just brush me aside? To ignore me like we never happened? And why did you stick your mom on the phone like a child instead of having a grown-up conversation with me?"

"I'm sorry, Blake, but you were a little drunk when you called, and it's not fun talking to you when you're blasted." She paused. "I know how complicated things are, but you have to stop acting this way, and no more flowers."

"What the hell, Beth Ann? Just come home and I'll stop drinking. We belong together and you know it!"

"No, Blake, we can't be together anymore. I know I've made mistakes, but I honestly haven't known how to handle this."

"I'll tell you how to handle it. You're my fiancée and you need to come home right now."

Tears stung her eyes. "I'm not your fiancée anymore, Blake. I'm sorry."

"Where the hell are you!" His voice was getting louder and louder.

"I'm in Salem. I told you when he was in the hospital that I wasn't coming back. I've told you over and over but you're not listening."

"I know what you said, and I've seen the damn gossip magazines, too. I saw the picture of him on his knees at the train station!"

"Oh, Blake, I'm so sorry you had to see that. I had no idea pictures were taken, but I'm being followed all the time." A thought occurred to her. "Are you having me followed, Blake? Have you been calling and disguising your voice?"

He laughed bitterly. "You know I don't hide it when I call you. What are you talking about?"

"I guess it's just the stupid paparazzi then. They even followed me up here to Gram's."

"I can't believe you took off with Kaylob and left me sitting here wondering where you are. That's just total bullshit. Just like saying, the paparazzi are following you up to Oregon. You have a big imagination."

"I said I didn't know who it was. And coming up here wasn't planned. Lisa went into labor and—"

"What's that got to do with your grandmother?"

"We came here after. I needed to see her. She missed me and I missed her."

"Yeah, I know a little bit about that myself. Well, he better not be touching you. I'll fucking beat him black and blue if he does!"

"Blake, please don't say things like that."

"How can you take a ring from him when you still have mine?"

Neither of them said anything for a few seconds, and she could hear his ragged breathing.

Finally, he said, "Beth Ann, you know you're the only woman I've ever loved. You said you loved me. Was it a lie? Did I mean anything to you?"

She could feel the pain in his voice and put her hand across her heart. "Of course you did."

"I deserve better, don't you think?"

"Yes, you do. I promise I'll come see you as soon as I get back home."

"I'm not giving up," he said, his voice breaking. "I won't lose you."

"Goodbye, Blake."

She wiped the tears from her cheeks after she hung up. Part of what he'd said was true. She had to go see him and give him his ring back as soon as she got home. But she hated breaking his heart.

Gram studied her face when she went back in the salon and said, "Sweetie, are you okay?"

"I had to call Blake. It didn't go well."

"Oh, dear. Is he okay?" Gram's face was etched with compassion.

Ashley was clearly eavesdropping while she continued to cut Gram's hair, but Beth Ann didn't let it bother her.

"He's very hurt and angry. I feel so guilty for hurting him."

Gram took her hand. "Oh, sweetness, he'll be okay. I'm sure he'll land on his feet. We'll pray for him this Sunday in church."

Beth Ann nodded. She wanted Blake to be happy with all her heart, so she would pray with Gram that he would find another true love.

When Gram's hair was done, everyone in the salon raved about her beauty, and it was as if years had been taken off her appearance. Their next stop was at a clothing store in a new mall across town. When Beth Ann parked in the large parking lot, she couldn't believe she saw the black car again in her rearview mirror. That really bugged her, but she decided to ignore the idiot because she didn't want Gram worrying and didn't want to spoil their fun makeover day.

Gram touched Beth Ann's arm as she was taking the keys out of the ignition. "Honey, I already have some dresses. I hate for you to spend all this money with your wedding and honeymoon coming up and all."

Beth Ann shook her head. "I want to do this, Gram. Please let me. If you don't, it will hurt my feelings and Kaylob's too."

Gram smiled. "Okay, you little plotter." She seemed to fade away into deep thought.

"Gram, are you okay? You look a hundred miles away."

I was just thinking about the wedding dress that Nicky and I picked out together. I still have it and I'll show you when we get back. It's still in the same box that it came in."

Beth Ann squeezed her hand. "Oh, Gram that is amazing, I can't wait to see it. I can't believe you've kept it all these years."

"I couldn't just get rid of it. I loved it too much."

They got out of the car and walked hand-in-hand to one of the larger stores anchoring the mall that was lined with clothes, perfumes and makeup. It took some searching in the ladies' department to find Gram's tiny size, but they finally found some things in the petite section. Beth Ann picked out a beautiful yellow dress with polka dots and a stylish belt.

The ladies in the store went on and on about Gram's lovely figure and how much she and Beth Ann looked alike. When one of the clerks asked if she was Beth Ann's mom, Gram's face lit up with delight when she informed the woman she was her grandmother.

"See, Gram, you look so young," Beth Ann said.

Gram waved off her comment and continued shopping. When they were done, she left looking radiant in an ivory dress Beth Ann picked out, along with a matching hat. She also found Gram a silk top the color of the ocean and a cute pair of slacks to match. Gram admitted she hardly ever wore pants, but enjoyed the comfort of the slacks. After leaving the store, Gram got her nails done and said, she felt like she was on the "Queen for a Day" TV show. Beth Ann remembered Gram watching that program and had to laugh.

As they got in the car loaded down with boxes and bags from their shopping spree, Beth Ann was thrilled that there was no sign of the black car. She guessed they had to eat and sleep sometimes, which reminded her of her own empty stomach after their fun filled day.

"Gram, are you hungry? I've been craving some ice cream."

"Let's stop at Creamy Cow," Gram said. "And this is my treat, young lady."

They both had Rocky Road and savored every drop. When they pulled up in front of Gram's house, Kaylob was sitting outside on the porch. As soon as he saw them, he ran down the steps to help carry all the bags.

"Gram, you look stunning!" He raised both eyebrows.

"Oh, don't be silly. I look like an old lady trying to make people think I'm younger than I am." She laughed and shooed him away while he took the bags out of her hands. "Only for my granddaughter would I do something so silly. She did buy me some beautiful clothes though, and I want to thank both of you for doing this."

Kaylob smiled. "We're happy to do it for you. Besides, I get to see what Beth Ann's going to look like when she's in her sixties. All I can say is— wow!"

Gram shook her head and hugged Beth Ann. "Your Kaylob is a charmer, no doubt about it."

"Tell me about it," Beth Ann said.

When they walked into the house, James exclaimed, "Wow, Mother, you look beautiful and yes, I turned your beans back on, and they've been simmering just like you told me. And mother, you are going to have men knocking down the door."

"Hush, James, that's the most foolish thing I've ever heard," Gram said, but the look on her face told them all that she was happy about the compliments.

Gram was making her best-in-the-world meatloaf with gravy and her amazing green beans and garlic mashed potatoes for dinner. The green beans had been simmering in her cast iron skillet all afternoon, and the aroma was making everyone's mouth water. Kaylob paced the kitchen like a famished lion and made Beth Ann laugh. He was used to smelling his own home-cooked meals, but this was one seasoned with a lifetime worth of real Southern experience.

Beth Ann decided to go outside and take in the beauty and sounds of the late afternoon. She took a deep, cleansing breath and relaxed on the porch swing while the breeze fanned its way through the yard. The fresh cut grass filled her senses of memories of long ago. God, how she loved that smell when she was at Grams.

Off in the distance, she could hear the laughter of children and dogs barking. Up until she turned eleven, she hadn't known what a real home was like. All the traveling across country with her parents had never allowed that, but being there at Gram's every summer had filled her with the sounds and smells of home and a real sense of belonging.

After all the stress of the past few months, life was finally beginning to unfold in a positive way. There was one more unpleasant task ahead, but after that, life would be smooth surfing.

When she went back inside Kaylob greeted her and took her hand while they headed towards the kitchen.

Gram was scolding her dad. "James, wash your hands before you sit at the table."

James looked at her and laughed. "Mother, I did." He laid down the newspaper.

"James, did you print that newspaper? You are not the only person who touched it? Should I try to name everyone, including my paperboy?"

He got up and rolled his eyes then held up his hands. "Washing, Mother."

Beth Ann and Kaylob sat down at the table and tried their best not to laugh, but found it hard.

After eating almost every morsel on her plate, Beth Ann reached down and felt her stomach.

"Gram, I'm going to get plump if I keep eating all your good cooking."

Kaylob laughed. "Nothing wrong with plump. As a matter of fact, I think it can be very nice."

Beth Ann looked at him and tilted her head. "Who do you know that looks good plump? What's her name?"

"Nobody." Kaylob held up his hands defensively. "I just meant there's nothing wrong with being plump, sweetheart. If you ever got that way, there would just be more of you for me to love, that's all."

Her dad cracked up. "Good save, Kaylob."

Gram narrowed her eyes at him. "James, silent now before you cause trouble!"

Her dad shook his head. "Why my middle name is trouble anyway."

Beth Ann and Kaylob tried to help Gram with the dishes, but she scooted them out of the kitchen. They went outside and enjoyed the brilliance of the blue sky as the last rays of sunset made its way across the lawn. Beth Ann could've stayed there in the swing beside Kaylob forever, but they had to get ready to go hear her dad sing.

The night on the town ended up being a nice surprise. Her dad's singing and talent on the guitar were even better than she remembered. They also got to meet his girlfriend, Vera, and found her to be a very sweet, grounded woman.

On their last day there, Gram knocked on their bedroom door bright and early. "Rise and shine, sleepyheads. It's time to get ready for church."

Kaylob glanced at Beth Ann and yawned. "Do we have to go to church?" he whispered.

"Well, you can go tell Gram if you don't want to go, but I'm going." She tossed back the covers then leaned over and kissed him on the cheek. "My Gram may be okay with us sleeping in the same bed because we already live together, but she's old fashioned about church."

Kaylob stared at the ceiling a few minutes then sighed and threw back the blankets to climb out of bed. It didn't take him long to get dressed.

Gram's church was only a few blocks away, so they walked since it was such a beautiful morning. On their way home, Gram said, "Kaylob, did you like church?"

"As a matter of fact, I did. Who knows, maybe I'll go again someday."

Gram smiled. "I know you're a good man and don't have to go to church to have God in your heart, but I'm glad you liked it. What really makes a good Christian is what one does when they walk out of that church door with only God watching."

"Amen to that," Beth Ann said, linking her arm with Kaylob's.

That last Sunday with her Gram was a fun filled day. Just eating leftovers and enjoying family time.

Saying goodbye to Gram and her dad was hard that Monday morning, but Beth Ann knew she would be seeing them again soon on her wedding day. Right now, she needed to get back and put in some days at work because they were shorthanded, and Kaylob had a medal ceremony to attend.

Beth Ann felt happy as they drove home, but in the back of her mind, she knew she had to go see Blake soon, and just thinking about it made her throat tighten. She hadn't told Kaylob about calling him and knew she needed to. Now was as good a time as any.

She scooted over on the seat next to him. "I have a confession to make."

He glanced at her then back to the road. "What is it, sweetheart?"

"I called Blake the day I took Gram to the hair salon. He's still very hurt and angry, but he's not the one who's been calling and hanging up. I need to go see him when we get back."

Kaylob's jaw clenched and his knuckles were white on the steering wheel, but he said nothing.

"Kaylob, please say something."

"I'll pull over at the next rest stop. I don't think I should be driving while we talk about this."

By the time he pulled over, the tension in the car was so thick you could cut it with a knife. He turned off the car but didn't look at her.

"I don't give a shit if he's upset, and I don't believe that he's not the one calling."

"He wouldn't lie to me about something like that, Kaylob. I have to go see him so I can give him his ring back—I owe him that much. And some of my stuff is still at his townhouse. I hope that when I do this, he'll finally be able to move on."

Kaylob continued to stare straight ahead. After another minute of silence, Beth Ann was relieved to see his face relax, as if he had come to a decision.

"Then go see him if that's what it takes to get him out of our lives for good."

Her lip trembled as she laid her head on his shoulder. "I'm sorry if this hurts you, honey."

"I'm trying not to be jealous, Beth Ann, but I can't help it. I know all this is hard on you and I'm sorry, but I don't understand why you're just now telling me you called him."

"I was going to tell you when I got home from shopping with Gram, but I honestly forgot." She lifted her head and gazed at him. "And there's something else I need to tell you. The paparazzi is still following me. I caught them taking a picture of me while I was out with Gram."

Kaylob's face went an angry red. "Those assholes followed us to Oregon? They need to be stopped and if I catch them, I'll teach them a lesson they won't forget."

She nodded and put her head back on his shoulder. "I would like to watch that."

The rest of the eight-hour drive seemed more like ten, but Beth Ann couldn't relax until she unpacked. As she was putting away their things, she felt the hair on the back of her neck stand on end. Something was off in their home. Some of the drawers weren't closed all the way, and things inside were messy. Maybe it had happened when Kaylob had his meltdown, but she was sure she had put everything back in place. And two of her new nightgowns and some panties were missing. Had she left them at Gram's? She didn't think she'd taken them.

She'd have to call Gram tomorrow and find out.

Chapter Nineteen

Two days passed and it felt good to be back at work, but even while she was with her students, Beth Ann couldn't help thinking about Blake and what facing him would be like. Maybe he wouldn't be mad anymore. Yeah, and maybe Kaylob would suddenly decide to give up eating cookies.

"Miss Beth Ann, did I hit the right note?" Eight-year-old Cathy asked, her eyes showing excitement. "I did like you said and used my diagram." She placed her hands on her diaphragm and looked proud.

"You did fantastic, and because you did so well I want to hear it again," Beth Ann said since she hadn't actually heard a single note.

Cathy beamed at the praise and waved to her dad who had just walked in and taken a seat. Beth Ann felt bad about the way she'd acted the last time he'd spoken to her. Just because he'd done business with Blake was no excuse for her to be rude to him.

When Cathy finished singing, Beth Ann took her by the hand and walked over to greet her dad. "Hello, Peter. It's nice to see you again."

"Hey, how's my girl doing?" He stood up and reached down to swoop Cathy into his arms and give her a kiss.

"Daddy, I sung from my diagram today, just like Miss Beth Ann told me. She said I was so good she had me sing twice." She giggled when he hugged her and nibbled on her cheek.

"Wow! Sounds like Miss Beth Ann is teaching you well."

Beth Ann smiled and touched his arm. "Believe me, Cathy is already talented." She noticed the way the man's eyes lit up. What a great dad.

After Cathy and her dad left, Beth Ann had to face the truth. It wasn't fair to her students to be so distracted, so she made a promise to stop thinking about other things and focus on the children. She would push away any other thoughts that tried to intrude.

When she got home, she was thrilled by the smell of Kaylob's cooking. And as he came out of the kitchen to greet her with his one and only sexy grin, she almost melted on the spot.

"Welcome home, beautiful," he said, giving her a kiss. "Did you have a good day?"

"Yes, but I'm so happy to be home." She tiptoed to put her arms around his neck and return his kiss. God, he was so fine.

She went to the bedroom to change and dinner was ready when she returned. The food was so good she didn't have- any problems eating every piece of barbecued chicken and salad he put one her plate, but she couldn't keep up with Kaylob. She watched him finish his third helping with a smile. The man could definitely put away a lot of food.

"Dinner was wonderful as usual," she said, standing up with her dishes. "Thank you for spoiling me with your wonderful cooking."

"You're welcome, sweetheart." Kaylob followed her into the kitchen with his plate and the small amount of leftovers. "So … are you heading over to Blake's tonight?"

She turned and put the dish down, searching his face for any trace of anger. "Yes, but I was going to help you clean up first."

He picked up the towel and slung it over his shoulder. "I'll do it. You go ahead and take off before it gets late. I get nervous when its dark and you're out driving."

She put her arms around his neck and kissed him. "I love you, honey. Thank you for trusting me to handle this on my own. And don't worry. I'll be back soon."

"I do trust you—it's him I don't trust." He sighed. "I may hate him right now, but I know you need to do this."

"Thank you for saying that."

He nodded. "Please drive carefully. I've been worrying about you a lot lately. I guess it's because of those crazy paparazzi out there."

"I will, and I'll be bringing home some boxes, so I'll need help bringing them in when I get home."

He flexed his arms for her. "I think I can handle that."

She laughed and kissed him again. "I'm sure you can, Mr. Universe."

It took her less than twenty minutes to get to the newer, more pristine part of town where Blake lived. She knocked on the front door and waited with a lump in her throat…No one answered even after she knocked again. Odd, since Dana usually answered the door. After standing there in confusion for a moment, she used her key to let herself in, figuring she would just leave a note and ask if he could send everything over to her.

Although Blake's penthouse had been her home for a while, walking into it felt like going into a stranger's house. There was no way she belonged there. She started to just turn around and leave, then she heard music winding its way down from the master bedroom.

"Blake, it's me!" she called up the stairs. "Are you here? Blake, hello!"

When she got no answer, she walked down the hall into the spare room to see if that was where he had stored her stuff. She saw only a few boxes, but wedding gifts were piled everywhere. On the top of everything else was the wedding dress box along with a professional photo. It was the one of them sitting in a gondola when they were in Venice. They had planned to use that for their wedding announcement. God, that made her feel awful. She picked up the photo, remembering the joyful moment it had captured. Now it was only an orphaned memory, one that would never be revisited. After a few seconds, she put down the photo and took a deep, cleansing breath. She was losing his friendship, and that really did hurt.

A noise behind her made her turn to see Blake standing in the door in his robe, propped against the frame. "So you finally decided to come back home."

He took a step closer and she inadvertently stepped back. "I told you this is not my home, Blake." She looked at the floor, unable to meet his gaze.

"Why can't you look at me, Beth Ann?"

"Fine." She forced herself to look up and wanted to hide from the pain she saw in his eyes.

"Thank you for that at least. Let's see, how long has it been since you went to Novato to plan our wedding?"

"Blake, I'm sorry. Please don't be like this. None of this has been easy."

"No?" He laughed bitterly. "Well, it's been a helluva lot easier for you, darlin. While you went on with your life as if I was never a part of it, I've had to pick up the fallout from what's left of my life. I gave you what you needed when Kaylob was gone, but he's back now, so the hell with good old schlep Blake! It didn't matter that you were wearing my ring or that we had a wedding planned, did it?" He waved his hand around the room. "You left everything to me—all the canceling, calling and explaining to all my friends and co-workers. Don't you think that since I'm the one that got my heart broken that maybe, just maybe, you could've done something to help out?"

"I'm sorry, Blake. You're right, I should've helped you."

His eyes darkened. "No, what you should've done was get your ass home and marry me!"

"That's not happening, Blake. You know that." She turned her back and started fidgeting with the bows on some of the gifts.

He put his hands on her shoulders and turned her back around. "We need to talk, and you need to face me!"

"Don't do this to me!"

She pushed him away with tears in her eyes and bent to pick up an unopened wedding gift. This was so unfair. First, she had to deal with Kaylob's emotions and now Blake's. Didn't anybody care what she was feeling? She loved Blake, but she was *in love* with Kaylob and couldn't imagine not spending her life with him. Now there were all these wedding gifts that needed to be returned. How could she take them home and let Kaylob see them?

"I have to get these in the car," she said, wiping her eyes angrily. "Do you think you could help me, please?"

He pulled the gift box out of her hands and threw it down. "No, you're not leaving yet. I'll deal with all this shit."

"I thought you said you wanted me to help you deal with everything."

"I meant making all the calls. That wasn't anything I could delegate."

"Oh, I guess not," she said.

He held her gaze. "You really thought it was okay to break up with me on the phone? After spending almost a year dating me, that's all I deserved, really? Tell me, Beth Ann, how could you do that to me?"

"I had no choice, Blake. I couldn't leave him. Don't you understand that?"

"No, I sure as hell don't! And you're not gonna just brush me off now. You did nothing but use me. Did you think I'd just walk away and not look back?" His face was a mixture of anger, pain and a few other emotions she didn't recognize.

"Blake, I'm sorry, I—"

"Screw your apologies! What did you want from me the most? Money, fame, or the new car I bought you?"

She knew he was hurting, but her temper finally ignited. "I didn't want any of it! I never cared about your money and you know it. And I never wanted that car. Donate it to someone who needs it!"

His eyes were filled with wounded rage. "You know, you were right not to come see me before now. All you're doing is driving a knife deeper into my heart, but what do you care? You got want you wanted from me, so just leave me the hell alone! I hope I never have to look at you again!"

That was more than she could take, tears flooded down her cheeks. It killed her to hurt him and lose his friendship, and now she knew he hated her. She covered her face with her hands and cried. Then a handkerchief appeared.

"I'm sorry, Beth Ann. I didn't mean what I said." He wrapped his arms around her. "Please don't cry."

She pressed her face into his chest. "I'm so sorry, Blake. I never meant to hurt you."

"I'm sorry I said all those stupid things, but you have to know how hard it is for me to think about him making love to you. It's killing me!"

"But he isn't," she said before she could stop herself. "We haven't made love, so don't let that torture you." She knew she shouldn't have told him that, but she was desperate to ease his hurting at least a little.

Blake's face was suddenly filled with what looked like hope. He picked up her hand and looked at Kaylob's engagement ring. "You're not going to marry him."

"I didn't mean that, Blake. I'm sorry for hurting you, but yes I am going to marry him."

"Bullshit, darlin. Ain't happening."

God, she'd only made things worse. "You have to accept it, Blake. You had part of my heart and you always will. I miss you every day. You're one of my best friends in the world and I don't want to lose your friendship. Can't you see this is hurting me too?"

He turned around and left without saying another word.

* * * *

All Blake could focus on, is what Beth Ann had just said, *best friends.* Jesus, she was a helluva lot more than a friend to him. What he wanted to do was kidnap her until he got her to see the truth—his truth. He climbed the stairs, went into his bedroom and called Johnny.

"She's here so could you load up some of her stuff I had in the den."

"Sure, boss." Johnny said. "Do we need to get her car keys?"

"No, she never locks her doors." Blake hung up and changed from his robe into his clothes.

"To hell with being friends!" He threw his wallet across the room.

While he was buttoning his shirt, he looked up to find Beth Ann in the doorway, watching him.

I'm so sorry, Blake. What can I do?"

He took a step toward her, memories of their lovemaking nights filling his heart. The way she smelled, the taste of her sweet kisses. Lord Almighty he wanted her.

"Let me make love to you," he said, reaching for her hand. "Let me remind you why we belong together."

Beth Ann took a giant step back. "No, Blake. I'm engaged to Kaylob and I love him. I would never do that to him."

"Oh, but you could do it to me! That was easy enough for you, wasn't it?"

"Blake, you need to remember that I was with Kaylob and engaged to him first."

"I don't give a damn about that! That was then this is now. And, darlin, you became mine."

"That was only because Kaylob was gone and we didn't think he was coming back. You know I was with him almost all my life. He was and will always be my true love." She looked at the floor with a sigh. "I'm sorry. I don't want to hurt you."

Blake didn't want to hurt her either, and he hated the pain he saw in her eyes. He just wanted her back, no matter what. He had to think of some way to make her see that she belonged with him, but right now, he didn't know what else to do but to pretend he was okay.

"I'm sorry too, Beth Ann. I don't want to fight with you. I'll have the rest of your stuff sent over. I packed up some of your clothes and Johnny and Lucky loaded them up in your unlocked car. That's a bad habit by the way. I need your address and phone number so I can send the rest of it over."

The gentleness in her eyes almost did him in. "Thank you, Blake."

She wrote everything down then turned to him with tears in her eyes. He reached out, took her hand, and walked down the stairs to the landing.

She turned to face him. "I have something I need to give you." She opened her purse and pulled out the engagement ring. "Someday you'll find a new love. You're a good man, Blake Tanner, and someday some lucky girl will win your heart. You'll see."

He took the ring and stared at it in his open hand. Some lucky girl had already won his heart, and it would never be free again. But he couldn't tell her that. It would only make things worse, and right now, he had to play it cool.

He tried to smile but failed. "Take care of yourself, darlin."

"I love you, Blake. Please always know that."

In that moment, he would sell his soul to have her back. "If you ever need me for anything…" Unable to finish, he caught his breath. "Call me."

She kissed his cheek then turned and walked out the door. He watched the door shut, knowing it was the last time he would see her for a very long time.

He walked to the bar on shaky legs where a bottle of scotch called his name, so he poured a full glass. It went down so fast it burned his damn throat. Again and again, he emptied the glass until the liquor was gone.

"Like hell it's over! We'll just see about that!" He punched the wall, ignoring the pain. "I have to find a way to break them up so she'll come back to me."

Another bottle of scotch called his name and he worked on it until his eyelids got so heavy he couldn't keep them open, and everything began to fade.

He tried to make it upstairs, but the room was spinning and he ended up on the floor. He didn't know how long he'd been lying there when Dana's voice woke him up.

"Blake, you'll get through this, I promise." Her voice cracked. "Johnny, help me get him up."

"It's okay, boss. We gotcha."

"Gonna get her back," Blake slurred. "Just *watch* me."

"Sure you will, boss." Johnny said, pulling him up from the floor.

He blacked out again and woke a few minutes later to find himself on the bed in his underwear. The room was dark and he was alone again, so he rolled over with a groan and went back to sleep. Sometime later, he opened his eyes and cried out with joy when he saw Beth Ann standing beside the bed. There she was the tiny redhead he had loved since childhood. He watched as she slipped off her clothes and smiled down at him and knew he had to be dreaming or hallucinating, but he didn't care. He pulled her into his arms and made love to her the way he'd done when she was his. It was always her, and always had been.

Tears slid down his face as he called out her name. "Beth Ann…"

* * * *

The pain from the emotional scene with Blake made Beth Ann have to pull over and compose herself before driving home, so it was well after eleven p.m. when she turned into the parking lot of their townhouse. She got out of the car, grabbed a few boxes and decided to get the rest in the morning.

When she turned around, a couple of guys she had never seen before were standing in the shadows off to the side, and it seemed as if they were watching her with more than mild curiosity. She tried to hurry past them but the shorter guy called out to her.

"Hey, can we help you carry something?"

Chapter Twenty

"No, thank you," she said. "My fiancé is coming out to get the rest. You can help him if you want."

"Sure, no problem." The man lit a cigarette and passed it to his friend.

Kaylob flung the door open as soon as she got to it, and she knew he'd been anxiously awaiting her return. He grabbed her and kissed her, and she returned it with relief.

"Just what I needed to feel your arms around me," she said. "There's more stuff in the car if you want to get it. And there were two guys out there who offered to help."

"Okay, I'll go grab them while I've got some help."

Beth Ann took the boxes to the spare room and decided to deal with her clothes in the morning. When Kaylob came in a few minutes later carrying one of the bigger boxes, he set them down then touched the frown lines on her forehead and gave her another kiss.

"Sweetheart, there was nobody in the garage."

"Strange," she said. "They asked if they could carry anything for me and I told them they could help you when you got there."

"Well, the rest of the stuff isn't going anywhere. I'll get it in the morning." He took her hand and led her over to sit down. "Was it hard for you to see him, baby?"

"Yes, he's very hurt." She sighed. "At least it's done."

"Do you want to talk about it?" He twisted one of her red curls around his finger.

"It can wait. We have to get up early for your award ceremony tomorrow and tonight I just want you to hold me."

"You got it." He wrapped his arms around her, and she melted into his embrace.

* * * *

Kaylob's award ceremony the next morning was touching and made Beth Ann so very proud of him. When they got home, he placed the medals away in his closet and didn't want to talk about them, so Beth Ann didn't push. Someday he'd display those medals. She was sure of it.

When Friday rolled around, she was more than a little thankful that she had only one week left to fill in at work, then she could get to the important business of planning her wedding. Plus, she and Kaylob had to meet Mitch at the Tony awards and she was really excited about that too.

That afternoon when she got home from work and entered the spare room of their townhouse, the rest of her stuff was there just as Blake had promised. That chapter was closed, and a mountain rolled off her shoulders.

Kaylob wasn't home and had left a note for her on the bed. He'd been gone a lot lately and was working on the surprise for their wedding. She picked up the note and was happy to see he hadn't gone far this time.

> *Hey sweetheart,*
> *I'm down at the pool. It's a beautiful day, so come on down. Behave yourself with your bathing suit. If we're going to keep our agreement and wait until our honeymoon, you can't torture me!*
> *I missed you today! Love you with all my heart.*
> *P.S. Come on, hurry up and give me my hello kiss. My lips await you.*

She held the note to her heart. How blessed could one girl be? On her way to her bedroom, the phone rang and she picked it up.

"Hello?"

Nothing but breathing.

Just as she started to hang up, a man's voice said, "You're so beautiful and smell so good. When are you going to wear that little pink dress with the rose over the pocket again?"

Before she could say anything, the dial tone came on.

Who was that? She knew it wasn't Blake but that voice was someone she knew or at least it seemed that way.

She needed to tell Kaylob and get their number changed. Maybe even call the police. Obviously, someone was watching her, and it wasn't just the paparazzi. A chill ran through her as she remembered the missing clothes.

146

Maybe she hadn't left them at Gram's after all. She'd call Gram tonight and find out for sure.

She tried to put it out of her mind so she could go enjoy the beautiful day with her gorgeous fiancé. It had been unusually warm for April, so a swim would feel great after a long week. She put on her least-revealing bikini so Kaylob wouldn't be tortured and covered it up with a colorful light jacket.

When she stepped outside into the hallway, she noticed movement from the corner of her eye and turned to see the same two guys who'd offered to help her the other night coming out of the townhouse next door, one of them carrying a bag. Funny, she'd never seen them in that townhouse before. Her stomach did a little flip, and a shiver ran through her. She suddenly wished she wasn't alone.

"Hey, strawberry," the big guy said, "you look sweet enough to eat." He licked his lips obscenely.

"Go to hell," Beth Ann shot back. She turned to go back into her townhouse and call the police, but before she could, a hand covered her mouth. She tried to scream for them to let go, but the hand over her mouth muffled everything. They dragged her toward the open door of the maintenance area at the end of the hall. The short guy threw her on the floor while the other one locked the door.

"Kaylob!" she screamed. "Help me!"

The bigger guy pulled her up and wrapped his arms across her chest from behind. "*Kaylob*," he mimicked in her ear. "He can't hear you, bitch, so shut up!"

The shorter guy flashed a knife in front of her then thrust it against her throat. She felt the icy blade pulse with her racing heartbeat and froze.

"Don't scream again or you get the blade," the taller guy said as he took the knife from the other guy.

She closed her eyes, hoping it was all a bad dream. Trillions of thoughts ran through her mind. Her legs wouldn't move. She couldn't scream and couldn't think. Fear gripped her as tightly as the assailant.

Are they going to kill me? Are they the ones who've been calling me? Oh God, please help me!

"Please stop this," she pleaded, afraid to struggle because of the knife at her throat.

The short one just stood staring at her, but the bigger guy brushed her face with a hand as rough as sandpaper, then handed the knife back to the other guy. "Junior, take this and stab her if she tries to fight or scream. Here, hold the loot too." He handed him the bag and Beth Ann realized it was probably stolen goods from the neighbors next door.

"Hawk, let's just get out of here. We don't need her. The jewelry we got must be worth at least a couple grand."

"Shut the fuck up, you fat ass!" Hawk said. "Just do what I tell ya!"

"I don't want to get caught and lose everything we got," Junior argued. "And I'm not fat!"

"We have a lot of money," Beth Ann said, hoping she could bribe them to let her go. "I have jewelry I could give you if you let me go. Please—"

"I told you to shut up!" Hawk pulled her head back by her hair. "We know you got money, you little snob. You think you're better than us?" He twisted her head around, slammed his mouth over hers and bit one of her lips. "I'll show you just how good I am."

"Please, you're hurting me." Beth Ann cried, tasting blood in her mouth. "I don't think I'm better than anyone, I swear. Why are you doing this to me?"

Hawk ran a finger down her cheek and neck and kept going. His breathing sped up as his rough fingers worked their way inside her jacket fondling her breast. "Hot, so steaming hot," he muttered, running his finger across her nipples. "I know who you are, bitch. I recognize you from the magazines, and I want a piece of your famous ass." He slid his hand lower to her bikini bottom. "Yeah, you got jewelry all right. Red jewels."

Oh, God, he has to be the one who's been calling. He's some kind of obsessed psycho!

"No, please don't." Beth Ann's voice wouldn't go above a whisper.

Hawk grabbed her jaw so hard that she tasted blood in her mouth again. "I told you to shut the fuck up and stop your goddamn begging or I'll slit your throat. Understand?"

She nodded as fear stabbed her. *What can I do to stay alive? Maybe if I don't fight him, I'll live through this.*

"That's a good little girl." He growled and pinched her breast so hard that more tears slid down her face.

She knew there was no way she could overpower these two guys, but she also knew Kaylob was not far away and he might come looking for her. Maybe she could somehow send him a mental distress signal. They'd always had a connection to each other, even when he was in Vietnam. She shut her eyes and silently called for Kaylob to come save her.

Hawk ran his fingers over her belly with a menacing laugh. "So firm—a dancer, right? You're a pretty little thing. I'm gonna give you something you never had before and make you forget all about that fiancé you talked about the other night."

He started to pull down her bikini bottom and she panicked. This was it. She was going to be raped and killed if she didn't do something, so she clawed at his hands to keep him from pulling off her bikini. He let go, but only long enough to slap her.

"You stupid bitch, you scratched me! Junior, get over here and hold her hands. I'm taking her first. You can have seconds." He stuck his hand down his pants and started pulling at himself and groaning in a way that made her gag.

God, this can't be happening. I have to get away. Please, Kaylob, can't you feel that I'm in trouble? Please hear me!

Junior held her hands but didn't look like he wanted to. "Hawk, let's get the hell outta here before somebody hears something and we get caught. She's not worth going to jail over."

"Shut your fucking mouth, you idiot!"

"Listen to him, please!" Beth Ann begged. "I won't tell anyone, I swear."

Hawk hit her again and again then covered her mouth with his filthy hand. The thought of where his hand had just been made her almost vomit.

"Shut your mouth or I swear I'll break your pretty little neck!" Hawk said.

She cried silently and looked up at him with pleading eyes, even though she couldn't see anything but stars after being struck so violently.

"That's better," he said, unbuckling his pants. "Now keep quiet and maybe I'll let you live." He ripped off her top, then he lowered his mouth and bit her so hard that blood poured from her breast. It was deep and she knew it. He was ripping her apart.

She inhaled deeply, fighting to stay conscious as a sense of defiance struck her. He might kill her, but she wasn't just going to lie there and let this beast violate her any more. She managed to lift her mouth high enough to bite his lip as hard as she could.

"Ouch, you bitch!"

He backhanded her again and more warm blood trickled down her face, but she ignored the pain and took the deepest breath she could manage so she could scream as loud as possible.

"Kaylob, help me! Please, hear me!"

Hawk was still slapping and punching her, but she barely felt the blows in her terror and fought back with everything she had. All of a sudden, it occurred to her that her hands were free. She saw the open door and realized Junior had fled, so she screamed again.

"Kaylob, please, help me!"

Hawk stopped hitting her long enough to reach over and close the door, then he laughed mockingly. "Nobody's coming to rescue you! And since Junior ran off like a chickenshit, which just leaves more for me!"

He forced her legs apart and was about to rip off her bikini bottom when the door crashed open and she heard the most beautiful sound she had ever heard—Kaylob's voice.

Chapter Twenty-One

"Beth Ann, what the hell—Jesus Christ! I'll kill you, you sonofabitch!"

Kaylob pulled Hawk off her and they crashed to the floor in the hall. Someone's hands pulled at her and she struggled at first until she felt something warm wrap around her. Then she heard a woman's voice telling her she was safe now. She couldn't see much because of the blood and tears in her eyes, but she could sense others around.

"You're gonna be okay now, sweetie," the woman said, pressing a towel against Beth Ann's bloody chest and hugging her. "Help is on the way."

She could hear scuffling sounds then suddenly remembered the knife. Did Hawk have it or did Junior take it with him? She had to warn Kaylob! She pulled away from the woman and tried to fight her way through the people surrounding the two fighting men.

"Kaylob, he's got a knife! Be careful!" Her knees buckled and she would have fallen if a man hadn't caught her.

"It's okay, miss. There's no knife. And your boyfriend can definitely take care of himself." He gently sat her down near the wall and tucked the towel around her.

Another man said, "Yeah, we better stop him or he's gonna kill the guy."

Two of the onlookers pulled on Kaylob's arms, but it took three of them to pull him off the would-be rapist.

"Let him go, buddy," one of the men said. "We'll hold him for you until the cops get here. He's not worth it, and your lady needs you."

Kaylob's face was a mask of rage as he fought to get away so he could beat on Hawk some more, but what the man said seem to get through to him. He stopped fighting and turned to look at Beth Ann.

"Baby …" He ran to Beth Ann and dropped to his knees. Tears streamed down his face as he wrapped his arms around her.

"Kaylob, I thought I'd never see you again." She reached for him and sobbed.

"My baby, oh my God, my baby." He cupped her face in his hands and moved the hair away from the blood. She could see his eyes widen as he touched her wounds and she could tell he was hurting just as much as she was.

All Beth Ann could think was *I'm alive. Thank God, I'm alive. I knew Kaylob would hear me.*

She felt Kaylob swoop her into his arms, then he turned to the lady who'd helped her. "I don't want her near that piece of shit a second longer." He glared at Hawk, being held down by the other men. "Can you send the police to our townhouse when they get here? It's right over there."

"Sure, honey," the lady said. "Go take care of her."

* * * *

When Kaylob carried Beth Ann inside their townhouse, the familiar aroma had never smelled so good. A warm feeling somebody associates with being alive after a traumatic event overwhelmed her, and she clung to Kaylob with an iron grip.

He placed her on the couch as if she were a fragile rose and gently pried her hands loose from his shirt, then he carefully pulled back the bloodied towel and flinched when he saw her chest.

"Beth Ann, we have to get you to a hospital."

"No, please, I only want to be in your arms," she said, holding on to him tighter, her tears returning.

He shook his head. "You've been beaten bad, sweetheart, and…raped."

"No, he didn't rape me. I kicked, screamed and fought him off long enough for you to get there and save me. But it was close, Kaylob. So, so close." She started to sob and couldn't seem to stop.

He held her until she gained some control, then he said, "I'll be right back."

He brought back a summer dress and a blanket. Gently, he slipped the dress over her head and wrapped her in the blanket, then he went to the kitchen and came back with a warm cloth. While he was wiping the blood off her face, a knock on the door signaled the cops and paramedics' arrival. They wanted to take her to the hospital and at first, she refused, but Kaylob finally convinced her to go.

"I want you to ride with me though," she said, clutching his hand.

"I'll be right there with you," he said. "I'll call Frankie to pick us up when they release you."

"Okay, but please don't tell my family yet. I don't want them to worry."

He didn't seem to like that idea but agreed to respect her wishes. At the hospital, they sent a female doctor in to see her and made Kaylob step outside the room.

"Hi, sweetie. I'm Dr. Hancock." She smiled at Beth Ann. "So there was no penetration according to the report, is that correct?"

Beth Ann nodded, and felt her lip tremble.

Dr. Hancock examined her then said, "You've got some really bad bruising and hematomas here, along with some nasty bites." She patted Beth Ann's hand. "We really should keep you."

Beth Ann shook her head and felt tears swimming in her eyes. "I just want to go home. It was so close. I mean, it could've been worse."

The doctor studied Beth Ann's face closely. "I know, but you still were assaulted and there could be emotional effects from this. You may want to get some counseling or go to some groups. We need to do about six stitches on your breast and give you a shot for infections. Human bites can be very serious."

Dr. Hancock wrote out a prescription and handed it to Beth Ann.

"I'm sorry this happened to you, sweetie. We're going to take good care of you and release you, but you need to do a follow up a couple of days. You have a minor concussion, but I understand your desire to go home."

"I promise to go to the doctor," Beth Ann said.

Dr. Hancock smiled. "Okay, we'll be processing you out soon, but no heavy work for the next two weeks. I only want you relaxing, got that?"

Beth Ann nodded and managed to fight the tears until the doctor left the room. Her innocence had been stolen. They hadn't raped her, but she'd been brutalized and demoralized. If she didn't have Kaylob, she didn't know what she would do.

He came back in the room and walked over to put his arms around her. "My baby," he murmured, stroking her hair. "Are you okay?"

"Now that you're here." She took his hand and held on for dear life.

After another hour, they were finally released.

When Frankie picked them up, his eyes widened and his face went pale when he saw her. Both her eyes were bruised, one almost swollen shut. Her lips were also swollen and had deep gashes, and she had bruising all over her face, neck, and arms. Even her leg had one bite mark that she hadn't even been aware of until the nurse had treated it.

After Frankie hugged her, he had a hard time letting her go, they got in the car then he told them he'd talked to the police and they'd caught both guys and had them in custody. Beth Ann would need to go down in the morning and

153

identify them. Beth Ann saw the look that passed between Frankie and Kaylob. They wanted to kill those guys and she knew it.

She didn't talk much in the car and they didn't push her. When they got home, she went to the couch to lie down, but Kaylob and Frankie stayed out in the hall. She wondered what they were talking about. After a couple of minutes, Frankie stuck his head in the door and told her goodbye. Kaylob sat next to her and she went to the only place she felt safe—his arms—then she fell asleep listening to his heartbeat.

When she opened her eyes, Kaylob was looking at her with tears. Before she could speak, he touched her swollen lips and said, "Please let me take care of you."

There was no way she could refuse him anything.

He scooped her into his arms and stood up. With her hands linked around his neck, she lay her head on his chest and let him carry her into the bathroom. He turned on the shower then went to get towels and fresh clothes for her. The only sound was the shower's steady stream and her own heartbeat.

Tenderly, he helped her undress and slipped out of his own clothes as well. "Take my hand, baby."

He helped her into the shower and just held her for a moment, the warm water blanketing both their bodies in a protective cocoon. Beth Ann would've been happy to stay there like that forever, but after a few minutes, he placed her on the shower seat, loaded the sponge with liquid soap and gently glided it over her bruises and gashes.

"Tell me if I hurt you." He winced as he ran the sponge over the bite marks that were again crusted with dried blood. When he came to the one on her leg, he gently ran the sponge over it then leaned down and placed a whispery kiss on the wound. "I'm so sorry those monsters hurt you."

She looked up at him and put her hand on his cheek. "I'm just glad to be alive and here with you. And we're lucky you came back just then and heard me scream."

His forehead creased as he looked at her. "It wasn't luck, Beth Ann. When I was at the pool, I got a strange feeling that you needed me for something. I didn't know what, but I knew I had to go find you. On my way, I heard you scream. So did others who were in the hall."

Tears mixed with the water on her face. "I was mentally calling out to you when they had the knife on me to keep me from screaming. I was trying to send you a message."

He smiled softly and swept the tears from her eyes with his thumb. "Just like when my heart called to you from that hellhole in 'Nam. I always knew our souls were connected."

God, he was so amazing. She had never felt so close to anyone in her life, and she knew he was right. Their hearts and souls were inseparable.

As she watched the blood flow down the drain from her wounds, she imagined that every ounce of pain went with it, and she had never felt closer to him as she did in that moment. As strange as it was, the silence between them was precious. How unbelievable that the worst thing that ever happened in her life had morphed into something so beautiful. His touch was like a gentle breeze blowing over her wounded and sore body, healing her soul with every caress.

When they got out of the shower, he sat behind her on the bed and brushed her hair, adding even more to the intimacy between them. She hadn't thought it possible to love Kaylob more than she did, but a sea of emotion overflowed her heart.

Later, while she lay in Kaylob's arms as they fell asleep, she realized how with every storm comes a rainbow. You just have to open your heart to the possibility of the rewards that pain can bring. She had found her reward at the end of the rainbow—strength, power, and a newfound joy of being alive.

* * * *

At the police department the next day, they told her the monsters who'd attacked her had confessed to everything but denied calling and claimed they'd never been to Salem. That confused her, but why would they lie about that after confessing to the attack? The police said they more than likely didn't want the judge to add premeditation to the charge. The detectives had been unable to find any type of black car in their possession and even checked with the rental companies, so that part was a mystery. At least the two scumbags would be locked up for a long time because they had been linked to other crimes in the area.

When Beth Ann went back to the doctor two days later, she told her everything would heal in time, but she did have bruised ribs and lungs. Dr. Hanson also said there was no way she could return to work for at least a month. After Beth Ann called her job to tell them, she also called Mitch to let him know she wouldn't be able to attend the Tony awards. He agreed to accept on her behalf if she won and said he would bring the award to her.

She hated to miss the event but couldn't bring herself to go with all her bruising and she also had no desire to be in a large crowd. She was dealing with her emotional trauma thanks to Kaylob, but she knew it would be a while before she felt completely comfortable around strangers again.

Days went by and things finally settled down. All the concerned phone calls from friends and family had tapered off for the evening, so she asked Kaylob to come sit by her on the couch and hold her.

"My pleasure, sweetheart." He sat down and lifted her feet into his lap. "Have I told you how much I love you?"

"Never." She tried to laugh but it hurt. "I feel completely safe here with you. You're my safe harbor and my hero."

The phone rang and Kaylob reached over to pick it up. "Hey, Mitch. Yes, she's here and she's doing pretty good considering. Hold on." He handed the phone to Beth Ann.

"I'm so sorry about what happened to you," Mitch said. "Thank God they caught those creeps!"

"Thanks, Mitch. They'll be locked up for a long time."

"I have some good news for you, sweetie. If you want to hear it." He had a hint of joy in his voice.

"Sure, I'm always up for good news," she said. "What is it?"

"You won kiddo! You're a Tony winner!"

"Oh, my God!" She stood and tried to jump up and down but winced in pain. "I did it, Kaylob! I won a Tony!"

Kaylob stood up long enough to kiss her but made her sit back down. "Ah, baby. I'm so proud of you."

"I'll make sure you get it soon," Mitch said. "You want me to bring it to you tomorrow?"

"No, just bring it to me after the wedding. We can have a celebration party then." She had happy tears in her eyes.

"Sure thing, kiddo. How are you really doing?"

"Fine, Mitch. Everything is healing, and I'm absolutely fine."

"Look I told the press and some of the reporters who were asking for your phone number that you were under the weather. So they shouldn't be calling you for interviews yet."

"Thank you Mitch." She said with a sigh of relief.

* * * *

Frankie was coming over to stay with Beth Ann on Monday morning because Kaylob said he had to get back to work on the surprise for their wedding. She did her best earlier while they ate to coax a hint from Kaylob, but he wouldn't give in.

Frankie's special knock on the door alerted her to his arrival. "You don't have to babysit me," she told him when she opened the door. "I'm really okay."

He arched an eyebrow. "What, can't a guy hang out with his best friend the Tony winner if he wants to? I always knew you were talented." He gently hugged her then waltzed into the living room holding Beth Ann's hand.

Her smile was ear-to-ear. "Thanks, Frankie. I told Mitch we'll celebrate after the wedding when he brings it to me. Right now I need to find a way to make Kaylob relax so we can go back to living normally again."

Frankie sat on the couch with her. "Are you okay?"

She knew he meant the attack, but she didn't think either of them could handle discussing the details, so she just said, "I'm still pretty sore and I do have nightmares. Not as bad as Kaylob though."

Frankie squeezed her hand. "I'm always here for both of you."

"I know that, Frankie." She leaned on his shoulder.

Their day together ended up being fun. They watched some old movies and took a short walk to a café for lunch. Beth Ann thought she saw the dark car again but hoped it was just her mind playing tricks on her.

A few days later, she finally convinced Kaylob to leave her unguarded in the townhouse, and she even felt empowered by going out alone. Again, she could have sworn she saw that same black car following her and decided it must have been the paparazzi after all. They'd be even worse now because she'd won a Tony. But to be safe she called to tell the police, and they assured her that the guys who'd attacked her were locked up with no chance of getting out. If it was the paparazzi like she suspected, maybe she should get a license plate number and have Frankie and Kaylob scare the crap out of them.

That Thursday night after she got ready for bed, Kaylob came in to kiss her goodnight, and she could tell things were falling back into place when he stayed to tickle her a little. Since the attack, he hadn't made a pass at her or even joked about it, and she knew he was worried about how she would react if he did.

She sat up and gave him an exaggerated pouty look. "Do you think we could sleep in the same bed tonight?"

His expression sobered. "Of course, sweetheart. Are you feeling afraid?"

"No, I just want you to hold me."

He smiled. "Okay, I'll be right back."

When he came back in the room a few minutes later, Beth Ann grinned. He was so darn cute in his white terry cloth robe.

"Could you please turn that light on?" she asked, holding up her book to explain why.

He walked over to the decorative light, dropped his robe, and began gyrating his hips while flexing his biceps.

"You like what you see, sweet thing?" he said, facing the lamp.

Had he lost his mind? "Kaylob, what are you doing?"

"You asked me to turn on the light. You think it's working?"

Once she got it, she doubled over in laughter. "Kaylob Shawn O'Brien, what am I gonna do with you?"

"Anything you want." He jumped onto the bed and began to kiss her face and neck.

She giggled and smacked him with the book. "Stop it, you goofball."

The next morning, she reached for him, but he was already gone. She found a note on the pillow.

> *Good Morning, Sweetheart,*
> *Had to run and take care of a few things to do with that surprise I promised you. I should be back by 10:00 and our appointment with the travel agent is at 11:00. Your breakfast is in the oven waiting for you.*
> *Don't open the door unless you know who it is.*
> *I love you, Kaylob*

When she got out of the shower, she thought she heard a noise, but realized it was her mind playing tricks on her. She stood in front of the mirror and examined herself critically. She no longer looked like the child or teen that people had often mistaken her for. Most of the fading bruises were turning yellow, although a few on her ribs and upper arms were still green. As she put on her lip-gloss, she grimaced because her lips were still tender and swollen, but overall she looked almost normal. Once she slipped on her new dress, she felt better.

Kaylob had left her eggs, potatoes, and biscuits with gravy. While she was eating, she heard the front door open and he walked over to kiss her on top of the head. Holy night, he smelled so good and was so irresistible that she wanted to stop eating and devour him instead.

"Beth Ann, you look incredible," he said, pulling her up into his arms. "How am I supposed to concentrate at the travel agency when you look like this?" His hand drifted to her thigh and lifted her dress enough for him to see the garter belt and stockings. He rolled his eyes and let out a growl.

She laughed. "Kaylob, you're turning into a bear."

"Yeah, I'm turning into something all right." He laughed and nibbled on her neck.

She convinced him to let her finish breakfast, then they headed out to the travel agency. As they walked in the door, the breeze caught some papers on one of the desks and blew them around. A little lady with gray hair and dark purple glasses jumped up and began scurrying about, trying to capture the papers in a pile. She punctuated the victory by placing a glossy glass paperweight on them, then she held up one finger while she finished chewing a bite of her sandwich.

"Go ahead and finish your lunch," Kaylob told the lady. "We can look around a minute."

The small office had two desks, a coffee area, and a few round tables with four oversized chairs. Along the wall, racks held different cruise brochures of exotic lands like Ireland, Spain and Mexico.

Kaylob picked up one and said, "I want to go meet the family I have in Ireland someday. You and I will have to go sometime."

Beth Ann grinned. "That's a good idea. You have some aunties and cousins there, right?"

Kaylob nodded. "My Aunt Lillian and some other family members. I've never met them but I want to."

Beth Ann remembered his mom talking to someone named Lillian when he was in the hospital and now knew it must have been his aunt.

The lady with purple glasses was still chewing her sandwich but motioned for them to come have a seat at her desk while she put the remnants of her lunch in a tiny refrigerator. A phone on the other desk rang just before she sat down again.

"I'll be right back," she said, rushing to pick up the phone.

Right back turned into fifteen minutes. They could hear the lady telling someone about rates for Disneyland. She tried to motion an apology to them and convey that she was trying to get off the phone. Finally, another lady came in from a back room and walked over to them.

"Have you been waited on?" she asked.

Kaylob pointed at the lady on the phone. "She got interrupted before we got started."

"Oh, then let me help you," she said with a big smile.

They looked at all the wedding brochures that mentioned wedding parties and chose the Maui Sunset package where the ceremony would be performed outside. The site overlooked the ocean and was simple but elegant. For their honeymoon, they both fell in love with the private island getaway home. Kaylob pulled out his checkbook, and Beth Ann leaned close to him with a catch in her breath.

"Can we afford this?"

He winked at her. "Don't worry, baby. We're gonna have the honeymoon of our dreams."

He paid a deposit on their entire package, and they signed all the papers without a hitch. When they got outside, he swung Beth Ann around as she squealed.

"Hawaii, baby! Can you believe it? I can't wait for you to be my wife."

"I can't wait for you to be my husband!"

They celebrated by going to lunch and spending the day at a little country fair. Her hero won her two stuffed animals and bought her cotton candy. They went on every single ride and took pictures of themselves in picture booths just like they did when they were kids. As they were walking to the car, Beth Ann looked at the pictures in her hand.

"I wish we hadn't lost all our childhood pictures like this," she said. "It would have been fun to have them all together."

Kaylob took the photos and looked at them with a sigh. "I know. My parents donated all my stuff, including the box you gave me with all our childhood memories inside. I wish they hadn't done that."

"It's partly my fault," Beth Ann said. "Your mom called me when you were declared dead and asked if there was anything in your room I wanted. At the time, I was just learning to breathe again after my breakdown and couldn't bear the thought of going through your room."

Kaylob took her hand and placed it on his heart. "It's okay, Beth Ann. I wish we had the box too, but we have all our memories right in here."

* * * *

A few days later Blake sat in his Palm Springs office, an hour away from the love of his life, wondering what the hell he was going to do. Beth Ann and Kaylob were getting married in June. Blake was determined that somehow, some way that marriage was never going to take place.

Melissa knocked on his door and peered inside. "Mr. Rutherford is back from Hawaii and wants to speak to you. He's on line one."

"Thanks, darlin.'" He picked up the phone. "What do you have for me?"

"Mr. Tanner, before I give you my report about the wedding location…" Rutherford paused. "You do know about the attack, don't you?"

"What attack?" Blake's heart lodged in his throat.

"The young lady you've had me checking up on, she was attacked, pretty bad from what I've heard. Assault and attempted rape by two men. She was beaten pretty badly and taken to the hospital, but she's been released."

"What the fuck?" Blake steadied himself against his desk as the room began to spin from his boiling rage. "I have to go!" He pressed a finger to the receiver, dialed another number and waited for him to answer. "Russo, what the hell? I just heard about the attack. Somebody could've fucking called me, you know!"

"She's hanging in there," Frankie said. "You could call her and... "

"What the hell happened, and where was Kaylob?" Blake demanded.

"Look, Blake, Kaylob's the one that saved her. I don't even want to think about what might have happened if he hadn't found her. You want me to have her call you?"

"No...she's been through enough. I don't want to put any more stress on her."

He hung up; his face and skin burning with fury. Every fiber of his being wanted to find the guys responsible and kill them, make them pay for what they did to his girl. He hurled a paperweight at the wall and raked his hands through his hair.

"Goddamn it!"

A second later, Melissa opened the door with a worried look. "Blake, what's wrong? What was that noise?"

His throat was too constricted to speak as he fought back the tears.

"Blake?" Melissa took a cautious step closer. "What's the matter? Please tell me."

He knew he couldn't speak without falling apart, so he grabbed his keys and bolted for the door. Bile rose in his throat as the thought of Beth Ann being attacked ran through his mind. He vaguely heard Melissa calling his name as he tore down the hall, blanking out the faces of strangers as they watched him. He needed to see her, needed to wrap her in his arms and protect her for the rest of her life. To hell with everything that he'd said to Frankie on the phone, he had to go to her even if it did cause stress.

* * * *

Preparations for the wedding were in full gear for the next few days. Lisa was coming to help Beth Ann pick out her wedding dress, and Beth Ann couldn't wait to see her. Denny wanted to come, but she was just starting a new modeling job and couldn't get away. Carol was going with them too, so Beth Ann knew she would have plenty of help finding the perfect dress.

When they got back to the townhouse after picking up Lisa from the Ontario Airport, Kaylob took one of her bags to the guest room and Lisa looked around with approval. "It's beautiful! So modern and I love the white couch." She ran her fingers over the material then sat down and patted the spot beside her. "Come talk to me. Are you okay, honey? I'm just going on and on and well... I just want to make sure you're really okay."

Beth Ann sat beside her. "I'm okay." She met Lisa's eyes and smiled. "Honest."

Lisa wrapped her arms around her childhood friend. "I hope they burn in hell for hurting you."

"Hey, ladies," Kaylob interrupted. "I'm gonna check the mail and get the rest of the luggage."

While he was gone, Beth Ann got up to show Lisa the guest bedroom where she'd be sleeping. When they passed the room Kaylob slept in, Lisa pointed at the clothes on the bed. "Who's here besides me?"

"Nobody except me and Kaylob."

"Whose clothes are those?"

Beth Ann shrugged and gave Lisa a coy smile.

"Okay, what's up?" Lisa walked into the room, picked up Kaylob's robe and blew a wisp of her bangs out of her face.

Beth Ann glanced down. "Kaylob is sleeping in here until we're married."

Chapter Twenty-Two

Lisa tossed the robe back on the bed then pressed her palm against her forehead. "What an idiot! Is he holding out again? He's such a buffoon. I'm gonna have a long talk with that man and his old-fashioned ways."

Beth Ann touched her arm and leaned closer. "No, we're both the idiots this time. We decided to wait until our honeymoon."

"Why?"

"We want the honeymoon to be special." Beth Ann walked over to his bed and sat down.

"Are you serious?" Lisa said. "I don't see you guys as having any issues with that. That must be torture for you both."

Beth Ann's silence was a cue to change the subject. Unfortunately, Lisa didn't take cues very well.

"Okay, then tell me this," she said. "Aren't you both tempted?"

Beth Ann sighed and stood up. "Come on. Let me show you your room. You'll have your own private bathroom because Kaylob uses ours."

Lisa rolled her eyes. "Uh-uh, subject changer, answer my question. Aren't you at least a little tempted?"

Beth Ann flashed an innocent smile. "Well, more than a little—"

"Horny!" Lisa chuckled.

Beth Ann's face flushed. "Don't say that!"

Lisa laughed and shook her head. "Oh, I forgot. Such words are not in your vocabulary."

Beth Ann smacked her arm. "Okay, yes, we're both a little needy." She tried to leave the room but Lisa caught her hand and pulled her back with an impish grin.

"I want to hear you say that word just once in your life. Come on, say it! *Hooorrrnnny.* Try it just once, it might feel good." She paused to laugh before continuing her goading. "I heard it on good authority that the remedy is even better. You're a full-grown woman, Beth Ann. Are you gonna be chicken all your life? It's just one word. Come on, you can do it!"

Beth Ann placed her hands on her hips and scowled. "Okay, fine. HORNY! *Hooorrrny* with a capital H! H-O-R-N-Y, horny, horny, horny!"

"Really? Is that so?" Kaylob winked at Beth Ann from the doorway. "I can take care of that for you."

She shot Lisa an indignant glare; her face flushed twenty shades of red. "I have to go pee."

Kaylob and Lisa cracked up as she rushed out of the room to save herself from their endless teasing. The doorbell rang as Beth Ann walked down the hall toward the bathroom.

"What the hell are you doing here?" There was no mistaking the anger sheathed beneath Kaylob's tone when he answered the door.

Beth Ann rushed to intervene. "Blake? What are you doing here?"

"I just heard. I had to see…" He choked back his words. "Never mind, you look okay. I shouldn't have come. I'm sorry." He turned and walked rapidly down the hall heading towards his car.

Beth Ann gave Kaylob a pleading look. "I need to go talk to him for a minute. *Please.*"

Lisa took Kaylob by the arm. "Hey, Hot Stuff. Come show me the new TV you guys bought."

Kaylob didn't look happy, but he nodded and followed Lisa to the living room.

"Blake, wait!" Beth Ann called after him and was relieved when he stopped, but he didn't turn around. She touched his arm when she caught up with him. "I'm okay, Blake. Really."

When he turned around, the anguish on his face made her reach out and hug him.

"Thank you for coming by to check on me." Her voice was just above a whisper.

He took a step back and took her by the arms. "Come home with me, Beth Ann. Please. I would never have let this happen to you."

"Kaylob didn't let this happen, Blake. I wasn't doing anything I didn't do when I lived with you. I was going out to meet him at the pool when they attacked me."

"Yeah, but the building we lived in had security that I hired to keep you safe. Come back home with me where you're safe, Beth Ann."

She shook her head. "I *am* home, and I'm safe with Kaylob. I'm right where I'm supposed to be." She shifted her gaze to the ground to avoid seeing the hurt in his eyes. "Thank you again for coming by, but I have to go."

She felt his eyes on her as she walked back to the townhouse. Once inside she closed the door and slumped against it. *I just wish I could make him understand and take away his pain.*

When she looked up, Kaylob was staring at her with worry in his blue eyes. She rushed into his arms where everything felt right. There was just no place in the world she would rather be.

* * * *

The next morning, Kaylob was already gone when Beth Ann got up. What kind of a surprise could take him away so much? After breakfast, she and Lisa headed out to a bridal shop on Gallo Drive in Riverside called Marion's Bridal Boutique. The owner agreed to open the shop early for them and even had coffee and muffins while they waited for Carol to arrive.

When she got there, they looked through a lot of dresses before Beth Ann found a sleeveless one she liked. She loved the sheer fabric that covered her chest and shoulders. A feeling of excitement warmed her as she stepped out of the dressing room, expecting lots of *oohs* and *ahhs* from her two friends, but what she got was a look of shock, as though she were the Bride of Frankenstein.

Carol walked over and hugged her. "Oh my God, Beth Ann. I had no idea you were hurt this bad. I've been a horrible friend."

Lisa's hand covered her mouth with tears swimming in her eyes. "I didn't know you were hurt this bad either." She touched one of the ugly bruises tenderly.

Beth Ann extracted herself from Carol's arms and looked at both of them. "I'm sorry you had to see me like this. I guess I'm just used to them. But look, they're fading." She showed them the bite mark on her leg and her breast.

That just made them look more upset.

"Honestly," Beth Ann said, "I'm doing really well. And I refuse to let those two beasts take away my happiness. The only thing I'm sad about is that Denny couldn't be here with us. Now you two stop worrying—that's an order. I'm the bride, so I'm in charge."

"Wow, listen to Miss Bossy," Carol said. "I like it." She and Lisa both laughed and embraced their friend, then Carol wiped her eyes and smiled. "Hey, enough of this. We need to find you a wedding dress."

After trying on what seemed like a hundred more gowns, Beth Ann finally settled on one with fabric that flowed down from the waist ending at the floor.

It was breathtaking. It left her shoulders and back bare—very sexy but not overdone. The little train cascading in the back added the perfect touch of elegance, which was ideal for Beth Ann.

Carol smiled. "It's beautiful, sweetie. I love it, and it looks like it was made for you."

Lisa nodded. "Look at this beautiful lady. This dress is perfect."

Beth Ann couldn't stop the joyful tears when she saw herself. "This is really happening. Kaylob is really going to be my husband."

They hugged again, and this time it was all smiles and laughter. Beth Ann knew they both understood what she had been through to get to this moment, and here it was, just a month away.

* * * *

The next few days went by in a blur of wedding activity, but Beth Ann managed to spend plenty of time with Lisa. On more than one occasion, Kaylob dragged himself in after seven p.m. with one excuse or another. Although Beth Ann smiled and rubbed his weary shoulders, inside she was beginning to wonder about his long hours. Especially since Lisa was visiting. Despite her happiness, a tiny seed of doubt began to grow.

Second to the last night of Lisa's visit, Frankie was over for dinner with them when the phone rang, and nobody was there when Beth Ann answered. A chill ran down her spine at the creepy silence just knowing someone on the other end was listening. She hung up and was glad that neither Frankie nor Lisa noticed her saying hello three times. Maybe it was Blake. She hadn't talked to him again since he stopped by to check on her.

Later that evening Kaylob got home way past his usual time. When Beth Ann hugged him, his scent was sweet smelling like perfume. No, it was more like paint or something else, something odd. She made a mental note to ask him later when they were alone.

That evening was a lot of fun, filled with laughter and reminiscing and Lisa sharing pictures of the baby. Beth Ann could tell she was missing her baby boy. Nevertheless, they had such a good time she lost track of how late it was. Once Frankie left, Lisa went straight to bed. Before Beth Ann did, she set the alarm for six a.m. She wanted to talk to Kaylob before he left in the morning.

When the alarm went off at the crack of dawn, he was already gone when she walked into his room. Now that little seed of worry in the back of her mind bloomed into a flower of doubt, and she remembered Gram mentioning something about sowing wild oats. She succumbed to temptation and rummaged through his things snooping for answers. All she found was some guilty feelings for not trusting him.

166

After breakfast, she and Lisa decided to do some more shopping on her last day there, so their first stop was at a lingerie shop, Sheer Lace, on Gateway Drive. When they got to the car and Beth Ann started to unlock the driver's side, she was surprised to find it *already* unlocked. She'd been doing her best to remember to always lock it and thought she had. Oh, well. Maybe Kaylob had opened it for something.

While sitting at a stoplight down the street close to their old apartment, Beth Ann glanced over and saw Kaylob walking down the sidewalk with his arm around a short, round woman, heading toward an expensive hotel on the corner. His truck was parked in front of the very building where Beth Ann had seen a vision of them while he was in Vietnam. She had peered through the window of the empty building and seen herself and Kaylob with a little girl and a golden dog.

Beth Ann sat there, frozen, staring at her supposedly loving, attentive fiancé, walking with his arm affectionately around another woman. She felt the heat ball up in her stomach before it began to radiate to her face. Could that woman be the mysterious caller?

Lisa saw them too and said, "Honey, I'm sure there's some explanation. No, I *know* there is. Please don't jump to any conclusions, okay?"

"Sure," Beth Ann said curtly. "I'll just assume it's no big deal my fiancé is leaving at the crack of dawn and staying gone every day for God knows how many hours, coming home late every night and is now groping some strange woman on the way to a hotel."

Lisa touched her hand. "There has to be some explanation. There *has* to be. You know he loves you and would never cheat on you. Even more so after what you've been through. He said he's been working on a surprise, so this must be something to do with that."

Lisa might as well have been talking to a busy signal. All Beth Ann could do was stare at Kaylob and the woman walking away until a car horn behind them goosed her back to reality.

"Sure, you must be right," she said as she drove away. She didn't want Lisa to tell Kaylob they'd seen him, so she pretended to believe it was nothing. She forced herself to act happy the rest of the day, and Lisa seemed to buy it hook, line and fish. Or was it hook, line and fishing?

Once they were done shopping, they headed back to the car to put all the bags in the trunk, Beth Ann stopped as a cold tremor ran up her spine, and she suddenly knew someone was watching her. She looked around and saw a dark car sitting with the engine running. Okay, she'd had it. She walked toward the car and had only gone a couple of steps before it sped away, squealing its tires.

"Who was that?" Lisa said as they got in the car.

"The paparazzi I guess. They must be hard up for stories. Those guys need to get a life."

Lisa frowned. "How annoying."

"You can say that again." Beth Ann started the car. "It was worse when I was with Blake, but it's picked up again since I won the Tony. There should be a law against it." She drove across town trying to take her mind off everything.

Kaylob came home later than usual that night, so tired that he didn't say much to anyone. Lisa had to get up early to get to the airport, and Carol had offered to take her since she had to leave for work at the crack of dawn anyway. At least Kaylob made sure to kiss Beth Ann's forehead and tell her he loved her before he went to bed.

He was gone again when Beth Ann woke up in the morning. After seeing him with that woman, she couldn't help snooping again to see if she could find any evidence, like lipstick on one of his shirt collars or something. But while she was digging through his hamper, guilt overtook her. Kaylob would never cheat on her. She was being stupid and paranoid, and it had to stop. She decided to do his laundry instead of being so ridiculous, so she gathered his clothes and took them into the laundry room, actually humming as she opened the washer to load his clothes. In that instant she felt a sense of peace, after what happened at Frankie's house of course he would never do anything to hurt her. What was wrong with her?

Just as she told herself that, a business card fell from his pants. It was from a deli with writing on the back.

I can do it all, and I do mean all. Call me and let's meet. How about at my house? Kendra

There were two phone numbers on the card, and it took everything she had not to call. Pride and fresh tears prevented it. No, she wasn't going to be one of those pathetic jealous women who did things like that. She put the card in her purse and made up her mind to talk to him about it when he finally wandered in, no matter what. Enough with all the secrecy.

She tried to put it out of her mind by staying busy, but after doing all the laundry, cleaning the townhouse and trying to watch TV, she still couldn't think of anything else. When Kaylob wasn't home by dinnertime, her mind was racing with all kinds of wild notions.

I need to get the heck out of here and go do something!

She hadn't eaten all day and decided to go out for something, and she was too upset to leave a note or answer the stupid phone when it rang just before she stepped out. When she passed a little bar only a few buildings down from her townhouse that catered to locals, she decided she wasn't hungry after all and wanted a drink instead.

As she entered the bar, the fading daylight seemed to be swallowed up by the darkness living inside. The décor consisted of framed newspaper stories on the dark lacquered walls, dotted with neon ads promoting vintage beers. The stench of stale smoke escaped the cushion as Beth Ann sat on one of the bar stools. The few other people there paid little attention to the newcomer, instead choosing to continue their no-frills relationship with the glass or bottle in front of them, and that suited her just fine.

The bartender gave her the once-over and said, "You look like a beautiful margarita girl to me.

She nodded in agreement even though she'd never had one in her life. While she drank her first margarita, she listened to the music coming from a jukebox in one of the dark corners, then she ordered another. Before she knew it, she was finishing her third one. The handsome bartender kept winking at her when he brought her drinks. He wasn't handsome like Kaylob, but who was? He was big like Kaylob though, only with dark hair. Nobody had Kaylob's beautiful blue eyes and dazzling smile.

When the handsome bartender brought her fourth margarita, she followed his gaze and saw a cop walk in the door and stare at her. Oh, great. She was probably going to jail. But he only came in, looked around and left.

"Whew, that was close," she said to the bartender who wasn't Kaylob. She crossed her hands in front of her and leaned toward him. "I'm getting married in…" She tried to count the weeks on her fingers and gave up. "I'm getting married *very soon,* and my fiancé is cheating on me with a plump girl. Can you believe that?"

He leaned on the bar. "I can't imagine anyone cheating on you, sweetheart, and maybe you should slow down." He pointed to the glass. "Margaritas can sneak up on ya. Would you like a cup of coffee, or is there someone I can call for you?"

She held up one finger. "Good idea! I'm gonna call my best friend F-F-Frankie. He'll tell me what I should do." She started fumbling in her purse. "My fiancé has been knitting his wild wheat before we get married like my gram warned me. What do you think about that?" She slapped her hand on the bar and almost spilled her glass.

The bartender moved it away from her. "I think you should call your friend Frankie now. Better yet, let me call him for you."

She was still digging through her purse. "Could you call him for me? I think he knows this pace."

"Sure, what's his number?" The bartender got the phone and waited.

After fumbling in her purse some more, she finally found Frankie's card and gave it to the bartender. Frankie was there in fifteen minutes. She heard him say her name and turned to look at him, but someone or something had pushed her off the barstool. Just in the nick of time, Frankie caught her.

"Frankie, I love you such much," she said, her arms around his neck. "That rotten fiancé of mine has been cheating on me!"

Frankie sighed. "I'm getting you out of here. Kaylob called me when he got home and you weren't there. He's worried sick."

"I don't care," she said. "I'm the one who's pissed off at him. Look at *this*." She handed Frankie the card she'd found in Kaylob's pants.

Frankie looked at it and arched an eyebrow. "I'm getting you home now. You need to talk to him."

"I saw him with the short round woman, and he had his tall arm around her. Can you believe that, Frankie?"

"No, I can't." He pulled her arms from around his neck and tried to hold her up straight. "Let's go so we can find out what's going on."

He guided her out of the bar, but she turned to wave at the bartender and blew him a kiss. "That's my friend, Frankie. He called you for me and told me I was beautiful."

"Yeah, good thing I came to pick you up and not Kaylob or you'd be in worse trouble."

He managed to get her home without having to carry her, and he knocked loudly on the door then opened it and took her to stand in front of Kaylob.

"I think she can stand," Frankie said, "but be ready to catch her just in case."

Kaylob's stern look was met with an erratic sway and a goofy smile from Beth Ann. When she saw Frankie grinning at Kaylob, she said, "Don't smile at him, Frankie. He's a wild weed player."

Chapter Twenty-Three

"I have no idea what that means, but I think it has something to do with this." Frankie handed the card to Kaylob. "I told you this would be hard and she might jump to the wrong conclusion."

Beth Ann turned too quickly to glare at Frankie and almost fell over. Kaylob had to catch her. "Frankie, you traitor!" She pointed at him. "You knew about this and didn't tell me?"

Frankie stuffed back a laugh. "I'm over here, Beth Ann." He waved a hand at her. "Kaylob, you might want to make her some coffee. The bartender said she had about three and a half margaritas."

"So you decided to get drunk, huh?" Kaylob steadied his pickled fiancé on her feet and glanced at the card then back at her. "What the hell were you thinking?"

"I was thinking about *you*, and you know what? I almost got arrested because of you!" She poked him in the chest. "A cop came in the bar and stared at me. I thought he was gonna fluff me and handcuff me, but he just smiled and nodded."

She tried to put her hands on her hips but they slipped off. She tried again with no luck and looked down with a huge sigh. "I must have lost weight. My hands won't hold on to my hips." She looked up and poked Kaylob again. "It's all your fault 'cause I didn't eat all day!"

Frankie let out a thunderous laugh and Kaylob covered his mouth. Beth Ann glared at them.

"I want you both to get that expression off your heads right now! This is not funny." She stomped her foot and lost her balance. "I'm gonna go back to the bar and have some more margaritas and talk to my new friend." She swayed and almost fell when she tried to turn around.

Kaylob caught her once again. "Oh no ya don't, sweet stuff. You're not going anywhere."

"You can't stop me, Mr. Playboy." She tried to wriggle free from his grasp.

"Oh yes I can," he said. "You're having some coffee and food, then you're coming with me so you can see what I've been up to."

Despite her inebriated state, Beth Ann was fully aware that they were trying not to laugh at her, and she was dead serious.

"Go ahead and laugh," she said. "But you're a two-timer and we all know it! I saw you walking with your arm around that lady! And you were heading to that fancy hotel."

Kaylob shook his head, then he swooped her into his arms and carried her to the sofa.

"Beth Ann, baby, listen to me," he said. "I haven't been sowing wild weeds, oats, or anything else for that matter. After all we've been through, how could you ever think I'd have an affair? Actually, how dare you think that? You're in so much trouble after I get you sobered up."

Her response was a blank stare, then her stomach did the bop.

"Bathroom!" she blurted, covering her mouth with her hand. Kaylob helped her up, walked her to the bathroom and shut the door. A few minutes later, he knocked.

"Beth Ann, you okay?"

"Just go away!" she shouted.

After ten minutes of praying to the porcelain god then brushing her teeth twice, she made her way back into the living room and collapsed on the couch. She could see Kaylob in the kitchen cooking. She was drunk, but not too drunk to realize that she may have jumped to the wrong conclusion, especially if Frankie knew what was up.

"Better?" Frankie asked, still looking way too amused for her taste.

"I still feel sick," she said.

Frankie grabbed a wastepaper basket and set it on the floor beside her, then he bent down to kiss the top of her head. "Here, Lucy. Desi's in the kitchen cooking. You're in big trouble now." He called to Kaylob, "I know she's in the doghouse, but go easy on her, Des." He was cracking up as he left.

After Frankie left, she held onto the wastebasket, as if it were an anchor that kept the room from spinning. Kaylob made hamburgers piled high with onions and French fries on the side. Gram always said onions would cure anything, but could they cure the trouble she was in now? She sure hoped so.

Kaylob made her eat everything before giving her a strong cup of coffee. Surprisingly, the food helped settle her stomach. She was able to make it to the bathroom again without colliding into an obstacle. After she finished brushing her teeth again, she washed her face and got ready to go wherever Kaylob was taking her.

While she was changing clothes, she wondered if maybe she should go out there and offer to forget everything and wait like a big girl for the surprise. Now that her head wasn't full of margaritas, she knew there was something innocent going on after all. Why hadn't she just listened to the part of herself that knew it all along?

Once she got brave enough, she walked out to the kitchen and sat at the breakfast bar. Kaylob was rinsing the dishes and loading them into the dishwasher, glancing up occasionally to look at her but not saying a word. Trying not to feel useless, she got the rag and wiped off the kitchen table, then she rinsed it and put it back over the faucet.

"Kaylob, why don't we just pretend this didn't happen and you can just surprise me like you planned?"

He raised an eyebrow then laughed. "Ha! I think not. We're leaving in a few minutes so you can see what I've been doing." He walked over and kissed her cheek. "I was gonna tell you next week anyway."

She was glad he wasn't mad at her, but then she felt guilty for ruining his surprise. She sat at the table with a sigh while he finished up in the kitchen then picked up his keys.

"Come on, let's go."

She stayed in her seat. "I have a headache. Can't we hold off one more day?"

"No way," he said. "We're going now. Grab a couple of aspirin and get your sweet ass out the door."

When they were both in his truck, he paused before he started it and stared at his hands on the steering wheel. "I'm not mad at you, but I am disappointed. You know how much I love you. After that whole ordeal with the lady at Frankie's and those guys attacking you, how could you think for one minute that I would cheat or lie to you?"

"Kaylob, I'm sorry. I tried to tell myself that same thing. When I found that card, I was going to wait until you got home and talk to you. But instead, I got drunk and..."

"I told you I was working on a surprise, and that's what I've been doing. I wish you could have had more faith in me and not gone snooping." He finally looked at her. "When you saw me yesterday, I was helping a dizzy pregnant lady carry a butt load of sandwiches. I wasn't cheating or having an affair. It was me helping someone who needed it."

She wanted the world to open up and swallow her. She was stupid and childish and an immature drunk. It wasn't helping that with every word he said it felt like a dozen gremlins were in her head pounding every nerve cell in her brain. If this was what a hangover felt like, why in the world did people drink? She looked at Kaylob and could see how much she'd hurt him by doubting his word. How was she ever going to make this up to him?

He started the truck and they drove in silence until he pulled up in front of an old building. She'd been too busy willing the aspirin to start working to pay attention until he parked, and when she realized where they were, it made her head spin. It was the place where she'd had the vision when Kaylob had been declared dead. God, had she been witnessing the future?

"Okay, here we are." Kaylob walked around and opened the truck door for her. "Come on, let's take a look."

Beth Ann couldn't move. The memory of the vision combined with her lingering intoxication made her feel faint.

Kaylob stuck out his hand. "Come on, we're going inside."

When she got closer to the building, she could tell it was being renovated. The dim lighting made it difficult to make out anything specific, but she could see there was lettering on the face of the building and work being done to the windows. Her heart fluttered and she froze at the memory of the vision of Kaylob carrying boxes, the little girl with blonde hair and the golden dog. Should she tell Kaylob about it?

"Beth Ann, hello." Kaylob tugged on her hand. "We're going inside."

She finally got her feet to move and watched him pull out a key to unlock the front door. They entered into a foyer lined with lovely seating covered in protective plastic. To the right was a podium, also covered in plastic. Behind the podium were stressed brick walls, dark swirl marble counters and frosted glass with etched roses in the corners. The carpet was an elegant black with silver specks, and in the far corner, she could see a partially constructed stage.

"I'm having that built for you." Kaylob gestured toward the stage. "Your singing can be the entertainment."

She was too astonished to speak as she looked around. The oak stage was big enough for a band and more than one singer. The bar on the right side of the dining area was long and stunning. You had to step up to get to it, but it had a beautiful marble top that ran across the whole length of the wall, and Beth Ann remembered that was where Kaylob had set the boxes in her vision. There was more glass with etched roses all around.

"I had seven roses put in every area on the glass. Do you know why?"

Of course, she knew what the seven roses meant. That was the number of days they made love before he left for Vietnam, and he'd sent her seven roses and named each one for their love.

Everything was just like in her vision.

He pointed towards the kitchen and they entered through the swinging doors. There propped against a stainless steel counter was a sign that Kaylob read aloud. "Seven Nights, Seven Roses Fine Dining. Our very own restaurant, named for our seven nights together and the Rose that's the love of my life."

"Oh, Kaylob…" She started to embrace him but he held her off with a smile.

"Wait, I'm not done showing you everything yet." He walked over to a drawer and pulled out a document that brought tears to her eyes. It was Kaylob's dream.

"I finally did it, baby. I got my degree in culinary arts." His eyes were bright with tears. "I've been going to school in the mornings and left early to study in my truck. Then I'd come and work here with the crew after school so we could get it done faster. I wanted to surprise you with making our dream come true—you sing, I cook."

"I'm so sorry for not trusting you, honey." She threw her arms around him and couldn't stop her tears.

He hugged her and nuzzled her neck. "Promise you won't ever doubt me again."

"I do promise, Kaylob."

He took her by the hand and led her to the adjacent rooms. "These are the theme rooms. When they're completed, they'll be for parties and special occasions. We'll also have rooms for wedding parties." He led her through some swinging doors into another room. "This is the game room for kids and adults. We're soundproofing it so it won't disturb the dining guests. When families bring their children, it'll be a place for them to play in case Mom and Dad want to have a few quiet moments."

There was even a garden area with additional seating and a waterfall. "Kaylob, everything is magnificent!"

He picked up a piece of tile from the ground, tossed it in the garbage then turned to look at her. "Now about that lady you saw me with. That's Tom's wife—the contractor in charge of this job. She's pregnant with their third child. I had my arm around her because she was feeling a little dizzy after walking down to pick up sandwiches for the crew."

"Oh, Kaylob. I'm so ashamed of myself. What can I say to make this better?"

"It's not what you can say, sweetheart. It's what you can do from this point forward."

She said, "Trust you," at the same time, he said *trust me.*

They both laughed, then his voice softened. "And the card you found in my pants was from Tom's sister. She runs an employment agency called 'Staffing Today' and has been helping me find workers. She's also married and has three children."

Beth Ann looked at the floor guiltily, but he lifted her chin with his finger and kissed her.

"This is my wedding present for both of us. I love you, Beth Ann."

She pressed her face against his chest and cried. "I love you too, Kaylob. I'm so sorry for not trusting you. I should have known better."

"We all make mistakes," he said. "I just hope that mistake I made by going to that woman's apartment won't make you lose faith in me forever." He held her away from him and lifted her chin again. "You are my life, my future wife, and the woman I want to have children with. Yes, I said children."

She cupped his face in her hands. "I promise to have more faith in you, and I won't ever get drunk again. I hope you can forgive me, honey."

He brushed his lips over hers and said three sweet words.

"I forgive you."

* * * *

Now that Kaylob finished school and the restaurant wasn't a secret anymore, they had plenty of time to spend together over the next few weeks. With all they had to get done for the wedding—choosing foods, registering and all the final details—time flew by like the roadrunner.

On Thursday, the week before the wedding, they had the entire day to do whatever they wanted. They decided to go back to the park where they had buried the unread letters to each other their first Christmas living in Riverside. Beth Ann had refused to even think of them while he was gone. In fact, she hadn't even stepped foot in that park. Their plan had been to open them on their twenty-fifth wedding anniversary. Looking at their initials carved in the tree brought back so many treasured memories—most good, but some bittersweet.

Like the night he'd told her he was going back to Vietnam and she'd run off in a storm. The sweet way he'd carried her to the car in the rain when he'd found her, that had led to them making love for the first time. What a journey they had been through and now a new journey was beginning. The one that would lead to their long-time dream.

Later that evening, Kaylob was watching TV and Beth Ann decided to go look through all the things she had bought for their honeymoon. The nightgown was white, very short and very see-through, holy hot stuff sexy.

A sudden urge struck but she sure as heck didn't want Kaylob to see, so she did a quick peek at the living room to make sure he was still watching TV, then she took off her clothes and slipped the little lacy gown over her head. Standing in front of the full-length antique mirror, she turned this way and that and decided the pose was all wrong, so she tugged with all her might and pulled the heavy mirror to the corner of her bed. She climbed up on it and pretended she was talking to Kaylob.

"Come over here, I want you," she said, puckering her lips and stretching out on the bed. The next pose was on her knees. "Come over here and let me devour you, Mr. Sexy. Come on. Let me kiss you all over." She giggled and a movement from the corner of her eye made her jump.

"You got it, baby." She looked up to see her fiancé leaning in the doorway, his arms crossed over his chest while he wiggled his eyebrows. Then he removed his arms pretending to unbuckle his pants. "I will do as you say." He chuckled.

She tried to scramble off the bed and grab her robe at the same time, but she ended up hitting the floor instead. While she was down there, she considered crawling under the bed to hide, but Kaylob pulled her up and into his arms before she had a chance.

"Are you okay?" He was trying not to laugh as he sat her on the bed.

Her face felt as if it were blazing. "Kaylob Shawn O'Brien, what are you doing sneaking up on me? You were spying on me!"

"Spying? First, I hear this dragging noise like someone is moving a monster trunk in here, then I hear a sexy voice demanding I get over here. I had to obey. It sounded serious."

"I thought you were watching TV."

"I was, but the show in here was a lot better."

She crossed her arms and glared at him. "How long were you watching?"

In reply, he moved the mirror back in place and said, "Devour me, baby!"

"You could've let me know you were watching!"

He came back and sat beside her. "No way. You're the boss, right, so I had to do what you were saying. Tell me, when were you planning on using those seductive moves on me? They were smoking hot, especially that last one where you landed on the floor." He threw back his head in laughter. "Reminds me of the first night we made love. Remember how you grabbed the cooking oil and thought you were getting ice water?"

She rolled her eyes. "For your information, I didn't grab the oil on accident. That book said to try using oil the first time. I thought of extra virgin olive oil because I was extra virgin."

Kaylob gaped at her a second, then he laughed so hard that he almost fell off the bed. When he managed to catch his breath, he said, "Are you kidding me?"

She stood up. "Laugh like a hyena as long as you want. I'm going to take a shower." She shoved him and he fell back on the bed.

"Oh, you want me on my back, huh?" He grinned and caught her hand before she could walk away. "Whoa, is that nightgown for our honeymoon?"

"Yes, so hands off." She turned to leave but he got up and pulled her back into his arms.

"Baby, you look amazing." His eyes drank her in.

She moved out of his arms. "Glad you like it honey." She headed toward the bathroom and, for a little preview of their honeymoon, she gave him her best strut. When she got to the door, she slowly bent over as if she was picking something up.

"Oh, lord have mercy." Was the last thing she heard him say before she walked in and shut the door.

When she got out of the shower, he was still on the bed looking pitiful, so she lay down beside him after putting on her regular nightgown. They talked about the wedding and all their plans for the restaurant, and she decided it was time to tell him about the vision she'd had of the little girl and the golden dog.

"You saw us in that same building?" he said when she finished. "And you saw us with a child?"

"Yes and a dog."

He smiled and pulled her closer. "So maybe we *will* have children."

"It was just a vision, Kaylob." She shook her head. "We've talked about kids before."

"True, but look at how you saw me in 'Nam and how I saw you too. Remember how I was feeling nervous before you were attacked? Beth Ann, we're connected in a very special way."

She leaned her head on his shoulder. He was right; they were connected in a way that even she didn't even fully understand. But still…a child? She just couldn't see herself as a mother.

Chapter Twenty-Four

A week later, everything was finally ready and the morning they had been waiting all their lives for had come at last. It was time to leave for their wedding in Hawaii. Family and friends started phoning at three a.m. to let them know they were ready and excited. Beth Ann and Kaylob were scheduled to leave at five a.m. and the excitement made butterflies swarm in her tummy.

Once they were on the plane, the noise of the engines mixed with her fiancé's heartbeat against her ear made it easy for Beth Ann to fall asleep on his chest. When she woke up, she looked up to see Kaylob staring out the window, his arm still around her.

"Did you sleep at all?" she asked.

"I nodded off for a while, but you've been asleep for hours, sleepyhead. Or should I say Sleeping Beauty? We're almost there."

He kissed her forehead, pushed the hair out of her face and completed his ritual of pushing a few strands of hair behind her ear. This beautiful man was finally going to be her husband. It was hard to believe the dream they'd shared since childhood was coming true.

When they landed and stepped off the plane, women in traditional grass skirts greeted them. Kaylob bent down to let one of the beautiful ladies put a lei around his neck, then he winked at Beth Ann and they both laughed.

After retrieving their luggage, they stepped outside the bustling airport and saw a tall man holding a sign that read: *O'Brien Party*. When Kaylob raised his hand, the man smiled and opened the door of the limo beside him.

"Welcome to Hawaii," he said.

Once the luggage had been loaded they left the airport, and the scenery changed from modern buildings to the more exotic fauna of a tropical island. Kaylob and Beth Ann were speechless from the beauty.

"Just ahead is the villa," the driver said. "It sits on top a hill with a stunning view of the ocean. You'll find it a wonderful place to stay."

The villa came into view and they could see he was right. The building was breathtaking, the grounds adorned with colorful trees and flowers that reminded her of a sunset.

"Oh, Kaylob," she said. "It's more amazing than I ever imagined."

"It *is* beautiful. But not as beautiful as you." He held her hand gently as the limo pulled into the circular driveway and stopped at the front door.

Once inside, they were greeted by more breathtaking sights. The lobby had a waterfall and filled with live plants and flowers of every color. Bamboo furniture lined the room, and a massive stone fireplace took up one entire wall. It was striking and elegant, but Beth Ann couldn't imagine that they ever needed to use it in such a tropical paradise.

As they approached the desk, a short man with a blue flowered shirt greeted them. "*Aloha ʻauinala*," he said cheerfully. "You must be the O'Brien and Rose party here for the *'aha'aina male*."

They both nodded, though they weren't quite sure what the man had said.

The desk clerk turned to another man on his right and pointed at the limo outside. "*Wiki wiki* luggage." Then he turned back to Beth Ann and Kaylob with a smile. "Don't worry about anything here at The Villa. We'll take care of you."

"Thank you," Beth Ann said. "We're so happy to be here."

Kaylob nodded and wrapped his arm around Beth Ann's waist. "We sure are."

The man picked up a set of keys and a small map then handed them to Kaylob. "Someone will be here soon to take you to your honeymoon *hale*. You'll be staying thirty days, yeah?" When Beth Ann nodded, he said, "Good. I promise you'll love it here. There will be a grocery list on the counter in your *hale* and another list of items you may require. Just check off what you need and we'll make sure you get them. There's a box on the gate for you to put the lists in. Raise the little flag and someone will pick it up and have your things to you by noon. Besides food delivery, we also offer twenty-four-hour room service. Do you have any questions?"

Beth Ann shook her head. "No, everything seems perfect." Kaylob agreed with a nod.

"Ah, here's your ride now," the man said, gesturing at the large glass front doors. A large islander pulled up on what looked like a cross between a golf cart and a prop for an episode of "Gilligan's Island." As they walked over to the doors, Beth Ann saw Kaylob check out the size of the man's muscular arms then look down at his own.

"My name's Brian," their driver said. "Nice to meet you." He shook hands with them then pointed to the cart. "Your chariot awaits. If you're ready, let's get you to your house."

Beth Ann stepped up to the strange car and Brian lifted her into it as if she were a feather, then he waved for Kaylob to step inside.

"We'll be there in about ten minutes," Brian said from the driver's seat. "There will be one of these carts at your house for you to use if you need to come back to The Villa or for anyplace else you want to go, but there are no cars where I'm taking you."

"Well," Beth Ann said, "we wanted seclusion, and it looks like we're going to get it."

Kaylob whispered, "Good thing because the honeymoon might get noisy."

She elbowed him and watched him chuckle.

As they took off to their honeymoon house they were serenaded by the sound of exotic animals and bird calls, they headed down the hill on a winding paved path no wider than two sidewalks. They turned a corner past a private beach, where the vegetation grew thicker and completely obscured The Villa above. In front of them, they could see an endless stretch of blue ocean dotted by sailboats and islands off in the distance. The aroma was a mixture of salty air and a sweet scent of blossoms that reminded her of what heaven might be like.

Finally, they reached a massive rock wall where they stopped and Brian got out. He pushed a few buttons on a large iron gate and it slowly opened. They continued down the path until they saw a house sitting at the edge of a beautiful beach. The deck that wrapped around the front of the house held inviting oversized lounge chairs, and a hammock big enough for two. Beth Ann covered her mouth and gasped when she saw all of it.

Kaylob took her hand. "Isn't it awesome, baby? I really didn't expect this."

She leaned over and kissed his cheek. "It's beyond my wildest dreams."

Brian led them inside where it seemed the ocean itself became part of the design. There were windows from floor to ceiling, and the floors were all made of bamboo. They walked down a hallway lined with photos of shells, waves, and sunsets. One photo especially caught Beth Ann's eye—a single footprint in the sand, surrounded by water.

She squeezed Kaylob's hand. "I don't know what to say, honey. I love it!"

The bedroom featured mirrors above the bed, a sight that seemed to make it difficult for Kaylob to find his voice for a moment. He managed to sum up his feelings with, "Wow! Beth Ann, look at that. You can practice your poses and devour me until your heart's content."

"Kaylob!" She elbowed him and blushed when he and Brian shared a wink.

The bedroom walls were covered in natural plants, and silky white curtains danced with the breeze. A hot tub with towels and wine glasses sitting on the edge graced one whole corner of the room.

Brian led them through a door on the left where they found an oversized bathroom. The shower had multiple showerheads and two seats, and behind it was a door that led to a private swimming pool.

Kaylob leaned toward Beth Ann and whispered, "I can't wait to see you in your new bikini, but you won't be in it for long."

"Oh, stop!" she said, her cheeks still warm.

Finally, Brian led them to the kitchen that amazingly had a transparent floor. "You may get to see dolphins swimming under your feet," he said.

Brian handed Kaylob a set of keys. "Your luggage will be here in about thirty minutes. The keys are to your cart, which is parked in the back. Enjoy your stay, and *aloha* 'til we meet again."

Beth Ann felt as though she must be dreaming. Everything was so incredibly perfect.

* * * *

After Brian Left and they were alone, Kaylob captured Beth Ann in his arms and kissed her deeply, then he took her hand and they headed to the beach.

At the ocean's edge, they removed their shoes and Beth Ann luxuriated at the feel of the warm sand between her toes. For a long moment, they stood in silence, gazing out at the vast blue sea blending into the sky on the horizon.

"Do you have any idea how much I'm looking forward to being your husband?" Kaylob asked. He leaned down to kiss her. "Not so long ago I **was** in the most horrible place..." He swallowed... "And now..." He glanced around. "I am in paradise with the love of my life." His voice cracked and he pulled her closer.

"Mr. O'Brien?" She stood on her toes and kissed the dimple in his chin. "The light from our love guided you home, and now, I'm the luckiest girl in the world." Emotions soared through her just thinking about the journey that had brought them to this moment.

For a short time, they held each other in silence then Kaylob sighed and nodded towards the house. "We should go inside in case our guests arrive."

As soon as they walked in the door the phone was ringing, so Kaylob dashed over to answer it. "Hello." He paused then turned to look at Beth Ann. "Really? They're all here? Yes, send them down." He listened a moment.

"Okay, three hours. We'll be there." He hung up and said, "We need to meet the wedding planner in three hours and everybody's here."

He grabbed Beth Ann's hand and spun her around playfully.

"I can't believe it's really here, baby. We're getting married!"

Beth Ann giggled. "Yay! We're going to the chapel of love!" she sang.

Kaylob pulled her into his arms and moved his lips across hers in a sizzling kiss. They were almost in trouble until they heard a beeping sound coming from somewhere. It took a few seconds to realize it was the staff delivering their luggage. Just as Beth Ann was directing the man to put the luggage in the bedroom, she heard more beeping and walked back to the living room to find caterers carrying trays of fruit, sandwiches, salads and pasta dishes.

It was amazing how fast they set everything up on the oversized tables outside on the lanai. Everything looked yummy as Beth Ann checked out the lemonade and a large tray of chocolate chip cookies that had Kaylob-drooling. Instantly, he was high tailing it toward the cookie tray, before she could intercept him, he stuffed one in his mouth and proceeded to grab a handful more.

She tapped him on the shoulder. "What do you think you're doing?"

"Brain surgery," he said, then he frowned when she removed six cookies from his hand and left him one. "Oh, baby, c'mon."

"Okay, fine." She turned and picked up several celery sticks. "Here you go."

He looked from the celery sticks to his fiancée, then he set them down and followed her forlornly away from the table. Within a few minutes, family and friends started showing up, and laughter permeated the air as everyone gathered around. When Beth Ann saw her brother Cole and his girlfriend Patricia, she almost burst with joy.

"Hey, Sis," Cole said. "I guess today's the big day, huh?"

She nodded and hugged them. "It's so good to see you, Cole. It's been a while."

"Too long," he agreed.

Beth Ann was telling Cole and Patricia all about the house when she saw Nickolas come in the door, looking dapper in a casual ivory jacket with a sky-blue shirt. Beth Ann and Kaylob hurried over to greet him.

He shook Kaylob's hand and hugged Beth Ann. "Is Maggie here yet?"

"Not yet, but soon," Beth Ann replied. "Let me introduce you to everyone."

Nicolas and John Patterson hit it off and starting talking about Korea.

Beth Ann's parents were already there, and Kaylob's mom and dad arrived next. As the party continued, Beth Ann kept an eye on Kaylob hovering near the cookie dish. She was talking to her mom and Stanley when she saw Kaylob talking with four people she didn't recognize. The younger of the two men was a tall, lanky kid with pale skin and dark eyes, and the girl looked like a runway model with dark skin and a body to die for.

Jean apparently noticed her daughter's preoccupation with the mysterious beauty. "My goodness, isn't she lovely? Do you know who she is?"

Just then, Kaylob waved for them to join him. "Let's go. I guess Kaylob wants to introduce us." Just as they were leaving, some friends of her mom and Stanley arrived and they had to excuse themselves.

Kaylob put his arm around her shoulder when she came and stood next to him. "Aunt Mindy, Uncle Steve, I'd like you to meet my future wife, Elizabeth Ann Rose. She's Beth Ann to all of us who know and love her."

His aunt and uncle hugged her and welcomed her to the family.

"And these are my cousins," Kaylob said. "Mary Ann and Jason."

Jason blushed slightly and Mary Ann gave her a warm smile. "Nice to meet you, Beth Ann."

"You, too." Beth Ann was relieved that the gorgeous creature was Kaylob's cousin.

The more of Kaylob's family she met, the more it struck her as odd that none of them looked the slightest bit like him. It was the same for Mary Ann. She didn't look like anyone in the family either. Beth Ann also wondered why no one from Ireland had come, but she'd ask him about that later.

While they were standing in the kitchen talking to several friends, the phone rang again and Kaylob excused himself to go answer it. A moment later, he motioned for Beth Ann to come talk.

"It's Gram," he said, handing her the phone.

"Hi, Gram!" Beth Ann said. "Where are you?"

"Hi, sweetness. We're here at the villa."

"Everyone's here at the honeymoon house," Beth Ann told her. "We're having pictures taken in a little bit and I'd like you to match me. Can you wear the yellow dress with the polka dots? And be sure to wear your hair down too, okay?"

"Okay, sweetie," Gram agreed. "I'll get cleaned up and be there soon."

Kaylob held up his finger. "Can I speak to your dad?"

"Gram, Kaylob wants to speak to daddy." She handed him the phone and heard him asking James if he could go around the side of the house and not down the pathway. He was explaining he'd be walking Gram down the path and that there was a surprise.

As soon as he hung up Beth Ann turned to Kaylob. "We have to get everything set up. Is the band on their way?" She felt anxious.

Kaylob smiled and pointed. "There they are now. Try to relax, sweetheart. It's all going to be fine."

Relax? Right. What did that mean? Since she'd started planning the wedding there was no such thing.

Kaylob kissed her cheek and headed out to greet the band members while Beth Ann talked to her older brother James and his wife Marsha.

"I'm so glad you're both here." She hugged James and his wife.

Just then, she noticed John Patterson walking toward her so she excused herself and went to meet him.

"John, I'm so glad to get a chance to talk to you and meet your wife," she said. "This must be her."

John introduced his wife Tina, and they had just started sharing stories when Kaylob walked up and said, "Gram's here, sweetheart. Sorry John, Tina, can I steal my almost wife away."

John nodded. "Sure thing, bud."

"Nickolas!" Beth Ann called a little too loudly as she waved for him to come over.

The entire party seemed to go silent, as if everyone knew something special was about to happen. While Kaylob went out to escort Gram inside, everyone gathered in the living room and Nickolas stood next to Beth Ann in the archway leading outside. She could tell he was nervous by the way he kept fidgeting beside her.

He reached for Beth Ann's hand. "I'm more nervous than I ever imagined."

She gave his hand a gentle squeeze then signaled for the band to play the special song they had prepared. Everyone, including the official photographer, pulled out cameras to capture the moment.

Through the floor-to-ceiling windows, the guests could see Kaylob walking Gram down the lighted path leading to the house. Gram paused a moment, tilting her head as the band started playing Moonlight Hawaii and You. Nickolas was staring at her with tears shimmering in his eyes. Gram was strolling with Kaylob towards the Lanai, when she dropped Kaylobs hand and glanced towards Beth Ann and Nickolas. At first, it didn't seem to register, but after she took a couple more steps, she stopped and gazed into Nicky's eyes. When she placed a hand across her heart, it was clear that age, time, and distance, didn't take away from her recognizing the love of her life. Her lip started to tremble and tears streamed down her cheeks.

"Nicky?" she finally said, just above a whisper.

The moment was so poignant that even the band stopped playing. The only sounds that could be heard were the ocean waves and people sniffling. Nickolas let go of Beth Ann's hand and started down the stairs.

"Maggie!" His voice broke.

He walked to her with open arms, and she met him in an embrace that seemed to sweep away all the years that had passed. Everyone witnessed as both their shoulders trembled and the two lost lovers came together at last. Beth Ann felt tears rolling down her own cheeks as she watched the incredible reunion unfold.

Kaylob spoke to all the onlookers. "Let's give them a few minutes of privacy, folks."

As the guests moved away, the band began playing again, "Moonlight, Hawaii, and You."

Beth Ann shared the story with everyone, and there was hardly a dry eye to be seen when she finished. Kaylob was kissing her cheek when her dad walked up.

"So that's the guy she's been in love with all her life," he said, pointing as Gram and Nickolas strolled arm-in-arm around the garden area.

"Yes, Daddy," Beth Ann said. "I'm sorry if you're hurt, but they deserve to spend the rest of their days together. They've missed so much already."

James smiled. "Honey, I'm not upset. I haven't seen Mother this happy in…well, forever."

"I can't say I have either," Beth Ann agreed.

When the band finished the song, they began playing a variety of music. Laughter again filled the air. Beth Ann looked around for Kaylob and saw him by the cookie tray talking to John Patterson while throwing back his head and laughing. Beth Ann had to giggle at that. It was just so cute and something he'd always done.

She had just stepped outside when Gram and Nickolas waved at her from the bench in the garden area, then they pointed at Kaylob who was now talking to Mary Ann on the front porch.

"Gram wants to see us," she told him when she walked up, giving Mary Ann a nod and noticing again how beautiful she was.

"Okay, baby. Excuse us, Mary Ann." He took Beth Ann's hand and walked toward Gram and Nickolas.

Beth Ann glanced behind them as they walked. "It's funny that Mary Ann looks nothing like anyone in your family, even less than you do."

Kaylob nodded. "She's adopted."

"Oh, I guess that explains it." Beth Ann tried to sound nonchalant. "So you two were close growing up?" She sure hoped they hadn't been kissing cousins.

"We were at one point, but we grew apart over the years."

When they approached the garden, Nickolas was sitting with his arm around Gram. They looked like a picture of pure and simple love. They both smiled when Beth Ann and Kaylob walked up.

"I can't believe you two did this," Gram said. "Thank you so much. I'm still in shock, but very happy." She dabbed her eyes with a tissue.

Nickolas nodded. "I want to thank you too for talking me into this." He stood and embraced Beth Ann then kissed her forehead. "You've made my life worth living again." He shook Kaylob's hand and added, "Thank you too, son. I mean it."

"I'm happy everything turned out." Kaylob put his arm around Beth Ann. "Thanks to my stubborn fiancée."

Gram reached out and took Beth Ann's hand. "We're coming in soon because I understand that you and Kaylob have a surprise of your own today and I don't want to miss that."

"We do?" Beth Ann and Kaylob said in unison.

"Yes you do," Gram said with a wink. "I love you two very much. Thanks again for bringing Nicky back to me."

As Beth Ann and Kaylob walked back to the house, she said, "What kind of surprise do you think she was talking about?"

Kaylob shrugged. "Beats me."

Once inside, Beth Ann was just about to take a bite of a sandwich when she heard their names being called. A moment later, Lisa was dragging them into the living room where she made them both sit on the floor in the center of the room. All the guests surrounded them, everyone pulling out cameras.

The two mothers, Jackie and Jean, stepped forward and handed Beth Ann and Kaylob a brightly wrapped box adorned with rainbows and butterflies. She and Kaylob opened it together, and she gasped when she saw what was inside.

"Oh my God! Kaylob, it's—" Her voice broke with emotion and she had to stop, so Kaylob finished for her.

"It's the chest you bought for me, baby. I thought it was gone!"

He opened the chest and they pulled out every picture, letter and trinket from their childhood still lovingly preserved.

"Honey, look," Beth Ann exclaimed tearfully. "The movie tickets from our first real date!"

Kaylob looked around at the gathered friends and family, wiping away a tear of his own as the photographer took pictures. "Thank you so much for this wonderful surprise. How did you ever get it back?"

Jackie handed him a folded piece of legal paper showing every step that had been taken to find the chest. It seemed as if the entire town had been involved, and Beth Ann had never felt so surrounded by love. The whole day was beyond fantasy, filled with the magic of an enchanted setting, reunited lovers and long-lost treasures. It was the kind of day they would tell their children about.

Wait, whose children?

Beth Ann glanced at Kaylob and could've sworn she saw the hint of a knowing smile, as if he knew what she'd been thinking.

Chapter Twenty-Five

Blake tried to relax in his private plane headed for Hawaii, but the reason for the trip combined with his eighteen-year-old receptionist's non-stop chattering in the seat across from him had him on edge. Her dad had talked him into taking her with him since she had never been and wanted to go. Now he had to make sure she stayed out of trouble.

A part of him knew this trip was a crazy thing to do, but the other part just didn't give a damn and told him to do it anyway. Of course he hadn't been invited, not that he wanted to be a guest at this so-called wedding. There was only one reason he was going and that was to stop that goddamn thing.

He stared out the window and fantasized that Beth Ann would see him and realize that she couldn't marry Kaylob.

"Blake, are you okay?" Melissa asked, pulling him from his daydream. "Are you sure you should be doing this?"

"No, little darlin, I'm not sure of anything," he said. "But I'm doing it anyway. Besides, you'll have fun in Hawaii. Think of all the boys you're going to meet. Just don't get too wild or your dad will have my head. I'm supposed to be watching over you, remember?"

"I don't want boys," Melissa protested. "You know I like more mature men. And I *don't* need a babysitter."

Blake laughed. "Sorry, you're right. I'm not your babysitter, but you'd better behave anyway. I'm still responsible for you since your dad talked me into bringing you."

"I'm not a kid!" she said, frowning. "I'm almost nineteen, and I happen to be a woman in case you haven't noticed. You're such a proper Texan."

Blake laughed. "I lived in Texas, but I'm from California. And, darlin, I never said I was proper, and you ain't even close to being a grownup yet."

If looks could kill, Blake would have been six feet under. Melissa sprung up from her seat and plopped down in the next one over.

Blake couldn't worry about her at the moment. He needed a solid plan. He had picked up a bottle of brown hair coloring and a fake mustache to help him sneak into the wedding, but then what? Should he wait for the pastor to say *speak now or forever hold your peace?* Or was that too cliché? Christ, his life had turned into a soap opera.

Melissa had apparently gotten over her sulking sooner than expected and had guessed what he was thinking, because she said, "You could pretend to be part of the wedding staff."

"Melissa, you're a whiz kid! That's brilliant."

"Kid?" she said. "You really think I'm a kid?" She got up and surprised the hell out of him when she put her arms around his neck and planted a kiss with tongue and all in his open mouth. He instantly felt himself responding, and that shocked him too.

"What the hell are you doing?" He pushed her away and removed her hands from his neck.

"I'm proving to you that I'm a woman," she said.

"Okay, fine. I hear you loud and clear. Now no more of that stuff!" He held up his hands in defense.

Melissa smiled triumphantly and returned to her seat.

Blake reclined his chair and looked out the window again. What the hell was she thinking, kissing him like that? She's just a kid, even if that kiss *had* been smoking hot. He shook his head and closed his eyes, imagining Beth Ann smiling at him with those beautiful brown eyes. In no time, the last three minutes were erased from his mind.

* * * *

Beth Ann and Kaylob met with the wedding planner at beautiful place right next the ocean. They needed to approve everything including the decorations for the ceremony. When Beth Ann saw the beautiful white flowing canopies tied back with lace and the flowers adorning a pond she was speechless. Then Sarah led them down a path close to the water to a flower-covered gazebo. Just beyond it, the ocean stretched out like God's carpet on the private beach.

"What do you think, baby?" Kaylob asked.

"I love it. It's perfect. Absolutely magnificent." She put her arms around his neck and kissed him. "Just like you."

Sarah also showed them the enclosed reception area where the band would play and the party would begin. It was all perfectly set up. Tomorrow morning at ten a.m. Beth Ann was going to become one with her future, her past, and her present. She couldn't imagine that anything could go wrong.

* * * *

After the rehearsal dinner, Beth Ann and Kaylob were each kidnapped by their friends and pulled in opposite directions. Beth Ann knew something naughty was up when the older ladies all declined to join them. Holy trouble, it was on its way. She could feel it.

They took her back to the Villa's main reception area. The music started and the lights dimmed as soon as they entered. Everyone was laughing and ordering drinks from the corner bar. Lisa handed Beth Ann some type of drink in a coconut shell.

"No, I don't drink anymore," she said, remembering her intoxicated outing the week before.

"Tonight you do," Carol said. "This is your girl's night out, a celebration party to do whatever you want before you tie the knot. So get ready for some fun!"

Beth Ann had heard about men having these kinds of parties before they got married, but this party for the girls was something new. Shelia and Denny came waltzing through the front doors and gave Carol a thumbs up. Beth Ann had no idea what was going on, but she knew it couldn't be good.

Everyone kept insisting she sample the drink in her hand. To her surprise, it didn't taste like alcohol. It tasted like coconut and cream with a hint of something else. Before she knew it, Beth Ann was on her second one, standing at the bar watching Lisa and Denny dance together. Debra and Frankie finally arrived and Beth Ann was happy they were there.

"Beth Ann!" Lisa shouted. "Get your sexy booty out here!"

Everyone applauded and called for her to get out there and dance, so Beth Ann had no choice but to go. It wasn't long before they were all acting like delinquents and having the best time.

Denny let out a whoop that caused everyone to turn and look at two well-built guys dressed in what appeared to be half tuxedoes. Everyone cheered as Lisa and Denny ran up and started dirty dancing with them. Beth Ann tried to exit the floor nonchalantly, but several of the other women took her by the arms and led her toward the barely-dressed men.

"Come on, Miss B!" Denny shouted. "It's time to let your hair down. Have some fun before you're an old married lady!"

The two men began peeling off their clothes. Beth Ann tried not to look, but curiosity won out as she peeked between her fingers and saw the male strippers in all their glory.

Someone yelled, "She lives, she lives!"

The next thing she knew, someone pulled Beth Ann to the middle of the dance floor and seated her in a chair. What the heck now? Then she saw a huge cake being rolled into the room, and she had a funny feeling it wasn't for eating. She also knew Kaylob wasn't going to like this.

Seedy strip club music spilled from the speakers overhead. Beth Ann waved her arms and tried to cover her eyes again, but she couldn't help laughing when she saw the top open and the strobe light show begin. A scantily dressed man emerged from the cake wearing a hat and a mask that partially covered his face, and nothing else except a G-string that left little to the imagination. To put it mildly, he was well endowed.

Holy beefy buns! Despite herself, Beth Ann found herself staring. His body was almost as fantastic as Kaylob's.

Lisa yelled, "Come on! Take a good, hard look!"

Beth Ann felt the heat crawling up her neck as she watched him work his way out of the cake then start to move toward her with his hips grinding seductively.

"Come on, Beth Ann," Lisa called. "Lighten up and have some fun! What do you think the guys are doing tonight? I bet right now Kaylob is dancing with some beautiful woman."

Heat washed over Beth Ann instantly. "Kaylob is with strippers tonight? He's dead. I'm not even married yet and already a widow." She started to get up from the chair, but the masked man grabbed her and began spinning her around the dance floor and laughing at what she'd said, which she thought was just rude.

He started to lean her back in a dip when she saw it. Holy birthmark, that was no stripper, it was her soon-to-be husband flaunting his bare ass around the dance floor. Oh, she intended to make him *and* her sneaky, underhanded friends pay for this. Their little scam was about to backfire on them.

Reluctantly, as if unsure of herself, she began to give in slowly to the seductive dance, then she stopped faking at being shy and grabbed a drink from a nearby table as if to boost her naughtiness. When the next song started, she moved her body rhythmically with his and gave him a sexy grin.

"I hope you don't mind," she said, her hand sliding over his firm buttocks. "You have the most incredible body I've ever seen. I just can't keep my hands off it." She swayed her hips with his and stepped even closer to him.

All her friends were cheering her on. "All right, Beth Ann! Way to go!"

She pulled off her top and wrapped it around his neck to pull him closer with just her shorts and bra on, she said, "you're *so* hot." She licked her lips. "And sexy." She ran her hands up and down his chest and traced a finger across his stomach. "I have a great big house and my fiancé is out tonight. Want to go back to my place?" She thought he was going to faint when she leaned over and touched her tongue to his chest.

"Elizabeth Ann Rose!" His body stiffened and he backed up, ripping off the mask.

Beth Ann doubled over with laughter. When she was able to straighten up, Kaylob was looking at her with his arms crossed over his chest.

"You knew, you brat!"

She giggled and pointed at his thigh. "Not in the beginning, but you should have covered your birthmark."

He removed her shirt from around his neck and pulled it over her head. "You were this close to being in the worst trouble ever."

She put her hands on her hips and scowled at his almost naked body. "You'd better get dressed before you catch a cold, Mr. O'Brien."

Kaylob motioned to Frankie. "Hey, bring my pants!"

Beth Ann watched him put them on and laughed. "Now everyone here knows your best features."

"What do you mean?" He looked puzzled.

She patted his butt. "Your buns. Best ones on the planet. Kinda appropriate for a chef."

They both laughed and Beth Ann stepped into his arms. Kaylob had made it the best girls' party ever.

* * * *

After a few dances with Beth Ann, the guys dragged Kaylob away for his bachelor party, but he didn't really want to be there. While the other guys were drinking and dancing with girls, he slipped away and took a stroll through the lush gardens bathed in moonlight. There was one very special lady he wanted to see before his wedding. He knocked lightly on her door, and her blue eyes opened wide with surprise when she saw him.

"Hi, Gram. I wanted to see you before tomorrow." Kaylob smiled but flushed when Nickolas walked up behind her. "Oh, hell, I'm sorry. I didn't know you two would still be together. I don't want to intrude."

"Nonsense." Gram waved her hand and pulled him inside. "I'm glad you stopped by. Nicky and I were just talking about you."

He told them what was going on at the bachelor party and that he wanted no part of it. The three of them enjoyed some late-night snacks and talked about the future. It was a great evening with a very special couple, and there was no place he would rather be than with Beth Ann.

When he got back to Frankie's room, he was there waiting for him. "Where the hell did you vanish to?"

"I enjoyed myself with another very beautiful lady."

Frankie knew him too well to buy it. He tilted his head and said, "Yeah, right."

Kaylob laughed. "I spent it with Gram and Nickolas. We had a wonderful evening."

"You are one strange guy, Kaylob." Frankie shook his head and put a hand on Kaylob's shoulder. "And a lucky one too."

"Don't I know it." Kaylob headed off to bed to rest up for what he knew was going to be the best day of his life.

* * * *

Blake stared out his window at the Villa. Since it was after midnight when he'd checked in, he hadn't run into anyone he knew from the wedding party. Now he was a brunette instead of a blond. Once he added the mustache in the morning, no one should recognize him. There was nothing he could do about the dimples and blue eyes, but he'd have to take his chances with that. He'd bribed one of the staff members with a good sum of money, and the guy had brought up some catering clothes and a fake name tag that would be his cover for the next day.

It was late and he was exhausted, but he couldn't sleep with the weight of the world bearing down on his heart. He wished like hell this was his wedding with Beth Ann. Since it wasn't, he was determined to make sure it didn't happen.

A knock startled him and made him look at his watch. Who the hell was at his door at two a.m.? He opened it to find a very sleepy Melissa.

"I can't sleep, Blake," she said, rubbing her eyes. "I had a bad dream and it scared me."

He opened the door all the way and sighed. She really was just a kid.

"Okay, come in. You can have the bed. I'll sleep on the pullout."

She came in and climbed up on the bed. "We could share. It's no big deal."

Maybe she wasn't such a kid after all.

"Oh, I think it's a big deal, darlin," he said. "And you should know better. Your daddy would pull out his shotgun. I'll take the couch."

She pouted and almost looked as if there were tears in her eyes. It reminded him of all the times Beth Ann had nightmares and what she went through.

He grabbed the spare blanket walked over and sunk down on the sofa. After what seemed like an eternity, he finally fell asleep around three and dreamed that the sunrise would find him back with the love of his life, no matter what it took.

* * * *

"Beth Ann, time to get up!" Lisa yelled. "Today's the day you've waited for all your life!"

"Okay, give me a—"

Before she could finish her words or even get up, a three-ring fashion circus descended on Beth Ann. Everyone came running in with dresses, makeup and food. Muffins on a tray smelled heavenly, and there was coffee and three kinds of fruit juices.

Lisa pulled Beth Ann out of bed and pointed her toward the shower with a smack on her bottom. "Hurry!"

She barely had time to brush her teeth after she got out of the shower when Lisa yanked her out of the bathroom and pushed her down in a chair.

"This is Ramona," Lisa announced. "She's the best on the island and can do magic. Let her do her thing."

The short lady with bright red hair said, "You want hair up or down?"

"Mostly down, but pulled back with curls around my face," Beth Ann replied.

"Ahh, *bueno,* Senorita Bonita," Ramona said, lifting Beth Ann's hair. "You will be taking your husband's breath away."

As Ramona was doing her hair, another woman began doing her nails. She felt like a model almost ready to walk down a runway.

Lisa held a muffin to her mouth for a bite. "Eat. You need something in your stomach." Beth Ann took a bite and her taste buds went to heaven.

When her hair was done, Ramona said, "Bella dama, you must look in the mirror."

Beth Ann looked at her reflection with tears in her eyes. Her hair was pulled away from her face with a beautiful gold-and-pearl beaded comb. Ramona had left wispy curls framing her face, and she knew Kaylob would love it.

"You're gorgeous," Lisa said with misty eyes. "Now it's time for the dress."

Her friends helped her step into the beautiful gown and zip it up, then Denny attached the flowing veil to her combs with Carol's help. Gram arrived just then carrying a small package.

"Oh my sweetness." Her hand went to her mouth. "You're the loveliest bride I've ever seen." She placed a black-and-gold antique box into Beth Ann's hands. "This is your something old."

Beth Ann opened the box to find a string of pearls that made her catch her breath. "Oh, Gram, these are beautiful. I love them."

"They belonged to your Great-Grandma Ann. She wore them on her wedding day. I've been saving them for you since you were born." Gram placed the necklace around Beth Ann's neck, and it looked as if it were made for the wedding gown.

Jean came in and started to cry as soon as she saw her daughter. Beth Ann embraced her and said, "Mama, I know those are happy tears."

"More than happy," Jean said, wiping her eyes. "I'm ecstatic to see my daughter so radiant and marrying her lifelong love." She handed another gift box to Beth Ann and whispered, "Something new."

"Oh, Mama, these are so perfect," she said when she saw the gorgeous set of pearl earrings. "Thank you so much…" These are divine. I love them."

"Well, I knew you were getting the necklace." Jean winked at Gram.

Beth Ann put them on and stood gazing in the mirror at the exquisite necklace and earrings that matched, as if they were a set.

"Okay, time for a gift from your maid of honor," Lisa said, handing her another package. "Well, it's actually from all of us. You needed something blue."

Beth Ann opened the beautiful blue box and pulled out a lacy blue garter with her future initials embroidered in it. Lisa helped her slip it on.

"Thank you all so much," Beth Ann said. "You're the best friends and family a girl could ask for."

Jackie stepped forward and hugged her. "We're not done yet. You need something borrowed too." She pulled a beautiful handkerchief from her purse. It was also embroidered with the initials L. R. "It belonged to my dearest friend in college."

Beth Ann tied the delicate lace hankie around her wrist and wondered if L. R. could be Lillian Kaylob's aunt that Jackie had talked to on the phone when he was in the hospital. But Jackie had said it was her best friend, her wondering was interrupted when a dear and familiar voice shrilled through the room.

"Oh my God!" Jack exclaimed. "Who is this goddess and where is my Beth Ann? You are the most beautiful woman I've ever seen, honey. You look so good I want to marry you." He pulled her into a hug.

"I love you, Jack, but you know Lenard would never let you go."

"Oh, poo on him. The old grumpy goose almost didn't let me come in here."

"Stop it. You know you two are stuck with each other."

"You're right, I'm all talk." He chuckled and hugged her again.

When it was time to leave, everyone in the entourage got in different carts for the short ride to the wedding. Beth Ann's was a special roomy cart that wouldn't mess up her beautiful dress. The wedding planner helped her out when they arrived at the location.

"Kaylob is out of sight so neither of you can see each other," Sarah said, pointing to a tent. "That's been set up for you. I think you'll be comfortable inside away from the elements."

After some last-minute touchups to her hair and makeup, it was time for Beth Ann to go join Kaylob at the altar. Sarah took her hand and they stepped outside the tent where all the bridesmaids were lined up ready to go in their soft pink dresses. Stanley and James came over and each took one of Beth Ann's arms. They were both her dads, and she wanted them both to walk her down the aisle.

The wedding music began to play, and she looked around at all the guests and family sitting in the chairs. Everything was perfect including the blue sky and warm sunshine, just as she knew it would be. The song being played was Etta James's "At Last," the lyrics were perfect for Beth Ann and Kaylob. The bridesmaids went first and walked slowly down the aisle as the groomsmen—handsome in their military uniforms, John Patterson among them—joined them from the right. They linked arms and walked down the stone path to the altar.

Beth Ann felt as if her feet were barely touching the ground as she walked down the aisle strewn with flower petals. She gazed around at the faces of all the people she loved, and joy washed over her. She and Kaylob were so lucky to have such wonderful friends and family.

Everyone was beaming back at her with love in their eyes, especially one set of blue eyes that belonged to a man wearing a caterer's uniform. Her heart tried to jump out of her chest and she stopped walking. No, the man in the catering uniform had brown hair and a moustache. It couldn't be Blake. Could it?

She stared at him and he returned her gaze. Oh, God, it *was* Blake.

For a few seconds, she didn't know what to do. Then she looked down the aisle and saw Kaylob waiting for her in a baby blue tux that took her breath away. He had his head down but looked up when Frankie nudged him, and when he saw her at the end of the aisle, his eyes widened and his smile swept across his handsome face. He was the most beautiful man she'd ever seen, inside and out, and she loved him more than anything in the world. She did the only thing her heart would allow her to do, and that was to walk to him and begin the rest of their lives together.

"Honey, you okay?" James asked and Stanley looked concerned.

"Yes daddy, I'm fine." She nodded and continued walking in step, passing friends and family, doing her best to forget those blue eyes watching her. She prayed he wasn't there to cause trouble. She'd been waiting for this day her entire life. When she passed her mom and Gram, they both mouthed *beautiful* as she went by.

At the end of the aisle, she handed her flowers to Lisa, then her dads gave her hands to Kaylob. In perfect harmony, they said, "We give our daughter to you, Kaylob Shawn O'Brien, with love and trust."

The pastor stretched out his arms and addressed the assembly. "These two partners have come together today to profess their love in front of friends and family, and to join together as one. Kaylob Shawn O'Brien and Elizabeth Ann Rose will now share their vows."

They turned to face each other, then Kaylob pulled a folded piece of paper from his pocket. He looked at her with tears pooling in his eyes.

"Elizabeth Ann Rose, I've loved you since the first day I met you. As I watched you grow into a teenager, your beauty almost made my heart stop, but all the while, you were becoming part of my heart. You are the most beautiful, caring, remarkable woman in the world. I love your beauty and your spirit and your passion for life. Your dreams melt into my heart and become my dreams. You are my love, my breath, and my very heartbeat."

He paused and put his hand over his heart, and she could see his lips trembling.

"You kept me alive when I thought I was dead. You held me up when I wanted to fall. You saw the good in me when I saw none. You are my water when I thirst, my air when I breathe, and every beautiful thing about life. I love you and I take you not only as my bride, but as my partner in life. I promise to respect you always and to treasure you as the beautiful woman you are. Thank you, Elizabeth Ann Rose, for giving me the chance to be the man I saw when I looked into your eyes." He let out a long breath and swallowed. "I, Kaylob Shawn O'Brien, take you as my life partner and my wife. I give you all of me, forever and a day."

Beth Ann had to take a minute to catch her breath and steady her voice. She hoped her tears weren't ruining her makeup, but there was no stopping them.

"Kaylob Shawn O'Brien," her voice broke. "I've loved you from the first day we met on the railroad tracks when you chattered away about my name, my age and flirting. You were the first boy I ever kissed, and you will be the last. Through the years you've held my hand through hard times, and you pushed me away through hard times."

She winked at him and they both laughed, along with a few others who got the inside joke.

"You've given me the kind of love I thought could only be found in romance novels and movies, and you've planted seeds from your love that are forever in my heart. I, Elizabeth Ann Rose, take you, Kaylob Shawn O'Brien, as my love, my life partner, and my husband. I will love you forever and a day and then some."

The pastor smiled. "Now that you have said the words that join you both in marriage, you may exchange rings as a symbol of your vows."

Frankie handed the rings to Kaylob—matching golden bands lined with seven diamonds each. Kaylob smiled as he slipped Beth Ann's ring onto her finger. "With this ring, I give you my heart and my love forever."

Beth Ann took Kaylob's ring and slipped it on. "With this ring, I give you my heart and my love forever."

The pastor said, "I now pronounce you life partners and husband and wife. You may kiss your bride."

"I love you, Mrs. O'Brien," Kaylob said as he kissed her to seal their love that was found, lost, and returned.

The pastor cleared his throat to end the kiss, then he said, "Ladies and gentlemen, I present to you Mr. and Mrs. O'Brien."

* * * *

Blake walked away from the ceremony, the air sticking heavily in his throat and his heart in pieces from watching Beth Ann marry another man. He'd been ready to stop her right up to the moment she'd stopped and looked at him, but there had been no way in hell to deny what he'd seen in her eyes when she'd looked down the aisle at Kaylob. He'd never seen her look at him that way when they'd been together, not even once.

He had to face the truth. She'd never loved him the way she loved Kaylob.

The truth may set you free, but all it did for him was kill whatever heart and soul he had left. His stomach turned and he barely made it to the bathroom in the nick of time before he threw up. Gasping and choking in the stall, he wiped away the tears that seemed to explode from his eyes.

When his retching finally stopped, he sat on the couch and ran a wet paper towel across his forehead. He wished there were a goddamn hole he could sink into somewhere. He covered his face and, for the first time in his life, admitted defeat. He'd lost the love of his life, his one and only. He would never love again. Sobs echoed through the bathroom, and his heart crash-landed somewhere outside his body.

The faint drumming of the music from the wedding pounded in his head and to nobody he yelled, "Shut the fuck up!"

Why the hell can't I stop crying? I'm Blake Tanner, I don't cry!

Bile rose in his throat again, and he almost didn't make it to the commode. Then when he did, all he had was dry heaves. Just like his life, full of nothing.

* * * *

Beth Ann was starving by the time they finished taking pictures, but she and Kaylob had to go stand in a greeting line at the reception next to their parents. When all the hugging and congratulations were done, she turned to Kaylob with pleading eyes.

"Can we go eat now?"

He gave her a wink. "I don't know, Mrs. O'Brien. I thought we'd go start the honeymoon now." Her stomach growled and he laughed. "Oh, okay. I guess we can eat something first."

The reception hall was stunning with flickering candles and flowers everywhere. After they ate, Kaylob walked up the steps to the stage, took the microphone and looked out at everyone.

"Don't worry." He held up his hand. "I'm not singing. That's Beth Ann's job."

Everyone cracked up.

"I chose the song for my first dance with my beautiful wife because when I was in the POW camp…" He paused a moment and took a breath. "…I used to hear this song in my head and would try to sing it. So this song is dedicated to the reason I'm alive, Mrs. Elizabeth Ann O'Brien."

He walked down the stairs and held out his hand. Beth Ann took it with tears in her eyes and gracefully moved into his arms while the lights dimmed and the opening strains of "Unchained Melody" filled the hall. Kaylob sang the words to her as they danced, and she knew there was no hope for saving her makeup.

They danced the next few songs with their parents, then Frankie and Lisa pulled them both onto the stage and handed them a microphone. As soon as the music started, they knew why. They had always sung the song together at parties.

Once things calmed down, Lisa came onstage with a glass of champagne in her hand and took the microphone. "Attention, everyone! I'd like to say a few words about this special couple." She waited for everyone to take their seats. "I've watched these two in love since I was eleven years old. I can honestly say that I've never seen two people love each other more. They've had a lot to deal with over the years and deserve complete and total happiness. Beth Ann and Kaylob, I love you both." She held up her glass for a toast.

Frankie took the microphone next. "I also knew from the moment I saw them together that it was something special, and it broke my heart because I knew I didn't stand a chance with her." Everyone laughed. "I want nothing but happiness for them for the rest of their lives. And I want to dance with the bride before the night is over if her husband will share her." He held up his glass. "To my two best friends in the world. Here's to your future of love and happiness."

The lights dimmed and Kaylob led Beth Ann over to Frankie for a slow dance. Frankie took her in his arms and pulled her close, his hands wrapped around her waist as she lay her head on his chest. She could hear his heart thumping and knew it was for her.

Frankie leaned close to her ear and whispered, "I picked a perfect song for us."

The music started, and the song was "I'll Be There" by the Jackson Five.

When the song ended, Kaylob appeared beside them and extracted Beth Ann's hand from Frankie's.

"Okay, that's enough," he said, his jaw clenching. "I'm beginning to feel jealous."

Beth Ann couldn't believe he was angry, but it sure looked that way. Before she could say anything, Kaylob let go of her and pulled Frankie into his arms, bending him backward into a low dip. The band started playing the Jackson Five's "Dancing Machine," and everyone rolled with laughter as Frankie and Kaylob moved around the dance floor. Frankie topped off the performance by taking a flower from one of the tables and putting it between his teeth.

Chapter Twenty-Six

An hour later, Kaylob was getting a snack and noticed that Beth Ann had a lot of guys lining up to dance with her. His face must've shown what he was thinking, because Frankie moved next to him and slapped him on the back.

"Do you know how many of those guys have wanted to dance with her since junior high?"

Kaylob looked at him and shrugged. "I guess I was so busy keeping an eye on Blake that I never noticed all the others."

"Well, now you know," Frankie said.

Kaylob watched as one guy after another glided his wife across the dance floor and decided it was time to cut the cake. He took Beth Ann's hand and said, "Cake time, sweetheart. Don't you guys have wives and girlfriends to get back to?"

The cake, decorated with fresh flowers from the island, tasted as good as it looked. They cut a piece and fed each other, tasting the frosting off each other's lips.

"Have you ever tasted cake so sweet, baby?" Kaylob whispered. "We've never fed each other cake before."

She got an odd look on her face, then she pointed at the cake. "Look at all the colorful flowers. What a great idea for decorating it. I love everything they did. And all the flowers have held up all day, can you believe it? Look at Jack and Lenard over there. They're so cute together."

Oh, yeah, she was rambling to change the subject. He studied her face and knew a switch-a-subject when he heard it. He knew why too—Blake must've fed her cake when they were together. He didn't like that one bit.

Beth Ann tiptoed to kiss him and said, "I need to go talk to my parents for a minute. I'll be right back."

Yep, that little redhead was an escape artist too. He decided to let the whole thing drop, because nothing was going to spoil this special day. She was his wife now, and that was that.

He decided to step outside to get some fresh air and stopped off at the restroom on the way back. One of the caterers jumped up when he walked in and went to the sink and started washing his hands. Kaylob strolled over to the urinal.

"You guys did a great job with the food," he said.

The guy kept washing his hands and didn't say anything. Kaylob moved to the sink beside him.

"Did you get to see the wedding? I'm the luckiest man in the world."

"Good for you. Maybe we should call in the -yippee-ki-y squad," the guy gave him a sidelong glance.

He turned off the water and turned to face Kaylob. Something about him seemed familiar, but before Kaylob could get a good look at him, he whipped around and headed toward the door. Just before he went out, he stopped and spoke without turning around.

"You're right. You're one lucky bastard, and you'd better take care of that little darlin'…or, never mind."

He opened the door and left.

Kaylob stared after him, thought about those blue eyes, that accent and knew it was familiar. Wait, could it have been…? Nah, that was crazy. Blake would never have been working as a caterer. Or would he?

* * * *

Lisa took Beth Ann by the hand and said, "Come on, it's time to go change."

Beth Ann had chosen a pink skirt and little white tie shirt for her after-the-wedding outfit. Lisa helped pull the combs from her hair, and Beth Ann could almost hear it yelling *freedom!* She looked in the full-length mirror then turned sideways to make sure everything was in place.

"Honey, you don't have anything to worry about," Lisa said.

"Do you think this is too revealing?" Beth Ann asked.

Lisa grinned. "Yes, but this is Hawaii. Kaylob's gonna flip when he sees how sexy you look. That skirt hugs all the right places."

As soon as they got back to the reception, Beth Ann spotted her husband in the crowd. He'd changed too into some white shorts and a beautiful Hawaiian shirt that was opened to show off his chest and bronzed skin. Holy honeymoon, she wanted him and wanted him now.

He walked over and took her hand. "Come on, they're waiting for us."

Outside, Hawaiian ladies were doing a synchronized hula dance and they led them down to the water's edge where lit torches lined a path. Most of the guests were already there waiting near a small boat with flowers and little lights strung delicately around its edges. Two of the dancing women placed leis around their necks and helped them into the boat. When they were seated inside on the blanket, their family and friends pushed them off and waved goodbye.

They sailed off to the sound of drums, seashell horns and women singing enchanted Hawaiian songs. They lay back on the blanket and gazed up at the sky filled with millions of twinkling stars.

Beth Ann pointed. "Look, honey, the stars came out to celebrate our wedding. Look at that bright one. I think it knows who we are."

Kaylob wrapped his arms around her. "That must be the one I used to put all my love in when I thought of you."

"Our very own special star," she said, turning over to kiss him and pointed. "Look, Kaylob, Wine and a scrumptious fruit tray."

After they sampled some of the delicious pineapple slices and mangos, both of them were ready to go back and start the honeymoon. Kaylob signaled with a flashlight for someone to come, and Brian arrived within minutes and towed them to the dock behind their house.

Kaylob swung her up into his arms, and they both thanked Brian. Then he held her and headed towards the house. Once they arrived, he carried her over the threshold.

"We're here, Mrs. O'Brien." He set her down and looked into her eyes. "You are one beautiful lady."

Beth Ann stood on her tiptoes and gave him a soft kiss. "Thank you, Mr. O'Brien. Give me just a minute to go freshen up and change."

"Okay," he said, his hand sliding up her waist to untie her shirt. "Hurry back, baby."

Holy midnight, his deep voice and sexy blue eyes had her heart pounding and her blood racing. Beth Ann walked to the bedroom on legs that trembled with nerves and excitement. She went straight to the closet and held up her sexy little white gown. Could she really walk out wearing this? Yes, of course she could. This was her honeymoon, and Kaylob was finally her husband. Besides, she had a silk robe she could wear over it.

When she came out of the bathroom, she heard music coming from the living room and smiled. He was such a romantic. She found him lying on the couch, his hands behind his head as he gazed up at the ceiling wearing nothing but his boxers. Good Lord, his legs were sexy and his rippled stomach was so hot it was boiling. Her throat was suddenly parched, and she found it hard to swallow.

He saw her and their gazes locked. Overstuffed seconds ticked by before he stood and walked over to her.

"Oh, baby." He touched the fabric of her robe. "You look like an angel."

She'd always dreamed of this honeymoon. Tonight was all about love and it dawned on her, it was time for all her shyness to be gone. She stood before this man who was finally her husband and slowly untied her robe and let it fall to the floor.

"Tonight I'm going to be a different kind of angel. Sit yourself down, Mr. O'Brien, and let me entertain you."

She pushed him onto the couch and watched his eyes grow large along with a few other things. He opened his mouth to say something, but all he managed was a long hard swallow.

Talk about perfect timing. The song on the radio was Marvin Gaye singing "Let's Get It On."

She pulled up a chair in front of him and moved slowly around it, showing him some dance moves he'd never seen her do before. His eyes darkened with desire when she let her sheer gown slide off her body. All those dance lessons had taught her a lot, but never had she imagined she'd use them to entertain her husband.

"If the spirit moves you, let me groove you," she sang as she skimmed her panties partway down and made him groan. Only then, did she move closer and let him pull them down the rest of the way. As she continued to do her routine and let him see *all* of her, in a way he never had, she saw him tremble with desire. Then she moved onto his lap where she finished her dance.

The second the song ended, he lifted her into his arms and carried her into the bedroom.

"Oh, baby." He lay her down on the bed and moved on top of her, moaning against her lips. "You're the sexiest woman in the world. And gorgeous doesn't even come close to how beautiful you are."

She reached up and linked her fingers through his hair. "I want you, Mr. O'Brien. Now!"

His mouth covered hers, and what he did with his tongue had to be illegal. She opened her mouth to give him more access, and a low moan came from deep within his chest and vibrated into every part of her. She wanted his boxers off and out of the way, but before she could slide them down, he started bestowing a trail of kisses down her neck to her stomach.

"Kaylob..." She knew exactly where he was going. He was giving her those sweet kisses that drove her through heaven's door. She surrendered all until she was quivering with desire and on the verge.

"Come on, Beth Ann," he paused to say, "Don't hold back."

"Kaylob, please." She tried to pull him back to her lips. "I want you."

"You want me how, sweetheart?"

She adjusted her body to show him and tried again to pull down his boxers.

"Uh-uh," he said with a devilish smile. "You have to tell me what you want."

"I want you here," she said breathlessly while she showed him where.

He slid his last stitch of clothing off and kissed her again as he lowered himself to her, touching her lightly. "Is this what you want, baby?"

"Yes!" She wrapped her legs around his waist and pulled him all the way home.

As he entered into the flames, he cried out, "Jesus, Beth Ann!"

Slowly at first then faster, he filled her completely with his love.

"Oh, Kaylob," she whispered against his lips.

"Keep your eyes open. I want to look into them while I love you."

He rained kisses across her eyes and her face as he took them both to paradise. The liquid heat of their love carried them over the edge not just once but many times throughout the night.

* * * *

Kaylob woke up at noon and found his wife still sleeping. She was almost always up before him, so he took advantage of the rare chance to gaze at her sleeping form. The sheet covered her body to her waist as she lay on her back. She started moving around in the bed then slowly opened those amazing brown eyes.

"Good morning, Mr. O'Brien."

He loved the music of her voice. The brightness of her smile sent chills into his heart.

"Hello, Mrs. O'Brien." He kissed her nose.

"How long have you been awake?" She started to pull up the sheet, but he held her hand.

"About twenty minutes, and I love this view." His finger traced from her cheek down to her collarbone, then he ran his finger across her breast lightly touching her nipple. She shivered as she looked at him from under her eyelashes.

"Kaylob..."

"Yes, baby?"

When she kicked the sheet all the way off and showed him what she wanted, he about lost it. She'd always been so shy, but there was nothing shy about her now.

Over the next few weeks, she showed him over and over what she wanted. Although their lovemaking was passionate and fierce, they also shared quite a few tears. Kaylob wasn't sure why. All he knew was that thirty days would not be enough time to satisfy his craving for her, and a lifetime wasn't long enough to share their love.

Chapter Twenty-Seven

Four weeks later back in Riverside, Jack started to unlock the door to Beth Ann and Kaylob's townhouse and found it already open. Funny, he could have sworn he'd locked it the last time he was there. Everything appeared to be in place. "Whew, I won't make that mistake again." He whispered.

He set down the casserole he was going to cook for the newlyweds as a welcome home surprise. About time they came home. He'd missed them like crazy and couldn't wait to see them. The oven needed to be set to 375° and he put the dish inside, glancing at the clock. It was about an hour before they got back. Things should smell heavenly by then.

"Where do they keep that vacuum?" he said to himself. Maybe the hall closet. "Bingo!" he sang out then decided he needed some tuney rooneys to make the work go faster. He switched on the radio, and the Supremes serenaded him with, "Stop in the Name of Love."

There was-nothing like singing while vacuuming he decided and lifted a throw rug to get it out of the way, then stood, feeling the hair on the back of his neck stand up on end. He stopped vacuuming, but before he could turn around, he felt a blinding pain in his head and knew he was falling.

What the hell! Did someone just hit me?

Just before he passed out, Jack heard an unfamiliar voice.

"She's going to be mine, and nobody will stop me."

THE END

Coming soon from Melange
The Journey of Elizabeth Ann Rose (prequel to Seasons of Love and War)
and
Book 4 of Seasons of Love and War
June's Stolen Rose

About the Author

Brenda Ashworth Barry's first book was a memoir titled, Healing the Voices Within, which was never published but sponsored on a local TV station and flew off the shelves at her Healing Center in Redding California.

Her most recent work is a six-part saga of star-crossed lovers separated by the war in Vietnam, entitled Seasons of Love and War. Brenda worked for over five years to bring the six-part Saga alive.

Brenda lives in Roseburg, Oregon, by the Umpqua River, and has raised four children three birth children and one adopted born in her heart. Her husband, who was in the military for 21 years, gave her help and encouragement while writing her novel. When she's not writing she can normally be found walking the trails with her husband and their little dachshund, or in their RV enjoying nature.

Twitter- @sunsetsky52
www.brendaashworthbarry.com
https://www.facebook.com/pages/Seasons-of-Love-and-War-Author-Page/411210412247684
http://brendabarry.blogspot.com/
http://brendabarryashworth.wordpress.com/

Other works by the author from Melange

Seasons of Love and War, Book 1 of the Seasons of Love and War Series